Dear Reader,

They say that people are the same all over. Whether it's a small village on the sea, a mining town nestled in the mountains, or a whistle-stop along the Western plains, we all share the same hopes and dreams. We work, we play, we laugh, we cry—and, of course, we fall in love . . .

It is this universal experience that we at Jove Books have tried to capture in a heartwarming series of novels. We've asked our most gifted authors to write their own story of American romance, set in a town as distinct and vivid as the people who live there. Each writer chose a special time and place close to their hearts. They filled the towns with charming, unforgettable characters—then added that spark of romance. We think you'll find the combination absolutely delightful.

You might even recognize *your* town. Because true love lives in *every* town . . .

Welcome to *Our Town*.

Sincerely,

Leslie Gelb

Leslie Gelbman
Editor-in-Chief

Titles in the Our Town series

TAKE HEART
HARBOR LIGHTS
HUMBLE PIE
CANDY KISS
CEDAR CREEK
SUGAR AND SPICE
CROSS ROADS
BLUE RIBBON
THE LIGHTHOUSE
THE HAT BOX
COUNTRY COMFORTS
GRAND RIVER
WHISTLE STOP

Titles by Lisa Higdon

TAKE HEART
WHISTLE STOP

~ OUR · TOWN ~

WHISTLE STOP

LISA HIGDON

JOVE BOOKS, NEW YORK

8-13-97 B&T 6.00

WHISTLE STOP

A Jove Book / published by arrangement with
the author

PRINTING HISTORY
Jove edition / July 1997

The Putnam Berkley World Wide Web site address is
http://www.berkley.com

ISBN: 0-515-12085-5

A JOVE BOOK®
Jove Books are published by The Berkley Publishing Group,
200 Madison Avenue, New York, New York 10016.
JOVE and the "J" design are trademarks
belonging to Jove Publications, Inc.

PRINTED IN THE UNITED STATES OF AMERICA

10 9 8 7 6 5 4 3 2 1

In loving memory of Lloyd David Ross,
who made every day a joy and
who would be absolutely appalled at the notion
of having a romance novel dedicated to him.
I miss you, Lloyd.

Special thanks to my brother, Jerry Bailey,
whose enthusiasm, generosity, humor, and
knowledge of computers made the writing of
this book an adventure.

Author's Note

Belle Plain was once a prosperous town in Callahan County, Texas. The town's demise was the result of a series of serious economic setbacks, one of which was its failure to secure the Texas & Pacific Railroad. My research of the area brought me into contact with many wonderful people who were anxious to help give the town a second life and a "happily ever after." The events in this book are purely fictional, offering another version of what might have been.

I would like to thank the following people for their time and patience—thanks to their reverence for history, Belle Plain will live on: Ben and Elaine Stephenson of Baird, Texas; historian Pat Coursey of Brownwood, Texas; Laura Jones of the Abilene Public Library; Mary Joy of Abilene, Texas; the late T. R. Havens, author of *Belle Plain, Texas: A Ghost Town in Callahan*; and Jim Rauchley, for loving Belle Plain.

Also, thanks to Virginia Brown for pointing me toward Texas, and to my beloved aunt, Katherine Hawkins Person for lending her name and grace to my heroine.

❖ 1 ❖

L UKE CANTRELL SWORE the only thing worse than the taste of his own blood was the rotgut whiskey he'd been given to wash it down. The liquor burned like fire in his throat and scorched a path toward his gut. Still, he wished he had a barrel of the stuff, enough to get himself stinking drunk—drunk enough to forget that he'd ever been anything but an outlaw.

"Go easy on that bourbon, boy." Johnson nudged him none too gently with a muddy boot. "I want you where you can ride."

To his own surprise, Luke actually wanted to laugh at the remark. If Johnson wanted him able to ride so damned bad, he shouldn't have paid three drovers to beat the hell out of him with barrel staves behind his hotel. But laughing would only accomplish two things: aggravate the piercing pain in his side and feed Johnson's anger.

Luke's only cause for reluctance was knowing that the aging bounty hunter wanted the five-hundred-dollar bonus for bringing him in alive. Luke had no desire to ride the remaining miles to Abilene puking blood or jarring broken bones. No, if he antagonized Johnson, he wanted to be sure one of them would end up dead.

Hiding his smile against the mouth of the bottle, Luke breathed a curse as the cheap liquor seared his split lip. "Who told you this kerosene was bourbon? I hope you didn't pay more than two bits for the whole case."

Johnson's eyes narrowed, and he snatched the bottle from Luke's shackled hands. "It's good enough for the likes of you and better than the good folks of Cutter's Creek are going to give you."

Luke didn't doubt that for a minute, not if they went to the trouble of hiring Caleb Johnson to track him clear to Texas. Johnson enjoyed the reputation of being one of the most accomplished bounty hunters west of the Mississippi, and if the price was right, he would even guarantee a live prisoner delivered for trial and hanging.

Johnson turned up the whiskey and took a quick swallow, unable to hide a grimace at the foul taste. Without a word, he corked the bottle and returned it to his saddlebag. He glanced back at Luke with a cocky grin. "Once you're delivered to the marshal in Abilene, I'll be able to afford fine French brandy. I'll even drink a toast to your hanging."

Once again, Luke was tempted to laugh. Johnson would toast his own mother's funeral for the sake of having a drink. This was the second stop they had made. Obviously his captor was suffering the effects of too much rotgut the night before.

He felt no pity for Johnson's misery, and he was quick to ask, "If you're so damned anxious to see me hang, why are you stopping here?"

"I ain't stopping here for the night," Johnson bit out, scowling as he clutched his belly. He had made several excuses for his nausea, blaming everything from alkaline water to tainted food at the hotel. "I only wanted to water the horses; we'll be riding into a little town called Belle

Plain by nightfall. I sent a wire to the marshal there before
we left town, and he'll have a nice cell waiting for you.''

He knew better, but Luke couldn't resist taunting, ''You
afraid I'll get away from you in the dark?''

''I'll rest easier knowing you're in a lock-up,'' Johnson
didn't refrain from admitting. ''You're worth a thousand
dollars, provided I haul you in alive for trial, but only five
hundred if I have to bring you in dead. I ain't too proud to
cover my ass for another five hundred dollars.''

With a groan, Luke let his head fall back on the dusty
ground, wondering if he would even make it to trial. More
than likely, a welcoming party with a new rope would be
waiting for him the minute he crossed the county line in
Cutter's Creek, and lynchings were never pretty. He wished
now that he'd listened to his mother; gambling, she said,
was evil and only brought men to bad ends.

It had certainly proven unhealthy for one poor bastard
who tried to bluff his way out of an eight hundred-dollar
pot with a pair of threes. Luke had been called a cheat
before, and he might have considered letting the man keep
his money, but once the fool went for his gun, Luke's
choices were gone. Just his luck, the sore loser turned out
to be the son of the man who owned the whole damned
town.

The clanging of a coffeepot lid and the aroma of frying
bacon drew his attention to the small campfire. Johnson was
hunched over the skillet, poking at the bacon with a fork,
and Luke felt the hollow space in his stomach rumble in
anticipation. He hadn't eaten since leaving the hotel yesterday, and Johnson had yet to offer him a scrap.

He watched his captor remove the skillet from the fire
and transfer the bacon to a tin plate that already bore thick
slices of bread. The bastard would love nothing more than
for him to ask for something to eat. Pride was useless to a
condemned man, but Luke wasn't quite ready to accept
defeat on that level. He might die hungry, but he wouldn't
die begging.

Johnson set the plate aside and poured himself a cup of coffee, but he didn't drink it. Instead, he removed his hat and wiped his brow, which Luke noticed was creased and beaded with sweat. Slowly, Johnson set the coffee on the ground and began to massage his left arm, a strangled curse escaping his lips.

Rising to his feet, Johnson crossed the clearing and stared down at Luke with a bewildered expression. Before Luke could decide what was happening, Johnson collapsed right in front of him. Luke managed to rise to a sitting position and turn Johnson over with the heel of his boot.

"Damn," he breathed, scrambling to his knees. Johnson was pale and his breathing was shallow, but he was still alive . . . for now. Luke fumbled through the man's coat pockets looking for the keys to the handcuffs and set about freeing himself.

He tossed the irons aside and wasted no time removing Johnson's holster, buckling it around his own waist. His mind raced for what to do next, but his hunger won out. Sandwiching the bacon on the bread, Luke ate quickly while gathering the saddlebags and canteens.

The horses were still saddled and picketed near the creek, and he gathered both sets of reins. He sure as hell wasn't leaving a fast horse waiting for Johnson when he came to. *If* he came to.

He hesitated, glancing back at the man's prone form. More than likely the bastard would die where he fell. Luke felt no remorse for that, but he contemplated the nuisance of being associated with Johnson's death. Too many people had seen them leave town together, and now the marshal in Belle Plain knew they were headed that way.

The shooting of a small-town poker player would eventually be forgotten, but being linked to the death of a reputed bounty hunter would be worse than having the mark of Cain. If the newspapers got hold of the story, every lawman in the country would be after him. Not that Johnson was well-loved by anyone, but the notoriety of arresting his killer would all but guarantee fame and, best of all, fortune.

Squatting beside Johnson's crumpled form, Luke swore every curse he'd ever heard. He glanced in the direction they had been traveling, north along the river, and decided on the best possible option.

If Johnson lived until they reached Belle Plain, he could claim to have found him on the trail and leave him with a doctor or some benevolent townsperson. If he died on the way, no one would know who was buried in an unmarked grave in the middle of nowhere. Either way, Luke would ride away a free man.

Katherine McBride stared out of the kitchen window, her mood as dismal as the shadows settling over the dusty streets of Belle Plain. She sighed and forced her attention to the task at hand. Now that it was just her and Tom, there were never too many dishes to wash, and he always helped with the chore.

A brother like Tom was a blessing. He was thoughtful and dependable, never drank or swore, and he was always pleasant company. He was sensitive to her somber moods and strove to cheer her.

Usually, his unceasing chatter took her mind off her troubles, but tonight he had chosen a subject that was a definite sore spot.

"I still don't see how you can blame Stuart for taking that job in California." Tom carefully worked the dishtowel over a dripping coffee cup. "He'll make three times as much money, and he won't—"

"I'll tell you how I can blame him," she cut him off, not wanting to hear the next sentence. "He signed a contract with this town! He agreed to three years, at a generous salary plus meals and lodging, and then he leaves after eight months without so much as a 'fare-thee-well.' I can't help it if he wanted to marry a woman who didn't want to be a lawman's wife.''

Tom lowered his eyes and finished drying the cup without another word. Katherine could have bitten her tongue. Her brother idolized the town's former marshal, and her words were a slap in his face more than that of the fly-by-night lawman.

''Stuart was a good marshal.'' He placed the cup on the shelf and reached for the plate she was rinsing. ''You ought not to carry such hard feelings.''

''I know he was your friend,'' she stated, wiping her hands on her apron. ''I'm sorry if you think I'm being unfair, but a man should live up to his obligations.''

Nodding in reluctant agreement, Tom did add one last defense of his hero. ''Sometimes life gets in the way.''

At that, it was Katherine's turn to nod in concurrence. The past six months had made her painfully aware of the unexpected trials life holds, but she hardly considered the marshal's dilemma worthy of leaving the whole town in the lurch. Instead of arguing further, she lifted the heavy basin of dishwater and asked Tom to open the back door. Once on the back porch, she drew a deep breath, filling her lungs with the cool night air.

''I expect we'll have some rain tonight,'' she predicted as she dumped the dishwater over the far end of the porch. ''The ground certainly could use a good soaking.''

She turned to find Tom watching her, his hands crammed in his pockets. He had been on the verge of broaching a subject all day and was still gathering his courage. She hung the dishpan on a nail near the back door and pretended not to notice his apprehension. She hoped his nerve would fail, and she wouldn't have to hurt his feelings, at least for one more day.

But he cleared his throat and faced her. ''Have you decided who's going to be marshal now?''

Since they were children, Tom had dreamed of wearing

a badge, and Stuart Carey asking him to be the town's deputy marshal had been the greatest thrill of his life. Katherine knew he hoped to become marshal now that the job was open, but she didn't have the heart to tell him that he didn't have what it takes.

Still, avoiding the issue would not change the outcome. She would rather hurt his feelings than see him killed. Drawing a deep breath, she simply stated, ''I think the best thing to do is appoint someone temporarily and then go ahead with the election in the fall.''

Tom only nodded, his disappointment plain to see as he held the door open for her. If Katherine failed to have him appointed as marshal now, no one would vote for him in an election. Wounded pride never killed anyone, she reassured herself, but inexperience behind a badge had slain many.

Without another word, she stepped inside the house, guilt gnawing at her resolve. She crossed the kitchen floor, folded the forsaken dishtowel, and hung it over the stove, ignoring Tom's crestfallen expression. She wouldn't allow her feelings for her brother to get him killed.

He heaved a sigh, lingering just inside the back door. ''I should be getting back to the office for a little while. That telegram said they would be here by now.''

''I hope they pass us right by,'' she retorted. ''The last thing we need is some no-account bounty hunter hauling outlaws into our town.''

''Katherine, don't you know who Caleb Johnson is?'' Tom was incredulous. ''Why, he's brought in over one hundred men—wanted for everything from armed robbery to murder.''

''A bounty hunter is not the same as the law,'' she reminded him. ''They have no desire for justice, only money. This Johnson will gladly let you house and feed his prisoner, but do you think he'll give you one cent of that reward money?''

"A marshal upholds the law; money doesn't figure into it."

"Money is all that matters to such men." She admired Tom's blind sense of duty, but his naivety made him an easy mark. "You just watch, Thomas McBride, this Caleb Johnson will only bring trouble this town doesn't need."

A flickering light in the distance was the only thing keeping Luke awake, that and the throbbing pain in his side. More than likely he had a few cracked ribs, but he was in better shape than Johnson. Slung across the back of his own horse like a sack of potatoes, the bastard was still breathing, but that was about all.

The sooner Luke unloaded his captor into the capable hands of a town doctor, the sooner he could make his break. He would simply fade into the darkness without calling attention to himself and be remembered only as a Good Samaritan who tried to help a sick man. By the time Johnson was coherent enough to remember what had happened, Luke would be a thousand miles from Texas.

Bolstered by the thought, Luke urged the horse on a little faster toward the glimmer of lamplight. The light began to take shape. The outline of a town rose out of the darkness, and he hoped there would be a doctor in one of the buildings silhouetted against the moonlight.

The road narrowed as he entered the outskirts of town. A dog barked, alerting its master that a stranger was in their midst. No lights shone behind the windows he passed, and he realized the hour was late.

The main street was almost empty, save for an occasional bandy-legged cowboy staggering down the wooden sidewalk. Luke scanned every building, hoping for a sign of life. In the distance, he could hear a bawdy piano, woefully out of tune, but even the promise of a brothel didn't tempt him to linger in town.

He rode down the street, hoping to catch sight of a physician's office, but the only signs visible proclaimed a mercantile, the livery, and finally a window filled with warm, welcoming light—the marshal's office.

Damn, he had ridden straight into the hands of the law, trying to save the life of the very man trying to haul him in for hanging. He glanced up and down the street, looking for a place to leave Johnson and make a run for it.

Luke heard the creak of new hinges, and a stranger's voice called out to him. "Evening, mister."

Luke felt the hair on the back of his neck stand on end, and he turned back toward the law office to find a lanky figure looming in the open doorway. Yellow lamplight spilled out into the street, and a match flared against the doorjamb. The man raised the tiny torch to the cigarette clamped between his teeth, illuminating a face that was much too young to belong to a marshal.

"Evening," Luke replied, never looking away, even when the match sailed into the dusty street.

"Been expecting you." The man drew deeply on the smoke, the end glowing orange in the shadows. "I see you had trouble with the prisoner."

Luke glanced at Johnson's limp form hanging across the back of the horse and managed not to react to the words. It hadn't occurred to him that no one in Belle Plain would know Caleb Johnson; that was why the bastard had sent a wire ahead.

The young man naturally thought he was Johnson, because surely no man wanted for murder would be fool enough to parade down the middle of the main street straight toward the jail. Luke hadn't figured on being mistaken for the bounty hunter, but decided against disputing the assumption. He'd leave the explaining to Johnson.

Still, he had to respond and make it sound good. Before he could think of an answer, the man broke into a fit of coughing, clutching at the door frame to keep his balance.

"Damn," he gasped, tossing the cigarette to the sidewalk. He coughed again, somewhat embarrassed, and crushed the glowing butt beneath the heel of his boot. "I reckon the makings were too dry."

Luke watched the pretense of a seasoned lawman fall away, revealing a green kid, no more than twenty or twenty-two, wanting to play marshal.

"I never did acquire a taste for tobacco myself," he offered, wanting to keep the boy at ease. "It's a nasty habit at best."

With a nod, he stepped into the street, his hand extended. "I'm Tom McBride, deputy marshal; you must be Caleb Johnson. I got your wire this morning."

Tom rounded the side of Johnson's horse and peered into the face of Luke's captor. "He doesn't look so good. What happened?"

"He passed out on me a ways back up the road," Luke decided to stick with the truth for now until he had a chance to sort out his lies. "Is there a doctor in town?"

Tom glanced up, somewhat surprised, and Luke remembered Johnson's deadly reputation. He quickly amended the question, "He'll be worth more alive, if I can keep him that way."

Nodding, Tom gathered the reins and turned Johnson's horse toward the end of the street. "Dr. Sullivan's office is this way. We'll probably have to wake him up, but he won't mind."

Luke prompted his horse to follow the deputy's lead, wanting to make sure Johnson was safely in the care of a physician before slipping away. He considered asking the doctor to bind his ribs first, but he would have to answer too many questions about how he had come to be so badly beaten.

The deputy stopped just outside a small frame house at the end of the street. He quickly scaled the steps and knocked on the door. A moment passed, and Luke saw a light flare in the front window. The door opened and a gray-haired man of small stature appeared in the doorway.

Words were quickly exchanged, and the doctor glanced in Luke's direction, his eyes wide with surprise. He hurried down the steps and peered into Johnson's face. "What happened to this man?"

"I'm not sure," Luke lowered the brim of his hat on his brow. "He keeled over by the campfire. He's still breathing, but that's about it."

"No bullet or knife wounds?"

"None that I saw."

The doctor nodded. "You fellas get him inside."

Luke dismounted and helped lift Johnson down from the horse. Tom staggered under the weight, and Luke couldn't stifle the groan as most of Johnson's bulk shifted unexpectedly to his shoulder.

"He's solid as a rock," the deputy observed, grappling for a better hold on Johnson's slack form. "Let's get him up the steps."

Luke nodded, wincing as pain shot through his rib cage, and he wished he'd left Johnson for the buzzards. Once inside the doctor's residence, they placed the patient on a narrow cot, and Dr. Sullivan wasted no time in examining him.

There was no response when the physician lifted Johnson's eyelids, and the old man frowned as he felt the patient's throat for a pulse.

"Is he alive?" the deputy asked.

With a nod, the doctor replied, "For now. Can't say it looks good. How long did you say he's been like this?"

Luke shrugged. "A couple of hours."

With an accusing look, Dr. Sullivan declared, "Moving him didn't do him any good."

"Neither would leaving him behind," Luke replied without hesitation.

"I'll just have to wait and see," Dr. Sullivan sighed. "No point in you two hovering over him."

"We'll check back with you after a while," Tom assured him, motioning for Luke to follow him outside.

Once they were down the steps, the deputy confided, "I don't think he's going to make it, but Dr. Sullivan will do everything he can. He doesn't like folks around when he's tending a patient."

Luke nodded, trying to think of the best possible way to part company with Tom McBride. "Don't let me keep you any longer, deputy. I'll just check into the hotel and get a bite to eat."

"Oh, you won't be able to get anything to eat this late," Tom warned him.

Luke hesitated. He had no intention of going near the hotel, and he'd only mentioned having dinner to make his departure sound plausible. Finally, he shrugged and said, "Doesn't matter. I can make up for dinner at breakfast."

The deputy's face brightened. "Tell you what, just come on back to my house and have some supper before going to the hotel. We had plenty left from dinner. Beef stew, apple pie—"

Shaking his head, Luke fervently groped for an excuse. "Your wife would skin you alive for bringing a stranger home to eat this late."

"I'm not married." The deputy would not be put off. "It's just me and my sister, and she'll be asleep by now."

Luke's first instinct was to refuse. He was anxious to get out of town, but refusing food after indicating that he was hungry would only arouse suspicion. He nodded in acceptance.

"You won't be sorry," Tom assured him. "My sister's one of the best cooks in town."

Katherine leaned back on the pillows she had propped against the headboard of her bed and seriously contemplated crying. There really wasn't much else she could do, but she rarely resorted to tears and only in the most dire of personal circumstances.

To anyone else, the demise of their hometown would be a very personal circumstance but, as acting mayor, Katherine had to maintain a sensible perspective on the entire situation. Anger toward her father flared unexpectedly, and she longed to toss the imposing stack of papers into the kitchen stove and burn the whole lot.

She had begged her father not to place Belle Plain in the running for a railroad stop, but he would not listen. He convinced every merchant and most of the townsfolk to invest their life's savings into a bond issue to build an impressive courthouse and a large jail.

"If we expect to be taken seriously by those railroad executives, we've got to look like a town on the rise," he had insisted. "If they come here and find some lawless little cow town, they'll pass us by without so much as a sidetrack."

Katherine drew a shuddering breath and began gathering the papers she had strewn across her bedspread. She shouldn't blame her father; his dream sounded good in theory, but she resented being left to shoulder the burden when the dream became a liability.

If Belle Plain wasn't chosen to be the next stop on the railroad, the town would go bankrupt, the citizens would be impoverished, and she would be held responsible. She would have refused the appointment of acting mayor in the wake of her father's death, but her brother would have been the next logical candidate. Poor Tom: she could never stand by and see him thrown to the lions.

Once the papers were sorted, she returned them to the top drawer of her dresser. No matter how many times she studied the documents, the conclusion was the same. Belle Plain would face the maturity of a twenty-five thousand-dollar bond, and the slim chance of luring the railroad to town was nonexistent now that the marshal had left.

"The railroad won't consider a town without law and order," Father had insisted. "Stuart Carey is the best lawman in these parts and worth every penny."

"Worth every penny," Katherine mimicked, slamming the dresser drawer shut. Her father's rough-hewn lawman had fallen head over heels in love with a sewing machine saleslady and handed in his badge to follow her to California. "I hope he spends the rest of his life sorting her thread samples."

She caught sight of her own reflection in the beveled mirror, and her expression grew more serious. She leaned toward the mirror, searching her face for telltale signs of her age. She had her father's fair hair and blue eyes, but her mother's gaunt features made her appear older than twenty-five. Tom had inherited Papa's coloring and good looks as well as his impulsive nature.

Always the serious one, she was the child everyone expected to do as she was told and mind her manners. Even as an adult, she rarely acted without careful consideration of the consequences. Never would she go traipsing off on a whim without a thought to those who depended on her, and she had little regard for those who did.

She pulled the worn flannel dressing gown a little closer around her, loving the feel of the threadbare material. It was her only self-indulgence; away from others, she gloried in the luxury of being wrinkled and faded. A gaping hole was still unmended over her elbow, and she decided against patching it altogether.

Downstairs, she heard the back door open. Tom was home early. She supposed his infamous bounty hunter hadn't shown, and she was glad. The last thing her brother needed was some gun-wielding scoundrel impressing him with stories of bandits and shootouts.

She heard the door close and the sound of boot heels on the kitchen floor. She hoped Tom would remember to wipe his feet, and she moved to open her door to call down a patient reminder. The sudden rise of voices stilled her steps.

"Have a seat at the table," she heard Tom instruct someone. "I'll make us a pot of coffee, and there's plenty of stew left from supper. You'd never get anything decent to eat at the hotel—not this late."

"I'm much obliged to you, deputy," a deep male voice met her ears just as she opened the door to her bedroom. "A home-cooked meal will be a treat."

"My sister's a real good cook, Mr. Johnson." An iron pan clattered against the stove, and the hinges on the cupboard creaked open. "You won't be disappointed, even if it is leftovers."

Katherine gripped the stair rail, not believing her ears. Tom had brought the bounty hunter home for supper! My God, the man was nothing more than a hired killer, and now he was sitting at her kitchen table.

Carefully, she made her way down the stairs, her slippered feet making no sound on the steps. She stood before the door leading into the kitchen and fingered the doorknob, trying to decide what to do. If she made a scene and insisted that the man leave, Tom would be humiliated, but the thought of such a detestable man in their home was more than a little unsettling.

The aromas of coffee perking and stew warming on the stove filled the kitchen, and she heard dishes rattle and silverware clink as her brother set the table for his guest.

"There's nothing like a home-cooked meal after a few days of trailing outlaws with nothing to eat but beans and jerky."

She almost laughed at Tom's words. What did he know about outlaws? The closest he'd come to making an arrest had been the time Mrs. Newman's dog made off with half of a baked chicken at the church picnic. He'd apprehended the hound before she could consume the bird, bones and all, thus saving the poor dog from a painful demise. The elderly lady had been so grateful that she promised Tom a puppy from the next litter.

The bounty hunter's voice drew her attention, making her forget about Mrs. Newman and her dog.

"I'll be obliged to you for making arrangements with the undertaker."

Arrangements. She shivered, more at the man's casual tone than his choice of words.

"I don't mind at all, Mr. Johnson," Tom assured him. "There's no undertaker in Belle Plain, but I'll see that he has a proper burial. There's no point in delaying your trip. If he does pull through, you can claim him on your way back."

Katherine could barely contain her angry gasp. The man had probably shot the prisoner deliberately and didn't even have the decency to see the man buried.

"You don't have to call me mister," the deep voice replied. "You make me feel like an old man."

Tom apologized, and they both chuckled slightly. How either of them could be jovial when a man was dying was beyond her.

"I don't know where my sister keeps anything," Tom stated in exasperation, opening one cabinet door after another. "Nothing is ever where it ought to be."

Katherine rolled her eyes. If a thing didn't jump out of the cabinet into his hand, Tom swore it wasn't there. Obviously, he meant to impress this bounty hunter with his hospitality, and she wouldn't spoil it for him. Her hand lingered on the doorknob, but she decided not to intrude.

Before she could turn back up the stairs, Tom jerked the kitchen door open, effectively dragging her into the room, still clutching the doorknob.

"Katherine, I was on my way up to ask you something." He gestured over his shoulder. "We have company. This is Caleb Johnson, the man I've been telling you about."

She could only stare at the man sprawled in one of her

kitchen chairs, and she felt like a rabbit rounding a corner and coming face to face with a hungry wolf.

"Well, say something, sis," Tom prompted. "You don't want him to feel unwelcome, do you?"

❖2❖

IF HE WAS surprised by her sudden entry into the kitchen, he hid it well behind a lazy grin. On the contrary, Caleb Johnson appeared to be absolutely enchanted by her embarrassment at being caught eavesdropping, and the only one oblivious to her predicament was Tom. Righting herself, Katherine released her death grip on the doorknob and forced her attention to her brother.

"I've looked everywhere," Tom insisted. "But I just can't seem to find those pickles Miss Lillian brought us when Pa died. I know we have a jar or two left. Didn't we have some of them just last—"

"I always keep the canned goods right here." Katherine jerked open the nearest cabinet door and produced an unopened jar of his favorite pickles.

"Thanks, sis," he said, taking the jar. Without a hitch, he turned back to his guest and made introductions. "Caleb Johnson, this is my older sister, Katherine McBride."

She flinched. Why did Tom always feel compelled to refer to her as his older sister? For pity's sake, she was his only sister, not that she should care what a man like Caleb Johnson thought of her.

Casually, the bounty hunter unfolded his tall frame from the chair and stood towering over them both. "Evening, ma'am. I hope we didn't disturb you."

He fingered the brim of his hat but didn't offer his hand, and for that she was grateful. His dark gaze slid over her, and she felt as if she were being appraised. She refused to look away and did a little appraising of her own.

The first thing she noticed was the trail dust clinging to his dark clothes and then the way those dusty clothes hugged his sinewy frame. The cut and fabric of his clothes were costly, not at all suited for arduous travel over rough, open country. Tom had described him as a seasoned tracker, and she wondered why he had set out on such a journey without more sensible attire. Finally, her gaze settled on the deadly pair of pistols holstered around his lean waist, each weapon tied low on his muscular thighs.

Schooling her thoughts, her eyes met his, and she wished she had not come down those stairs. His were the most wicked eyes she'd ever seen, the color of whiskey and temptation, and she could feel them lingering on her face like a physical touch.

"Yeah, sis, I thought you'd be asleep by now." Tom turned back to the stove, carefully stirring the steaming pot of stew. "What are you doing down here, anyway?"

To ask if you've completely taken leave of your senses.

Instead, she lied, "I came down for a drink of water."

Johnson's expression didn't waiver, but Katherine swore she saw a flicker of amusement in those luring eyes as they took in her flannel-clad form, noting every faded inch. Any proper lady would be mortified to meet a complete stranger in her dressing gown, but she was more angered than humiliated. How dare this assassin make himself at home in her kitchen and cause her to feel like an interloper?

The coffee was ready and Tom filled two cups. "Well,

I'm glad you had a chance to meet Caleb. It's not everyday a legend walks into your kitchen.''

"Good evening, Mr. Johnson." She forced her most reserved tone, refusing to play along with Tom's hero worship. "I trust you had a safe journey."

A halfhearted smile touched his full lips, and she realized how handsome he must be beneath the dark growth of whiskers and unkempt mane of black hair. His hair would be shiny and silky straight, if washed and combed properly.

He sank back into the chair, and she didn't miss the weariness in his eyes. She felt a twinge of grudging sympathy for him, and she could only guess how difficult it must be to escort a dangerous fugitive across open country. No wonder he hadn't taken time to attend his hair or beard.

As if he read her thoughts, he ran his hand along his shadowed jaw. "I hope you'll excuse my appearance. I had no idea I would be meeting a lady."

"I understand you've been on the trail for some time now," she replied, imagining the feel of his beard grating against her own palm. Her face grew warm, and she took two steps backward toward the stairs and the safety of her room. "Please make yourself at ease, and I'll leave you gentlemen to finish discussing . . . business."

A sudden knock at the back door drew everyone's attention, and Tom rushed to see who was there. Katherine didn't miss the way Johnson's hand fell to his holster, as if he expected the devil himself to be standing on the other side of that door. She held her breath as Tom turned the knob, wondering just what sort of danger had followed this man to her own back steps.

"Deputy, you'd best get down to the Millers' house."

Relieved, Katherine recognized John Dillard's voice and the usual Saturday night complaint, and she felt silly for allowing her imagination to get the better of her common sense. Dora and Mel Miller ended every week by fighting like cats and dogs, and she should have known that would be the reason for the sudden knock.

"They're going at it good tonight," John reported. "You can hear dishes bustin' all over the place."

Tom glanced anxiously toward his guest at the table and then back at Katherine. She knew exactly what he was going to say before he could ask. "Sis, will you see after Caleb's dinner? I'll be back quick as I can, but I reckon he'd rather not have to wait until then to have his supper."

Deep inside the pockets of her faded robe, Katherine clenched her fists, wishing she could tell Tom to play waiter to his own company. Dillard stood just inside the door waiting for Tom: he would love to tell everyone in town that Katherine refused to serve their company so her brother could do his job.

"Why, of course, I will, Tom." She refused to glance in the direction of their guest. "After all, you are the law."

She was the kind of woman a man longed for when he wanted to remember what it was like to feel decent again.

Luke watched the golden braid swing across her back, keeping time with the gentle sway of her hips, and wondered how long her hair would be when unbound and loose about her shoulders. Her skin was like sweet cream, smooth and pale, marred only by a slight flush just above her cheekbones.

It had been a long time since he'd sat at a kitchen table while a pretty woman prepared his meal, and this one was prettier than any he could recall. She had that sweet, wholesome look, and he couldn't keep from watching her. It was easy to let himself pretend he was some miner or factory worker coming home to his sweet little wife.

Easy, that is, until she turned around and fixed her contemptuous gaze on him. She looked at him as if he were a snake slithering over her kitchen table, poised to bite her if she ventured too close. Her blue eyes narrowed slightly, and he didn't miss the flush that crept up her throat when she realized he'd been watching her.

"More coffee, Mr. Johnson?" she asked. A slight tilt held her chin.

"Thank you, ma'am, I'd like that." All he really wanted was to crawl into a real bed and die, but his presence rankled her, and he couldn't resist pushing her a little further. "Your brother told me what a fine cook you were, but he didn't do you justice."

"Thank you." She managed to refill his cup without letting so much as the hem of her faded blue robe touch the table. She replaced the coffeepot on the stove and began fidgeting with the frayed end of the belt knotted at her tiny waist.

The deputy's claim that his sister was a good cook hadn't been idle bragging. The food was the best he'd eaten in months, and he finished two large bowls of stew before she offered dessert. When he accepted, she placed a pie tin containing half of an apple pie on the table along with a clean plate, knife, and fork.

"You don't have to be embarrassed," he finally said as he served himself a generous slice of the pie that was still slightly warm. The heady aroma of cinnamon rose from the chunks of baked apple, reminding him of home as drops of juice from the filling oozed onto his plate and fingers.

She rounded on him, her expression perplexed. "Embarrassed? Embarrassed by what?"

"That ragged dressing gown." He licked the stickiness from his thumb and reached for the steaming cup, savoring the first fresh coffee he'd had in days. "Believe me, I've seen worse."

Too late he realized he'd gone too far when she said, "I suppose you have seen worse if you're in the habit of coming into people's homes uninvited in the middle of the night."

"I was invited," he reminded her. "And it's hardly the

middle of the night. For a Saturday night, especially. If you had a beau, you'd still be holding hands on the parlor sofa."

Anger flushed her face, but her voice was steady. "My personal life is none of your business."

"Whose business is it?" he countered. "I'm willing to bet you're prettier than half the women in this town. So, there has to be a reason no one is calling on you."

With more force than necessary, she placed his dishes in the basin. "I will not explain myself to the likes of you."

"Ah, a bad temper," he concluded, draining his coffee cup and reminding himself that she was referring to Johnson. He shook his head in mock disdain, quite enjoying her barely contained fury. "Never cared for a woman with a nasty disposition, either."

"I certainly hope I bear no resemblance to the sort of woman you would care for." She twisted a faded dishrag in her hands, and the color in her cheeks heightened. "Painted harlots and dance hall hostesses are more to your liking, I'm sure."

He laughed at that. High-toned and proper, Miss McBride surely considered that a dreadful insult, when it was the God's honest truth. Whores were less complicated and certainly more accommodating, but he couldn't resist matching wits with her. "Every now and then, I like to treat myself to a prickly old maid; they're always a challenge but worth the effort."

The crimson stain drained from her face, and the only hint of color was the seething blue fire in her eyes. If looks could kill, Luke knew he would surely be a dead man. Her lips moved, but no words came forth, only a shallow gasping sound.

Before he could decide whether to apologize or leave, forsaking dessert, gunfire erupted in the street outside without warning, and she started, turning desperately toward the back door. Luke was instantly on his feet, the wooden chair grating sharply across the kitchen floor.

Damn, how could anyone be after him so soon? Johnson must have come to and warned the doctor.

"Tom!" she cried, and he was barely able to stop her before she jerked the door open.

"You want to get yourself shot?" he demanded, catching her around the waist. He couldn't tell her that the shots were most likely meant for him. She would only panic more than she was already. "Just stay put, and you won't get hurt."

"My brother's out there!" she insisted, struggling against his grip.

"Your brother's the deputy marshal," he reminded her as she squirmed against him. She was firm and soft all at the same time, and she filled his arms as if she were made for him. His palms ached to feel the weight of her breasts, but he didn't dare start her screaming.

He did tighten his hold to stop her squirming, which only resulted in crushing her more closely against him. "He can take care of himself."

"No, he can't," she countered, and tears filled her eyes as she swiveled her head to look up at him. "Mr. Johnson, please, he can't take care of himself. You will help him, won't you?"

Luke was unprepared for the way the shimmering of unshed tears in her eyes hit him, and he loosened his grip on her. If those shots were meant for him, he sure as hell didn't want her in danger.

"All right, but you wait here."

"You no-good cheat!"

"You're drunk, Charlie. Put the gun down, for Pete's sake."

Luke rounded the corner and saw a scene he'd witnessed too many times. Two men faced each other, weapons drawn, prepared to kill or be killed over a few dollars wagered in a card game. Tom McBride stood between the two men, his eyes wide with panic.

"Fellas, please, take it easy," the young deputy implored. "We can work this out."

"You'd best get out of here, Tom," one man ordered. "There's no point in you getting hurt."

"There's no need for anyone to get hurt," Tom insisted. "Just put your guns away and tell me what happened."

"This son of a bitch cheated me, and I aim to get my money back!" the one called Charlie shouted.

"Like hell I did!" his adversary countered. "You're just a piss-poor card player."

Luke raised his weapon and fired into the air, startling all three men. "Drop the pistols," he ordered, his aim steady. "You heard the deputy."

The second man's hand hovered near his holster. "This ain't your fight, mister."

"Don't make it your last," Luke warned.

The man hesitated, glancing back at his foe. "He cheated me out of six weeks' wages!"

"Is that what you'd like on your headstone?" Luke felt nothing but contempt for the drover. "If you're man enough to put your money on the table, be man enough to lose it." Reluctantly, each man tossed his pistol into the dust, and Luke motioned for Tom to gather the weapons.

"Better lock 'em both up for the night," he advised Tom who hurried to scoop the pistols from the ground. "All it will take is a few shots of bourbon, and they'll be right back where they started."

The deputy nodded, finally drawing his own weapon and directing the dejected duelers toward the jail. "Come on, fellas, things will look better in the morning."

Luke turned to find several people gathered, watching him with avid interest. Katherine McBride stood at the end of the street, a heavy woolen cloak huddled around her shoulders, and her eyes were wide with disbelief.

Luke holstered his weapon and looked away. The last thing he'd wanted to do was draw attention to himself, and here he was, putting on a show for the whole damned town. The few onlookers murmured among themselves but slowly turned toward their own homes, leaving only Katherine standing before him.

"You saved his life," she stated in a voice that was little more than a whisper. "You saved all their lives."

"I'm no hero," he reminded her. "Besides, there was no money in it."

Before she could respond, the old doctor rounded the corner as if expecting to find the street littered with wounded men. "I heard shots!"

"Just a dispute over a card game. No one was hurt," Luke said, hoping to dismiss the doctor's concern. He hadn't planned on seeing Dr. Sullivan again, but he did remember to ask, "How's the prisoner?"

Dr. Sullivan approached him. "He didn't make it. Never even opened his eyes."

The rain had stopped, and Luke was grateful for that, at least. There was nothing he hated more than graveyards, but he had to get through the charade of burying Caleb Johnson while the townsfolk still believed the dead man to be a wanted outlaw named Luke Cantrell. Once the grave was filled and the marker in place, he could head south, a free man.

The procession was meager; Tom McBride, the town preacher, and he were the only pallbearers. Katherine McBride followed in dignified silence. Luke could tell her pride was still smarting from last night's confrontation. Most likely Miss McBride was not accustomed to losing her self-control, especially while wearing her dressing gown.

When they reached the open grave, Tom motioned for

the casket to be placed on the ground. The men stood back, and the preacher fished a prayer book from his pocket and cleared his throat. Katherine clasped her hands before her, never so much as looking in Luke's direction, her expression stoic as the scripture was read.

"There is no man that hath power over the spirit to retain the spirit; neither hath he power in the day of death." Preacher Meeks' voice was strong and sure, and Luke felt that the words were directed at him. "Neither shall wickedness deliver those that are given to it. Amen."

"Amen," Katherine and her brother repeated.

The preacher motioned to two men standing nearby, and they hurried forward with shovels. The first spade full of dirt made a hollow sound, scattering across the washed pine of the coffin. Luke swallowed hard, watching the gaping grave fill with dark, moist earth.

"Mr. Johnson, you knew the man, perhaps you could say a few words about him."

Luke jerked his eyes toward the preacher, barely recognizing the alias bestowed upon him by the bounty hunter's death. He shrugged slightly, not at all prepared to deliver his own eulogy. Tom and Katherine exchanged curious glances, and finally he said, "Luke Cantrell is a man better off dead."

Meeks' eyes narrowed slightly, and Katherine gasped out loud.

"How can you say something like that?" she demanded, her eyes cold and contemptuous. "What if you were the poor soul being buried with naught but strangers to mourn you?"

A smile threatened at the irony of her question, but only for a moment. Before he could reply, the undertaker speared the crude, wooden marker into the soft earth with the name *Luke Cantrell* lettered in bold, sprawling script.

"I don't suppose a man like you can comprehend the sadness of such a plight." She knelt before the marker and placed a bouquet of dewy wildflowers on the soft mound of dirt. "After all, death is your commodity."

"Katherine," her brother admonished, helping her to her feet. "Dr. Sullivan said the man's heart gave out; Caleb had nothing to do with his death."

"Maybe not, but he'll stand to profit, just the same." She brushed the dirt from the front of her dress and stepped back from the grave. "I pity you, Mr. Johnson."

"Don't bother." Luke's voice sounded hard, even to his own ears, but he would not be lectured on morality while standing over his own grave. "Save your pity for someone who needs it, Miss McBride."

Katherine shrugged away from her brother's grasp on her arm, unable to look away from the bounty hunter's retreating form leaving the cemetery. "Let me alone. Do you see now what sort of person he is?"

"A lost soul if ever I saw one," Pastor Meeks said, replacing the prayer book in his coat pocket. He shook his head. "Great is the harvest, but the laborers are few."

"It would take a force of a thousand to bring that one back into the fold." Katherine drew her heavy woolen shawl more closely about her shoulders.

Pastor Meeks took her hand and admonished, "Have you said so much as one prayer for his soul?"

Taken aback, Katherine nodded reluctantly. Thunder rumbled in the distance and the pastor made his excuses and hurried home, leaving her and Tom alone.

"We'd better get going ourselves." Tom scanned the dark clouds gathering in the east. "Before we get soaked."

Katherine turned toward the far corner of the cemetery, a second bunch of flowers in her hand. She stood over her father's grave, admiring the marble headstone that had only been in place a month. She'd spared no expense, sending all the way to Dallas for the monument. She knelt and placed the flowers in the ornate vase designed for that purpose.

"He'd be proud of it, sis." Tom placed a gentle hand on her shoulder, and she immediately covered it with her own. "Real proud."

"I wish we could have done the same for Mama." Tears threatened and she tightened her hold on his hand. "She did without so many things."

"Never without love." Tom drew her to her feet. "Papa wanted to give her the world, but she was happy with a roof over her head and two healthy children. She said so many times."

"It wasn't enough." The memory of their mother's faded clothes and blistered hands haunted her. "She deserved better."

"She did," Tom agreed, leading her out of the cemetery. "She truly did."

They hurried down Hall Street toward the house that had been home for eight years. They had found prosperity in Belle Plain, and their father's knack for politics and blarney had given them influence. The first raindrops of the storm chased after them, and they just cleared the front porch before the downpour began.

Katherine barely had time to revel in escaping a soaking before she noticed Joe Perry seated in their front porch swing, his right foot balanced across his left knee. He rose to his feet and crossed the porch.

"Where have you two been?" he demanded. He held out his palm to reveal a gleaming pocket watch that read two o'clock. Impatiently, he snapped the watch closed. "I've been waiting over half an hour. I told you I would drop by today, and my time is valuable."

"You said you might drop by sometime after church," Katherine countered, her mood soured further at the prospect of bickering over the town budget. "My time is just as valuable; from now on set a definite time for us to meet, and you won't be kept waiting."

"We were at a funeral," Tom offered by way of explanation, both for their absence and Katherine's mood.

"A funeral?" Joe removed his hat. "Anyone I know?"

"No one any of us knew," Tom explained. "A gambler being brought in to Abilene on murder charges. He died on the way."

"I see," he replied, glancing apologetically at Katherine. "I'm sorry if my patience is short, but I am anxious to get this town's business in order. First and foremost, what are we going to do now that there's no marshal?"

Katherine glanced at Tom, not wanting to discuss this in front of him. "That is only one of many things we have to consider. I have all the papers in order on the dining room table. Why don't we go inside and get our business out of the way before the whole day is gone?"

"You two go ahead," Tom said by way of excusing himself. "I've got prisoners to see after and a good bit of paperwork to fill out myself."

Katherine didn't miss her brother's subtle reminder that he was already doing the work of the marshal. She watched him cross the street, avoiding puddles as he turned toward the center of town, reminding herself that last night's episode could have turned deadly had it not been for Caleb Johnson. The thought of the bounty hunter's arrogant indifference toward the death of his prisoner quickly cooled any gratitude she might have felt for his presence. Still the possibilities of what might have happened had he not stepped in to stop the argument left her torn. She would be glad to see Caleb Johnson leave town, but she hated to see the only semblance of protection for her brother go with him.

Joe Perry cleared his throat slightly and Katherine whirled in his direction. "Joe, I—I'm sorry," she stammered. "My thoughts are somewhat scattered today."

"Perfectly understandable," he assured her, tapping his hat against his trouser leg. "Why don't we get to that budget so that I can be on my way?"

"Of course, let's get started." She hurried to open the front door and invite him inside.

Katherine offered to make a pot of coffee, but Joe had the good manners to insist that she not go to so much trouble. Instead, she poured two glasses of cold buttermilk and led him toward the dining room. The long table was covered with stacks of ledgers and financial reports.

She seated herself across from him and waited patiently while he studied the figures she'd prepared. The rain beat hard against the dining room windows, and she jumped slightly when thunder boomed overhead. Unaffected by the storm, Joe continued to scan the various ledgers, comparing them to her reports.

"Well, everything certainly seems to be in order," he finally declared, discreetly wiping buttermilk from his heavily waxed mustache with his index finger. "You certainly have a talent for figures."

"Thank you," she managed.

"I hate to think what a mess this town would have been in if it weren't for you." He shook his head and chuckled. "We all figured you were helping Will, but we never knew how much."

"I don't want anyone to know," she insisted. Her father had been a brilliant politician but a poor administrator. For the past three years, Katherine had prepared the budgets he presented to the town council. "He still deserves their respect."

"I meant no disrespect." He placed the papers aside and studied her across the table. "The councilmen know William McBride made this town what it is, but they also know you're the one who made a lot of it possible. Otherwise, they never would have insisted that you serve as mayor."

"It's only temporary," she reminded him. The assurance of a fall election and that no one would expose her father's haphazard style of leadership were the only reasons she accepted the position and the responsibility. "You might find yourself in the job before much longer."

"Oh, no," he laughed. "My little law practice keeps me quite busy, thank you. Besides, I'd need your help more than Will did. You have an excellent mind for figures."

She shrugged. "I like numbers; they make sense."

"And they don't lie." He took a deep breath and brought up the subject she'd hoped to avoid. "The bond will come due in August, and there's still no word from the railroad. You know how bad this could be."

"Yes, I know." She folded her hands on the table. "You were convinced we would have no problem securing the stop."

"Your father convinced me. He could talk a bird out of a tree, but he's gone now."

Katherine tried not to react, but she deeply resented all the town's problems being laid at her father's grave. Not once since he was appointed as chairman of the town council did Joe ever speak against the hope of attracting the railroad. Not that Papa would have listened. She had been the only one to warn him of the risks.

"Hiring a new marshal is our most pressing problem right now." He took advantage of her silence and pressed on to another subject he knew she would rather avoid.

"It took three months to find Stuart Carey," she pointed out. "Not that he was a godsend, but we can't settle for just anyone. Tom will do the best he can in the meantime."

"His best will not impress those railroad men." He leaned forward, speaking in a loud whisper even though Tom was a mile away. "It's all over town how Tom stood like a scared kid, pleading for those two drunks to act nice."

''There are times when rational discussion can solve problems.''

''Katherine, Belle Plain stands as good a chance as any other town for the railroad, but we've got to have law. Tom can't do it; you'd better find someone who can.''

❖ 3 ❖

KATHERINE EYED THE top of the hotel staircase, loath-ing the task before her. Just up those stairs, at the end of the hall in room twelve, was the only hope she had of saving Belle Plain: an arrogant bounty hunter whom she'd all but called an infidel. She'd known it last night, the moment she saw him, pistol drawn, facing two gun-wielding drovers without a flinch. Caleb Johnson was the perfect candidate for interim marshal. He was the only candidate. If only she'd remembered that fact today at the cemetery and held her tongue.

His indifference to the dead man had so appalled her that she'd forgotten her manners and her dilemma. Belle Plain had to have a marshal, even it was the devil himself. Surely, Mr. Johnson would delight in refusing her request, and she would be forced to listen to his arrogant account of her surly ways and sharp tongue.

The weight of the basket on her arm slowed her pace, making each step more difficult than the last, but she hoped the food would supersede an apology. She gripped the rail-ing and forced herself up the staircase. She was doing this for the town, not herself. Finally she stood before the door, catching a glimpse of her own reflection in the highly polished brass numbers nailed to the door. She'd taken pains with her appearance, and she feared he would notice the cologne and earbobs and recognize them for what they were. Was there anything more pathetic than an old maid playing the coquette?　Her arm was like lead when she raised her hand to knock. There was no answer and for a moment she thought he might not be in the room. From somewhere down the hall she heard a woman's stifled laughter, high-pitched and bawdy.

"For the love of God, Maddie, do you want everyone in town to know you're in here?"

From three doors away, Katherine couldn't recognize the gruff scolding voice, and the name Maddie meant nothing to her. The woman laughed again, though not as loud, and Katherine felt a blush sting her face when next she heard the man's coarse laughter.

Hotel rooms were intimate places, and suddenly she wished she had not come here. She could leave a note with the clerk, inviting Mr. Johnson to dinner tomorrow night. That would be much more proper and safer. She glanced back down the hall, knowing her courage would fail her if she waited another day.

"Who's there?"

Immediately, she recognized his deep voice and turned to face the gleaming brass numbers. She hesitated. "Katherine McBride."

"The door's open. Come in."

She turned the knob slowly, and peered inside the spartan room. A narrow bed was wedged in the corner, facing the room's only window, and beside the bed stood a servicable three-drawer chest.

It occurred to her that she had never been inside a room at the hotel, and she was surprised by the stark decor. She glanced about the room, wondering where Caleb Johnson was.

To her mortification he stood shirtless before the wash-stand, working a towel over his cleanly shaven face. His dark hair was combed back, gleaming wet in the lamplight. A trickle of water snaked across his neck, and she watched it inch down his broad back. Mesmerized, she couldn't look away as the shining droplet coursed over his bare skin only to disappear, absorbed by the waistband of his trousers.

He turned slowly, his expression growing pleased when he found her watching him. She swallowed hard at the sight of his bare chest, his skin a dusky golden hue, marred only by a series of nasty bruises mapped across his midsection.

She couldn't help but gasp at the sight, and she nearly let the heavy basket fall to the floor. Righting herself and her burden, she placed the basket on an unadorned table near the door. "What happened to you?"

He only shrugged as he tossed the damp towel on the washstand. "I was outnumbered."

"Shouldn't you see Dr. Sullivan?"

He shook his head, reaching for a roll of clean linen bandages. "My ribs just need binding for a few days. I could use some help, though."

She hesitated, glancing back toward the open door and into the hallway. "I only stopped by to—"

He grinned slightly, his teeth white and even. "I promise not to bite you."

Goaded by that, she took the length of linen in her hands, studying the angry bruises on his abdomen. Not for one minute would she allow Caleb Johnson to think he intimidated her. "Are you sure nothing is broken?"

"It doesn't hurt to breathe," he offered, raising his arms to allow her better access to his midsection. "I've been busted up worse than this."

His flesh was warm and damp beneath her fingers, and she dared not meet his glance. The tang of soap and shaving

lather tickled her nostrils, and she couldn't prevent herself
from inhaling deeply. She cleared her throat hoping to dis-
guise her ragged breath as a cough. "Does this happen
often?"

"Too often to suit me."

He spoke softly, and she could feel the words feather
against her face. She focused her attention on the task, but
even that was a pitfall. Each time she circled his waist with
the bandage, he drew nearer, and she could feel the heat of
his body beneath her fingers.

She glanced up to find their faces mere inches apart.
"Perhaps, you should find another line of work," she suggested, hoping for an innocent lead-in to her proposition.

"What would you suggest?" he whispered, his words
husky as he let his arms fall to his sides. "I'm not the type
of man to work behind a store counter or wait tables. Death
is my commodity, remember?"

She swallowed hard. He smiled slightly, but she would
not be distracted. "There are plenty of opportunities for
someone with your . . . experience."

He reached out and fingered one of the garnet earbobs,
his hand brushing slightly against her throat. "Here in Belle
Plain?"

She gave the bandage a sharp tug, causing him to swear.
It was her turn to smile as she tied off the length of cloth.
He inspected her handiwork with grudging approval.

"What's in the basket?" he asked, reaching for a clean
shirt draped across a chair.

"I brought your dinner. My brother told me that you
refused his invitation to have supper with us tonight." At
that, he glanced toward her, and she confessed, "He said
it was because of my rudeness."

"I make you uncomfortable, Miss McBride, and I didn't
think you'd want me at your dinner table."

She neatly folded what was left of the length of bandage.
"I never said you made me uncomfortable."

"You didn't have to," he caught her hands in his. "A man can tell, even when a woman doesn't want him to."

"I'm sure the sort of women you're accustomed to are quite easy to read." She pulled her hands from his. "Don't judge me by their standards."

"Whose standards are you judging me by?" he countered, catching her gently by the arm. "You sized me up with one look."

"Was I wrong?" she demanded, ducking away from his touch. "You track men for money, preying on their misfortune without thought of the consequences."

Luke's opinion of bounty hunters was far worse than hers, and he was hard-pressed to deny her accusations. But if he was to have any chance of escape, everyone in Belle Plain had to believe he was Caleb Johnson, so he was forced to defend his own enemy. "I have my reasons," he finally replied. "Besides, if I don't do it, folks would just pay someone else. Why shouldn't I have the money?"

"Why should anyone?" she countered. "We're not barbarians. The law should deal with those wanted for crimes, not men looking to collect reward money. Has it ever even occurred to you that some of the men you've captured may have been innocent?"

Luke chuckled at the irony of her question. "Believe it or not, the thought has occurred to me."

"Very well, laugh all you want, Mr. Johnson. It only proves you have no sense of decency or respect for the law, and you would never consider anything more important than money." She turned to leave, her expression resigned. "I should never have bothered you."

"What exactly is it you want from me?"

"Want?" She paused near the door.

"You didn't fix yourself up and bring me supper out of kindness, and you're not the type who goes looking for a man." He crossed the room, covering her hand with his own as she reached for the door. Snatching her hand away, she relinquished her hold on the door.

"You want something . . . what is it?"

Necessity won out over pride. "I need a marshal, Mr. Johnson, and you're the only man for the job. "

"What's your hurry? Surely, you could stick around a few more days, just until I hear back from Abilene."

Luke shook his head as Tom McBride sealed the envelope containing the meager personal effects of the man buried in the Belle Plain cemetery. "Wish I could, but I don't have the time to spare."

Indeed, he was anxious to put as much distance between himself and Belle Plain as possible. He'd never been one to take good fortune for granted, and he intended to take his leave while freedom was securely in his grasp and before Katherine McBride could again approach him about being marshal.

"On the trail of another outlaw?" The deputy's eyes all but sparkled at the thought, and Luke couldn't help but resent his admiration of Caleb Johnson.

Had events not turned in Luke's favor, he might very well be the one whose razor and spare change were being sealed over to the state to be claimed by any surviving family. Of course, there would be no one asking after the welfare of Luke Cantrell, and he doubted Johnson had any family.

"It never ends," he replied, rising from the chair opposite the desk. "I appreciate all your help, deputy."

"I appreciate *your* help," Tom countered. "Don't think I don't know that you saved my neck the other night."

The humble expression on the young man's face almost made Luke ashamed of deceiving him the way he was. If the truth were ever revealed, Tom McBride would be a laughingstock, but he wasn't willing to hang to protect the deputy's feelings.

"You get used to dealing with those types," he reassured him. "They have too much to drink, win a few hands of cards, and think they're ready to take on the world."

Tom nodded, as if promising to be more careful the next time. Luke had to look away, pretending to study the wanted posters neatly displayed near the door. He didn't want to think about what might happen to Tom McBride the next time he stumbled into a gunfight, and he didn't want to care.

"I need you to sign off on this package with me, as a witness that it was sealed by more than one person."

Luke hesitated before taking the stub of a pencil from Tom. He had made sure that Johnson's pockets were free of any identification in the event his body had to be buried in the wilderness, and he was in sole possession of the arrest warrant bearing his own name.

For all he knew, Johnson could neither read nor write, but he refused to brand himself an ignorant by making an *X* on the paper.

He scribbled the initials *C.J.* across the seal of the envelope. The deputy only grinned when he tossed the pencil on the desk.

Tom placed the envelope inside a small safe and locked it away. "You'll be the envy of every lawman east of St. Louis when word gets out how easy a time you had bringing that one in."

"I doubt many folks will be that interested in . . . Cantrell." Luke managed not to stumble over his own name. "He's small potatoes."

"He *was*." Tom opened the second drawer of the desk and produced a printed notice. "No need to post this now, but I reckon it's already posted in every other town in Texas."

Luke accepted the paper, scarcely believing his own eyes.

MURDERER WANTED—DEAD OR ALIVE!!
LUKE CANTRELL

The smaller print went on to relay an elaborate account of what had actually been a minor skirmish, portraying him as a cutthroat who had cheated and killed a man in cold blood for what money he had left. The father of the dead man was posting a reward of his own, with no strings attached.

"Ten thousand dollars!" Luke looked up in disbelief.

"Isn't that something?" Tom practically beamed. "And you were worried about losing a five hundred-dollar bonus because he died."

"But the folks in Cutter's Creek only put up one thousand—for a live prisoner," Luke insisted, distinctly recalling Johnson's words.

"This must be a separate reward, offered by an awfully wealthy man who didn't take kindly to his son being killed over a card game." Tom folded the notice and concluded, "That much money would send a blind man looking for Cantrell."

"And everyone I ever knew," Luke said more to himself. He didn't regret his vagabond life, but he couldn't claim one friend who would value his life more than a reward of that size.

"That's for sure," Tom agreed. "You can bet every bounty hunter in the state is making plans for that money. Just wait until they hear you brought him in without even knowing about it."

"How long will that take?"

Tom shrugged. "Don't really know. I'll send a wire off to the sheriff in Abilene, and he'll notify the marshal in Cutter's Creek. Might be a month before word gets through and they send your money."

A month. A month wasn't so bad. He could lay low for that long.

"Those old boys on the trail won't know until they ride into town somewhere. We had a fella come through here back in the fall; he was trailing a bank robber who had already been caught, sentenced, and paroled. It's a good thing we told him he was too late, or he probably would have shot the man for a reward that had already been paid. Yep, it looks like Belle Plain is the only place where no one will be looking for Luke Cantrell."

Tom went on to tell other accounts of the ironies of men wanted for crimes, but all Luke could think of was the fact that the name Luke Cantrell would be on the lips of every bounty hunter, county sheriff, and truant officer for five hundred miles.

"You're sure a lucky man, Caleb." Tom carefully placed the notice in the desk drawer."

Katherine felt her pocket for the key that would unlock the door to her father's office and slipped inside the dark room. She raised the shade of the window that faced the alley, allowing ample light into the room without signaling to the entire town that someone was in the mayor's office. Slowly her eyes became accustomed to the dimness, and she began her search of the mahogany desk for the file regarding the marshal's office. Several men had responded to the advertisement she had placed in the Denver paper, and she was certain any one of them would be willing to accept a belated offer.

She had always felt her father had made a hasty choice by hiring Stuart Carey. In his letter, the flashy lawman had included a newspaper clipping bearing a photograph of himself alongside Wyatt Earp in Dodge City, and her father had been sold.

"That's what we need in this town!" he declared, ignoring her pleas to check references and consider other applicants. "A lawman with a ready-made reputation will make the railroad sit up and take notice."

Behind a stack of blueprints, she caught sight of the file

and retrieved it. She hurried to sort through the papers, mostly scrawled in barely legible script. One man was just out of the Cavalry, another serving as a deputy in Nebraska.

She wasn't certain she knew what to look for in a candidate, but any man in that file would be a better choice than Caleb Johnson. Searching this file is what she should have been doing last night instead of trying to coax him into the job.

She hated the fact that she was allowing his refusal to irritate her. She had made a business offer that he declined, and that should be the end of it. If only he hadn't laughed.

Katherine flipped through a few more letters, trying not to dwell on being dismissed like an impetuous child. How foolish she'd felt, standing there in the hallway of the hotel with the door to his room closing in her face.

"You'll need more than earbobs and fried chicken to lure me into playing lawman," he'd advised her just before the door closed completely, and she had heard him laughing inside the room.

Forcing her attention to the papers on the desk, she assured herself that he had laughed at the idea of being marshal, not at her. Still, age and maturity hadn't eased the sting of being the brunt of classroom teasing, and she was ever cautious to present a flawless image. Never again would she be mocked because of her faded clothes or scuffed shoes. She was a lady of prominence now, and she wouldn't let the likes of Caleb Johnson cause her a moment of self-doubt.

Reading through the letters, Katherine decided that the applicants all had one thing in common—they saw being a Texas marshal as means of advancement and of attaining notoriety. Each letter bore accounts of shoot-outs with bandits and Indians. Two men claimed to have killed the same fugitive: one in Arizona, the other in Montana.

Finally, she selected the man recently discharged from

the Army. She would write a letter to him tonight, insisting, of course, on a letter of recommendation from his former commanding officer. That decided, she replaced the remaining applications in the folder, this time in order of their qualifications. She might very well have to contact more than one man before finding a marshal.

She couldn't help but regret that Caleb Johnson had refused to even consider taking the job. He could have started right away, eliminating the need for a search. She supposed it was for the best, considering his scorn for the law, but she doubted that even Stuart Carey would have put himself between Tom and two pistol-wielding drunks.

Leaning back in the chair, Katherine could only wonder what kind of man would track men for money and then risk his life for no reason other than saving the life of a stranger.

The kind I need to keep Tom from getting killed.

Luke stepped out of the marshal's office and turned toward the hotel, trying to decide what the hell he was going to do now. With a king's ransom on his head, there would be no haven for him, not even in Mexico. Lawmen and bounty hunters alike would be on his trail, and nothing as trivial as a foreign border would stop them from trying to collect the reward.

Ten thousand dollars. Few people he knew would ever see that much money in a lifetime, and turning in a wanted man would be child's play for such an amount.

He stepped aside as a woman leading a little boy hurried past him on the wooden sidewalk. She glanced at him with obvious apprehension and recognition, drawing the child closer to her side as if to shield him from so much as Luke's sidelong glance. By now the good folks of Belle Plain were well aware that the notorious bounty hunter, Caleb Johnson, had ridden into their town to bury a prisoner and his presence was not welcome.

Better that than having them know who he really was.

The irony of the situation wasn't lost on him, and he wondered if somewhere the devil himself was posting the notice for Johnson to see. Ten thousand dollars right in his hand and the poor bastard didn't live to collect it or even know about it. What could be more hellish than that?

He leaned against the storefront, making a quick appraisal of the town. Three saloons bracketed the main street, two smaller ones side by side facing the larger. Experience told him that the larger one would offer a better opportunity for a profitable game of poker, while the others would cater to the more carnal needs.

As his vision traveled farther down the street, the nature of the businesses grew more decent. The marshal's office served as a buffer between the respectable trade and the saloons. Past the law office there was a seamstress shop, two general stores, and the hotel. Beyond that stood the church, and from there Main Street branched into various side streets where upstanding men went home every night and slept in the same bed every night with the same woman.

He thought of Katherine and wondered if she had supper on the stove by now. He could picture her arranging fresh flowers for the table or smoothing the linen tablecloth. He'd sent the basket of dishes back to her by way of the hotel errand boy, keeping the linen napkin with the letter *m* neatly stitched in a pale shade of blue. It was somehow comforting to know that little bit of cloth tucked away in his bedroll had her touch on it. He would look at it and remember eating at her table, and he would always wonder what might have been if he had stayed in Belle Plain. It was something he might never have considered had she not asked him to, and he wished she had needed anything but a marshal.

The thought brought a curse to his lips. He'd nearly cut his throat on his razor upon hearing her voice beyond his hotel room door. His pride let him believe she'd come to his room for more than conversation, only to learn she wanted him to play lawman. Even now, the idea was ludicrous. He'd spent his adult life sidestepping the law, avoiding trouble at every turn. Now he was the most wanted man in west Texas, and he needed a place to hide.

More townspeople filed down the sidewalks, eyeing him with varying degrees of curiosity and disdain. He took little comfort in knowing that bounty hunters enjoyed no more respectability than gamblers.

In the alley facing the law office, he caught sight of Katherine McBride slipping out of a narrow doorway. She glanced toward the street and hurriedly closed and locked the door. She held a bundle of papers close to her side, and her face was etched with concern.

The building bore no sign and appeared to be brand new and empty as a tomb. He glanced toward the ornate rooftop, guessing the building had at least three floors, maybe four. What would a town like Belle Plain need with such a fancy building?

She turned toward the residential area, her steps quickening as she neared the intersection. Without stopping to consider why, he crossed the street and fell into step with her.

"Good afternoon, Miss McBride."

She came to a halt and glared up at him, clearly annoyed at being caught off guard.

"A lot on your mind?"

"No more than usual." Her reply was curt. "I thought you were leaving town today."

"Sorry to disappoint you," he said. "Looks like I'll be here longer than I had thought."

She took a quick breath as if to speak but thought better of it. She tightened her hold on the bundle of papers and asked, "To what do we owe the honor?"

He grinned. "I wish you thought of it as a pleasure rather than an honor."

She stiffened. ''You're right. What would a man like you know about honor?''

She resumed her steps without a backward glance, and he laughed aloud in spite of himself. The clicking of her heels on the sidewalk faltered slightly but never stopped.

He turned back toward the hotel, wondering if Caleb Johnson wasn't the one laughing now.

* 4 *

"DEALER TAKES TWO." Luke drew two cards from the ragged deck and considered his hand. Three queens and now a pair of tens. Luck was with him tonight. "I'll open for ten."

The intense frowns and audible groans around the table assured him that his opponents had not drawn the cards they needed or that they had thrown away a good hand. Keeping his eyes focused on his cards, he tossed two blue chips into the center of the table.

"Too rich for my blood," a drover complained as he tossed his own cards facedown on the table.

"I'm in."

"Me, too."

Four blue chips joined the pair Luke had wagered. He scanned the faces of the three men facing him in a semi-circle. They all looked hopeful but not certain.

"I'll see your ten and raise you ten." A man across the table gulped down a shot of whiskey, wiped his mouth with the back of his hand, and tossed four blue chips into the pile. "You still in?"

Luke grinned slightly, reaching for his own drink. To his displeasure, he was growing accustomed to the cheap liquor served in the cow town saloons. He could barely recall the last time he'd had decent brandy, and he vowed not to forsake his preference for the finer things in life.

The whiskey burned, but not unpleasantly, pooling warmth in his belly. He would be sorry tomorrow, but at least he had the comfort of knowing the drinks were bought with money he'd won, not earned.

He placed his glass on the table, testing the patience of the man who'd raised his bet. "I'm in, and I'll raise you another ten."

The chips clicked against one another. The man licked his lips and unconsciously glanced at his cards, signaling a waning confidence in the hand he'd been dealt.

Finally he tossed in the pair of chips needed to remain in the game and said, "I call."

Undaunted by the implied challenge, Luke neatly laid his cards on the table. Three queens gazed up from a green felt background, as lovely a sight as he could imagine.

The man tossed his own hand, three sevens, on the table. "That's the fourth hand you've taken so far. What are you doing? Dealing off the bottom?"

"Just lucky, I suppose." Luke reached to gather the winnings, paltry though they were, but the drover slammed a ham-like hand over his.

"I ain't gonna take being cheated," he bellowed, and silence fell over the saloon. "Not by the likes of you."

Luke didn't miss the quick assembling of cowhands behind his opponent. One false move and a brawl would ensue. "You must think you're one hell of a cardplayer. A blind man wouldn't have to cheat to win against you."

Snickers rose from those gathered around the table, angering the man further. He sprang to his feet, sending the wooden chair skidding across the room.

"Settle down, Zeke," the bartender advised. "Joe, go

fetch the deputy before he tears the joint to pieces.''

Luke never took his eyes from the man as he casually raked his winnings into the pile he had already accumulated. The bartender's quick summons for the law assured him that Zeke was known for letting his temper lead him to violence.

"Poker's just not your game," he finally said, hoping to dismiss the man and the dispute. "Let's call it a night, and maybe you'll win your money back another time."

The man lunged forward and upended the table, sending cards and whiskey glasses flying. The other players scattered, but Luke merely moved away from the eruption and sized up his opponent. Zeke easily outweighed him by a good fifty pounds, but it was mostly fat, which made him slow and clumsy. Luke held the advantage of a clear head and cool temper: he was also the winner.

"You'll be sorry for cheating me." Zeke snatched a half-empty bottle of whiskey from a nearby table and broke the end off against the wall. Wielding the nasty looking weapon, he advanced toward Luke with a certainty he'd lacked for poker.

Luke was reluctant to draw his gun too quickly, painfully aware of the similarities between this night and the fateful evening in Cutter's Creek. Once again, he'd matched skills with an inept opponent and now faced another deadly confrontation, only this time there would be nowhere to go if he was forced to leave town.

"Somebody stop them before there's a killing!" The woman's screeching distracted Zeke only long enough for Luke to make his way around the table.

"Come on now, Zeke." Luke knew reasoning with an angry drunk was a waste of breath, but he hoped to give the man time to think. "I'll buy you a drink."

"With my own damned money?"

Tom McBride rushed through the swinging doors, his gaze finding Luke immediately. Without hesitation, he palmed his revolver and faced the combatants.

"Put that bottle down, Zeke," he ordered. "What's going on here?"

"You'd better mind your own business, youngster," Zeke advised, brandishing the jagged remains of the bottle at Tom. "This is a private matter."

"Not anymore." Tom stood his ground. "You've destroyed private property, and you'll be locked up for it."

"Locked up?" Zeke laughed at the thought. "By who? You?"

"That's right." Tom closed the distance between himself and the larger man, losing his advantage. Zeke tossed the bottle aside and lunged at Tom, slamming a huge fist into his face. The impact sent him toppling, upending another table in a flurry of cards and poker chips. Blood gushed from the deputy's nose, and his shirt was instantly stained bright red.

Tom scrambled to his feet, slightly dazed, and realized too late that his pistol had been lost in the fall. Zeke laughed and, at last, drew his own gun.

Luke cursed a thousand times and seized a toppled chair, smashing it across the man's back. Stunned, Zeke turned to find the source of the assault, but Luke drew his weapon before he had time to react.

"Get your hands in the air. Make one wrong move, and it'll be your last."

"Don't shoot, Caleb." Tom managed to find his handcuffs. "He's just drunk."

The color drained from Zeke's face. "Caleb? Caleb . . . Johnson?"

"That's right," Luke replied as Tom snapped the irons in place. The fear in the man's eyes was almost enough to lend a note of pride to the claim. "The one and only."

For the second time, Katherine read over the letter she had written to her chosen candidate for marshal, satisfied that everything was explained in detail. She'd made no grandiose claims regarding the town's prominence, nor did she downplay what would be expected of whoever accepted the job. In closing, she had asked for an answer by the end of the month.

There was no time to waste in finding an experienced man to fill the position; already the town was attracting seedy characters. Even tonight, Tom had been called away to settle a disturbance at the saloon.

Glancing up at the clock, Katherine tried not to worry, but she knew how easily an argument can escalate into bloodshed when whiskey was involved. Capping the ink bottle, she laid the letter aside to dry. She would post it first thing in the morning and hope to receive a prompt reply.

The front door rattled, and she heard Tom's key turn in the lock. Thankful for his quick return, she rose to meet him in the parlor. The door swung open none too gently, and she gasped at the sight of her brother leaning against Caleb Johnson, the front of his shirt stained with blood.

"Tom!," she managed, catching hold of the doorjamb. "My God, you've been shot!"

"Not exactly," the bounty hunter replied, a sardonic grin lending a touch of evil to his face. "Just a bloody nose."

"A bloody nose?" She hurried into the parlor, anxious to see for herself that Tom's injury was not serious. "What happened?"

"A drunk didn't want to be arrested." Caleb released his grip on Tom's arm, and the younger man swayed on his feet, grabbing the back of a chair to keep from falling. "He just got the wind knocked out of him."

"I think it's a bit more than that." She reached to touch his cheek, his left eye already swollen nearly shut. "Oh, Tom, your poor face."

"Let me alone!" he shouted, holding up a palm to ward

off her touch. "I'm man enough to take a punch in the nose."

Horrified, Katherine could only stare up at him. Tom had never so much as raised his voice in her presence. Now he was furious—with her!

"I will not leave you alone when you come home covered in your own blood." She finally found her voice, her own anger rising to match his. "I want to know what happened."

"Caleb told you what happened." He shouldered his way past her. "I *am* the law in this town, and I'll do what's expected of me, even if it's not always pleasant."

He glared at her a moment longer and then turned without another word to storm up the stairs, slamming the door to his bedroom behind him.

Without hesitation, she turned on the bounty hunter. "This is your doing, no doubt. What did you do to cause this?"

His eyes narrowed, and she couldn't prevent the shudder that coursed through her body as he closed the distance between them. "I kept your brother from getting killed for the second time in as many days."

Their faces were mere inches apart and with the slightest intake of breath she could smell the whiskey clinging to his words. Her own eyes narrowed, and she didn't back down. "It was your fight he was trying to break up, wasn't it?"

"I beat a man at cards, and he called me a cheat. I was willing to let it go, but he wanted satisfaction."

"I could very well have lost the only family I have left for the sake of whiskey-drinking gamblers." Images of Tom being beaten whirled in her mind, but she rejected any sense of gratitude toward the man who had again come to his defense. "Forgive me if I don't seem gracious."

"I saved your brother," he reminded her, advancing another step.

"From a danger you created," she countered, determined not to back away. The fabric of his shirt brushed slightly against her bodice, and she swallowed hard, her courage faltering. "Would you be so proud if he had been shot?"

She moved to put a safe amount of distance between them, but he gently seized her by the shoulders, forcing her to look at him. "Don't blame me for your brother playing lawman. If he can't handle it, why does he have the job?"

Guilt surged unexpectedly. Why, indeed? Tom was much too young and inexperienced to be a deputy, and Caleb knew it as well as she.

"I didn't think it would ever come to this," she confessed. "The last marshal appointed him as deputy, and my father thought it was a wonderful idea. Besides, there was no danger in just being the deputy at the time."

"But . . ." he prompted.

"But the marshal left town, with no one but Tom to take his place," she finished.

"What about your father?"

Her throat constricted, and she barely managed to say, "All of this happened after he died."

The challenge in his eyes softened, and she could feel the heat of his palms burning through the material of her dress. She didn't want his pity, but she sensed something else beneath those dark lashes—empathy.

For a moment, she glimpsed pain in his eyes, and she wondered what life had taught him about losing people. He drew her against him, and she was helpless to resist when he lowered his mouth to hers.

The first heated touch of his lips was a shock, but his kiss was gentle despite the force with which he held her. Firm and enticing, his mouth moved over hers, and she sank against his solid frame, welcoming the feel of his arms about her.

Whatever emotion she'd glimpsed in his eyes quickly changed to desire, but she didn't pull away. She'd forgotten what it meant to be held and to lean on the strength of another, and she began to wonder if she had ever known.

Instinctively, she raised her palms to his broad chest, but no thought of protest would form in her mind. Instead, her hands slid over the crisp cotton of his shirt to rest at the nape of his neck. The silky length of dark hair brushed over her knuckles, sending shivers up her arms, and his arms tightened around her.

His mouth was warm and coaxing, and she couldn't resist combing her fingers through his hair. The kiss grew urgent, and she gasped when his tongue crossed the barrier of her teeth. She shivered at the taste and feel of him, and her lips parted, welcoming the intimacy.

Immediately, he raised his hand to cradle the back of her head, guiding her response as she hesitantly returned the kiss. His other hand splayed across her back, urging her nearer. She complied, groaning at the feel of her breasts crushing against his broad chest.

Slowly, he eased his mouth from hers, raising dark eyes to study her face. She felt bereft of his touch and actually leaned toward him, seeking the feel of him. An arrogant smile touched his face and he said, "I'll take that as thanks for saving your brother's hide."

His words were like cold water thrown in her face, and she immediately wrested herself from his arms. He then turned, still smiling, toward the door. She could only stare at his retreating back, so angry she couldn't speak.

She gripped the back of the same chair Tom had leaned on for support, her knees buckling. Her face still tingled from the rasp of his whiskers against her skin, and the taste of him lingered on her lips.

Only when the front door closed none too gently behind him did she find her voice. "Damn you, Caleb Johnson," she managed, but even as the curse escaped her lips she prayed he would not leave Belle Plain.

*   *   *

Katherine tried not to look at Tom's battered face across the breakfast table, but her eyes would not remain on her plate. She hadn't slept much the night before, and she suspected he hadn't either. She should have insisted on tending his injuries, but she had left him alone with his wounded pride. Her own ego had been equally as bruised, and things did not seem better this morning as she had promised herself they would. The upheaval of emotion—fear, anger, and passion—had left her dazed and exhausted, yet she couldn't rest.

Each time she closed her eyes, her thoughts returned to the kiss she had shared so willingly with a hired killer. The thought made her shudder, and she was frightened by how eagerly she had responded to his advances.

She glanced at Tom. He had barely spoken to her this morning and was now focusing his attention on the food before him, ignoring her altogether. Well, she had just as much right to be angry with him. After all, he was the one who brought Caleb Johnson into their home, and he had probably encouraged the man to remain in town.

She laid her fork aside and faced him. "You could have been killed last night. What on Earth were you thinking?"

"Things just got out of hand, that's all." He winced as he raised his coffee cup to his bruised lips. He set the cup down and reached for a spoon with swollen fingers. "You shouldn't worry like you do."

Katherine shuddered at the sight of his skinned knuckles, and she didn't miss the way he held his side with the other hand. Belle Plain was by no means a wild and wooly town, but men had been killed in the saloons.

"How can I not worry?" she asked, still shaken by the thought of losing her only brother, her only kin. Tom's anger was still tangible, and she feared that the first seeds of resentment had been planted between them. "I'm sorry if I overreacted."

He nodded curtly, his attention focused on the plate of

eggs and biscuits. "Like I said, you shouldn't worry like you do."

A sudden knock at the back door silenced her response. She rose to answer the door, dismayed by his cool dismissal of her concerns.

She opened the door to find Joe Perry facing her, a polite smile on his face. "Good morning, Katherine. I know it's early, but may I come in?"

"Of course." She moved aside to let him into the kitchen. "Have you had breakfast?"

"Yes, I have." He removed his hat and placed it in her outstretched hand. "But I would like some coffee, please."

Katherine retrieved a cup and saucer from a nearby cabinet as Joe seated himself across from Tom. Her brother glanced up, and their guest's eyes widened at the sight of Tom's bruised face.

Joe thanked Katherine for the coffee and reached for the cream pitcher. "I won't bother to pretend I don't know what happened last night, Tom. I suppose we can only be thankful no one was killed."

"You mean that I wasn't killed."

"Tom," she chided softly.

"The man's behind bars," Tom reminded them both. "And he'll be charged with resisting arrest and assaulting an officer of the law, along with destruction of private property and public drunkenness."

"Public drunkenness?" Joe mimicked, stirring his coffee. "My, my, that should be the clincher. He'll think twice before causing trouble in this town again."

"There's no need for sarcasm." Katherine was quick to defend her brother. "I don't suppose you could have handled the situation any better."

"No, I couldn't, but I'm not the deputy marshal." He favored Tom with a sympathetic look and insisted, "I realize this responsibility was thrust upon you unexpectedly, but I see no reason why you should risk your life when no one expects you to.''

''I can handle the job.'' Tom did not look up from his breakfast.

''I don't doubt your capability,'' Joe insisted. At that, Tom did level an accusing look at them both, but Joe would not be silenced. ''You lack experience in dealing with these matters.''

''Joe is right, Tom,'' Katherine hesitated.

''So, you think I should just quit.'' He shoved his breakfast away only half-eaten, and reached for his own coffee. He drank deeply, and this time it was Katherine who winced as he held the cup firmly to his swollen mouth.

''Not at all,'' Joe said. ''What I'm suggesting is hiring an experienced person to act as marshal until you have a chance to adjust to things.''

''I don't need a nursemaid.'' Tom rose from the table, glancing sideways at Katherine. ''No matter what my sister thinks, I do know what I'm doing, and I can handle the job.''

Without another word, Tom retrieved his hat and gunbelt hanging on a peg near the door and stalked out of the house. He didn't slam the door, but he shut it soundly enough to rattle the window panes. Joe didn't look up from his coffee until Katherine spoke.

''Where would we find someone willing to act as marshal, Joe?''

''This Johnson chap, what about him?''

''Caleb?'' Katherine asked, warmth rising in her cheeks. She should have known Joe would have learned all the gossip about the notorious gunman. ''He's a bounty hunter.''

Joe sipped his coffee, waiting for her to elaborate. When she said nothing, he asked, ''Would you object to having him in the job?''

''He doesn't seem the type who would be interested in

such work.'' She didn't want Joe or Tom to know she had already considered the possibility, and she wanted no one at all to know that she had called on Caleb at the hotel, only to be dismissed.

"Frankly, I agree, but we need a man who can keep order in town and keep your brother from getting killed. I can't think of anyone better qualified, and he's right here in our pocket, so to speak.''

"I doubt he would consider the offer,'' she stated.

"You don't mind if I approach him about the matter, do you?''

Of course she did. If Caleb told Joe Perry that she had visited his hotel room, everyone in town would know by the next morning. She already had enough worries about the kiss they had shared before the front room window, but she couldn't object very strongly without an explanation.

"Katherine, we have to do something,'' he insisted, not waiting for her answer. "The men from the railroad are due here in less than a month. We can't let them think that we are without competent law enforcement.''

"Tom is competent,'' she stated, despite her own fears. "He's just inexperienced.''

"I doubt they'll see much difference between the two.'' He rose from the table. "You know I respect your opinion, but a man like Johnson behind the badge will set a tone in this town. I don't see that we have much choice.''

"Ask him if you like,'' she answered, praying that Caleb Johnson had enough decency not to discuss their meeting. "I doubt you'll have any luck.''

The hotel restaurant was filled with breakfast diners despite the late hour. The din of conversation quieted as Luke made his way to a back table, and he could feel the curious glances following him across the dining room. A waiter materialized to fill a cup with coffee and offer him a menu.

Luke glanced over the limited choices and made a hasty

selection. The waiter quickly noted the order and hurried toward the kitchen. The other diners resumed their conversations, only they now spoke in hushed whispers.

He tasted the coffee, pleased to find it hot and strong. He was relieved to have been spared any ill effects of the cheap whiskey, but his gut still burned from the previous night's turn of events. He'd nearly gotten Tom McBride killed, and then he'd given in to the temptation of Katherine's beauty.

Hell, women like that were beyond his understanding. Pretty words or flowers did nothing for them, but get them riled and they turn hotter than fire. Ladies . . . they keep their passion packed away with their anger: scratch one and you generally find the other.

One by one, those seated at nearby tables slipped quietly from the room, leaving their meals mostly uneaten. Logic told him that it was Johnson they meant to shun, but he knew about these upstanding folks, or at least he knew their kind. Even as Luke Cantrell, he was nothing more than a gambler, and they wouldn't have their delicate sensibilities fouled by his presence.

He took a deep gulp of coffee, savoring the way it burned his throat. He was growing accustomed to more than cheap liquor and cheaper women. He was getting used to being treated like trash. The man he'd become was far from the son his mother had raised in Santa Fe. His mother had been respected by everyone in New Mexico, and her family name carried weight with cattle barons and politicians alike. The governor of the territory had even attended her funeral, offering consolation to her grieving husband, Luke's stepfather.

The burning in his gut grew as memories beset him. The past would not be changed by anger or regret. Still he was haunted by the day he lost not only his mother, but his home and station in life.

At least his stepfather had been honest, immediately in-

forming Luke that from then on life would be very different
for him. His mother's death gave clear title of her home,
property, and fortune to her husband, and Señor Lira felt
no obligation to provide for another man's child. Sixteen,
his stepfather felt, was old enough for a boy to become a
man and earn his own way.

There had never been a moment, no matter how hungry,
tired, or frightened he was, that Luke had ever regretted
leaving, refusing to be a cowhand on the ranch that origi-
nally belonged to his mother and her father before her.

"Your breakfast, sir."

Luke glanced up to find the waiter eyeing him with open
curiosity. He made no comment as the plate of eggs and
bacon was served and his coffee refilled.

He ate without really tasting the food. He hadn't thought
of home for a long time, and he had never given any
thought to how things might have been if he had stayed.
Even the pittance he would have received from his stepfather would be more than he had now. Hell, even his own
name was lost to him now, written on a marker in the Belle
Plain cemetery.

"Mr. Johnson?"

Luke's hands stilled over his breakfast, and he glanced
up to find three men standing over his table. His only response was, "Yes?"

"We'd like to talk with you, if you don't mind."

He shrugged and gestured for them to be seated at his
table. They exchanged relieved smiles and sat down, one
man motioning for the waiter to bring more coffee.

"You've caused quite a stir in our town, sir." The man
acting as spokesman for the trio paused long enough for
three coffee cups to be doled out and filled. "Everyone in
Belle Plain knows the name Caleb Johnson."

"I don't know yours."

"Pardon me," the spokesman offered with a sheepish

grin. "I'm Joe Perry, this is Jacob Pruitt, and that is Frank Talley."

Each man nodded in greeting, sporting an accommodating smile. Luke pushed aside the remains of his breakfast and reached for his coffee. The waiter hurried over to gather the dirty dishes and place the check on the table.

"With your permission, I'll take care of that." Joe Perry hesitantly reached for the slip of paper, and Luke offered no protest. "We have a proposition for you, Mr. Johnson."

"I'm listening." Luke had been asked to leave many such quaint little towns after cleaning out a band of drovers and causing a fight, but never so politely.

"Last night was a perfect example of how quickly things can get out of hand here. We are thankful that no one was hurt."

Again, he nodded, wondering which tactic Perry would use. There was the usual "if you stay, there will be more trouble" or the ingenious "it would be in the interest of your own safety to leave town."

The other men quickly chimed in their gratitude that no one had been hurt. Perry continued as spokesman.

"We have to ensure that nothing like that happens again."

Luke reached for his coffee. "Just how can I help you with that?"

"We want you to be the marshal of Belle Plain, Mr. Johnson, and we'll make it worth your while."

He grinned, remembering the anger on Katherine McBride's face when he left her house. He also remembered the way she had returned his kiss, and he realized how quickly reasons for staying in town were mounting.

It was enough that he needed a safe haven until the death and burial of Luke Cantrell was common knowledge, but suddenly he wanted more. If he was going to stay on in Belle Plain, it might as well be with a little rank and privilege.

He motioned for the waiter to refill his coffee and leaned back in his chair. "I'm listening, gentlemen."

"Katherine, how could you not tell your two best friends about this man?"

Glancing at Patsy Reynolds, Katherine was surprised she and Charlotte Alston had waited this long to question her about Caleb Johnson. The moment they had sat down to lunch, Charlotte wasted no time in expressing her hurt and resentment over missing out on the best gossip going around town in two years. Especially when Katherine was right in the middle of the situation and knew all the details.

"That's right, dear, you shouldn't keep such things from us." Charlotte said. "If it hadn't been for Mr. Percy at the bank, I wouldn't have known anything about your Mr. Johnson."

"He's not *my* Mr. Johnson," she insisted, stirring a bit more cream into her coffee.

Patsy smiled knowingly over her coffee cup. "He's been seen leaving your house two nights in a row, and he hasn't even been in town a week."

"Both times he came home with Tom."

"Lannie Morgan says she saw him outside the general store, and that he is so handsome it's absolutely wicked." Charlotte Alston leaned over her own cup, lowering her voice dramatically, and pressed, "What's he like, Katherine, up close?"

Katherine nearly dropped her own cup, causing it to rattle against the china saucer. She couldn't think of a better description of Caleb Johnson than wicked. An idle moment would have her thinking about the feel of his embrace and the taste of his lips.

He had kissed her like a man who had kissed many women, and she had responded like a woman who had not been kissed much at all.

"I don't think much of him," she finally said. "He's no gentleman."

Delighted by the answer, Charlotte exchanged a knowing look with Patsy Reynolds. "Those are the best kind, don't you think?"

"We'll never know at this rate." Patsy rose from the table, with more difficulty than expected. She braced her hands against the small of her back, and dug her fingers into the aching muscles. "I can't believe this baby has another month to torment me."

Indeed, Patsy's misery had been the reason for today's visit. Dr. Sullivan had given strict orders that she was to have complete rest, and Katherine and Charlotte had spent the entire morning doing the housework that had gone undone. Every inch of the tiny frame house bore evidence of their labor. The floors were scrubbed clean, the laundry ironed and put away, and the only dirty dishes in the kitchen were the ones they were eating out of now.

Katherine couldn't help but stare at her friend's bulging stomach, barely hidden beneath yards of fabric. Patsy clasped her abdomen and gently stroked. "There he goes again."

Without warning, she took Katherine's hand and placed it, palm down, against her hard belly. A sudden movement caused her to gasp, and Patsy laughed when she tried to pull her hand away. "He's just getting started."

Twice more the baby lunged against Katherine's palm. "How do you know it's a he?"

"It has to be a boy; I can't imagine a little girl acting this rowdy." Patsy crossed the kitchen. "I want to show you both what Justin's grandmother sent me."

She returned to the table with a package tied with ribbon. She opened the box and retrieved a length of white material. "This christening gown has been in their family for four generations. Can you imagine Justin in this?"

Charlotte and Katherine fingered the delicate material, admiring the intricate needlework.

"I just can't thank you two enough for all your work." Patsy sank back into her chair and admired her sparkling kitchen. "Justin does what he can, but he's so tired in the evening. I know he'll be happy to have something for dinner besides fried eggs and canned peaches."

"We brought enough for several days," Katherine assured her. She glanced at her friend's half-eaten plate of food. "You should try to eat a little more."

She shook her head. "I couldn't eat another bite! You must have spent two days cooking."

"Hardly. The ham baked overnight, and I fixed the beans and potato salad last night."

"And the cabbage, and the bread, and the chicken?" Patsy then turned to Charlotte. "The cakes and pies were your doing. At this rate, Justin will be as big around as I am."

They laughed at that, and Katherine took her hand, reminding her, "You would do the same for us."

Charlotte covered the two clasped hands with her own. "Sisters, remember?"

The three women sobered as the memories of days not so long ago surged unexpectedly. They had been gangly teenage girls whose families had ventured from different towns to an unsettled area in hopes of a better future. A strong bond had formed between them that withstood the test of time—loss of loved ones, marriage, and soon children.

Tears welled in Patsy's eyes, and Charlotte rose from the table, turning away to dab at her eyes with the hem of her apron. "Goodness, what a sight we must be. Katherine, do I look as pitiful as you do?"

Smiles came at the barb, and she replied, "A couple of scullery maids, that's what we are."

Wearing their oldest dresses, they had made quick work

of dust and dirt, and their clothes were smudged from neckline to hem. Even the fireplace had received a thorough scrubbing, but it had put up a good fight.

"I'm going to slice this apple cake," Charlotte returned to the table with the cake in hand. She wiped at the smudges of soot on her face. "I say I've earned the first slice."

The mood lightened considerably, and Katherine insisted that Patsy try to eat at least a small piece of cake. She tasted her own serving, savoring the filling of tart apples and cinnamon. "Your mother must have made this. No one can match her apple cake."

Charlotte grinned, serving herself a generous slice. "I don't suppose that brother of yours has mentioned anything about asking me to the dance next Saturday?"

"You know Tom is a little shy."

"Well, I don't like the fact that he thinks he can wait 'til the last minute, and that I'll be waiting."

"You *will* be waiting," Patsy assured her. "Everyone in town knows you've already turned down Henry Matthews and his brother."

"For someone who has doctor's orders to stay in bed, you certainly know everybody's business." Her indignation was short-lived. "I'd rather stay home than go with either one of those two."

"What about you, Katherine?" Patsy studied her. "You will be there, won't you?"

"I don't know. Perhaps."

Charlotte's eyes brightened. "You can get that Johnson fellow to take you!"

"Caleb Johnson? At the Founder's Day dance?" Katherine couldn't even imagine it.

"Oh, I think it might lend a little excitement, and Lord knows we could use some of that in this town."

❖ 5 ❖

*K*ATHERINE,

Sorry I missed you this afternoon. I have business near Baird and won't be back until late. Your worries about a marshal are over. Caleb Johnson has agreed to stay until we can find a permanent man for the job. I wanted to tell you before I left town; I knew you would be delighted with this news.

Joe Perry

"Miss McBride, this is an unexpected pleasure."

This time Katherine held no misgivings about knocking on that hotel room door. She would have come straight over to confront Caleb Johnson after reading Joe's note had she not been such a wretched sight. A clean dress and neatly combed hair gave her the confidence she needed to face the bounty hunter and let him know he wasn't needed as marshal.

She ignored his sarcasm and stepped into the room with the conviction of a temperance worker, grateful at least to find him wearing a shirt this time. She made no attempt at pleasantries and came right to the point of her visit.

"What sort of game are you playing, Mr. Johnson?" she demanded, folding her arms across her chest.

"I'm playing your game, Miss McBride," he said, his hand cupped around the doorknob. "Only I've made a few minor adjustments in the rules."

"You told me that you had no interest in *playing* marshal," she reminded him. He closed the door, and her courage faltered. She groped for a little self-righteousness to steady herself. "I don't consider the safety and well-being of the townspeople to be a game."

"Neither do I," he countered. "But I find myself with a little time to kill in your town, and Mr. Perry has made me a very interesting offer."

As chairman of the town council, Joe did have the authority to hire his choice of marshal, and she had not adamantly opposed his intention to approach a man she was so certain would refuse the job.

"You're not doing this to spite me, are you?"

He had the gall to appear affronted. "Not at all. If anything, I'll be doing you a favor."

"A favor?" She didn't believe that for a minute.

"You and I both know it's only a matter of time before Tom runs in front of a bullet. He's green, and he can't handle being marshal."

She had to look away, nodding with reluctance. "He would never forgive me if I had the job taken away from him."

"That's not what you're doing." He stepped away from the door, joining her in the center of the room. "I'll play marshal long enough for him to learn the job and learn that it's not for him."

Katherine looked up. "What do you mean?"

"If Tom is no lawman, the sooner he realizes it the better."

The possibility had not occurred to her. Tom might just

listen to a man like Caleb Johnson, someone he admired and whose opinion he would surely respect. "You would convince him of that?"

"Yes, ma'am, I would." There was a note of sincerity in his voice she had not heard before. "Tom needs to learn that there's no glory in wearing a badge. The most he'll get is a hero's funeral."

Katherine shivered at the thought, remembering the terror she'd felt at the sight of Tom's bloodstained shirt.

"When I leave town, you won't have to worry about your brother getting himself killed." He paused long enough for the idea to settle in her mind and added, "Provided you hold up your end of the bargain."

"What are you talking about?"

"I'll stay on here in Belle Plain, and I'll be marshal, but I won't tolerate the contempt of your good citizens."

He crossed the room to the dresser where a whiskey bottle had been placed. He pulled the cork and poured a generous amount into a glass. "They look at me like I'm a stray dog walking down the sidewalk."

"There's nothing I can do about your sordid past and deadly reputation. You brought all of that with you." She watched as he tossed back the liquor without so much as a grimace. His Adam's apple bobbed slightly, and she swallowed as well, remembering the taste of whiskey on his lips.

"There's an old saying, Miss McBride." He replaced the glass on the dresser. "The love of a good woman can turn a man around."

Her breath caught in her throat, and she waited for him to say who or laugh and dispel the notion. Instead, an almost solemn expression flickered across his face, and his dark eyes remained fixed on her face.

"You're joking," she whispered, taking a step back.

He advanced toward her, his long stride equaling two of hers. "I've never been more serious."

She bristled. "You expect me to barter my flesh for a town marshal?"

"You flatter yourself. Do you think I'd go to this much trouble just for a quick tumble?" He laughed at the thought, a deep chuckle rising from his chest, but his amusement was short-lived, and he grew serious again. "What I want is respect. Just once more in my life I want people to look at me with respect."

She was indignant. "I don't see how I can help you with that."

"How can they not respect the man courting their mayor?"

It was her turn to appear affronted. "Joe shouldn't have told you about that."

"He was very talkative—told me all about your high-priced marshal taking off for California and leaving the town in a bind."

"He told you how much we paid him?" She was surprised at Joe. Surely he knew they could hire another marshal for half of what her father had offered Stuart Carey.

"I never have come cheap," he informed her.

"If the money suits you, then leave me out of it."

He only shook his head. "Carey had the money and the respect: I want both."

"What about my honor?" she demanded, it was her only argument. "I won't agree to anything that might . . . compromise my reputation."

"I'm not asking you to. I don't have trouble finding women willing to . . . compromise themselves." He flung the words back at her. "Just make sure you're on my arm where folks can see you. A few parties and dinners should do it, we could even throw in a Sunday picnic for good measure."

When she didn't answer right away, he added, "You said yourself, I'm the only man for the job. Otherwise, it'll be Tom facing a town full of drovers and gamblers all alone.

Just tell Joe Perry that you don't want me in this town, and I'll be on my way.''

"Once Tom understands that he doesn't need to be marshal, you'll leave?''

"The very day.''

She scanned his face but found his expression unreadable. What choice did she have? Joe had left her with no leverage in the deal, and to refuse his demands could cost her brother his life.

She held out her hand. "Very well. I suppose we have a bargain.''

His large hand swallowed hers and shock waves ran up the length of her arm. He smiled, and Katherine knew she was making a gentleman's agreement with the devil himself.

Luke had never seen the inside of a jail cell in his entire life. Despite all the time spent in the seedier parts of various towns, somehow he'd managed to avoid arrest and incarceration. His wits always kept him just shy of the reach of the law, just as his skill with a gun had kept him alive.

Even in Cutter's Creek, he'd managed to get out of town before the law could catch up with him, and Caleb Johnson had died before locking him up.

It was inevitable, of course; a livelihood earned by the turn of the cards usually landed a man behind bars for some offense, real or fabricated by a sore loser.

Never did he dream his first visit would be on the right side of the law and the bars. He gazed up toward the ceiling where the steel bars speared into the stone building. The "inmate facilities" consisted of three cells, each containing two cots on either wall. Between the cots was a wash basin with a towel folded neatly over the pitcher. Without so much as one barred window, the tiny rooms were as smothering as they were plain.

He was struck by how cold everything was. A man

wouldn't expect to feel welcome in jail, but the absolute absence of any personal objects would make a man feel stripped of his identity.

Even his pretense of being Caleb Johnson had not eradicated his sense of who he was. He was still Luke Cantrell, and he had his own things to prove it. Tom had painstakingly explained the process of collecting all of a prisoner's personal effects—belts, spurs, and never forget the contents of their pockets. Even their cufflinks, if they wore them. This was something Luke never wanted to experience, and his determination to remain a free man only strengthened. Even if it meant taking advantage of the fact that Katherine needed a marshal. He had spent the previous night second-guessing his bargain with her, fighting off the guilt he felt for the way he had manipulated her with her concern for her brother.

Now, standing inside the confines of a jail cell, he felt completely justified. What good would it do Katherine if he left town and rode into the hands of yet another bounty hunter? His hanging wouldn't discourage Tom from a career as a lawman, and he had no delusions of nobility.

From behind him, the steel door slammed, making an eerie, hollow sound that settled into his bones. Luke whirled around to see Tom grasping the bars. He rattled the door loudly but the lock was secure.

"Pretty impressive, don't you think?" Tom's gaze followed Luke's to the top of the bars. "My Pa pulled a few strings and got these from the fella building a penitentiary over in Arkansas. Those bars are solid steel, not iron, so we don't have to worry about jailbreaks."

"Where is the key?" Luke demanded.

"Right here." Tom inserted the key into the lock and the sound of the clicking tumblers was a relief. The door swung open, and he grinned at the concern on Luke's face. "We'd look pretty foolish . . . locked in our own jail."

Tom turned from the cell block and went back into the

outer room. The law office was neat, though sparsely furnished. A row of chairs stood along the far wall, and a shiny black cookstove took up most of one corner, providing both heat and a means to prepare meals. From time to time, food for overnight prisoners would have to be provided, but mostly, coffee was all that was required on a daily basis.

"Over here is where the bulletins are posted." Tom crossed the room and stood before a wall neatly papered with various notices depicting the likenesses of outlaws wanted for crimes ranging from petty theft to murder. "A lot of folks take the wanted posters for granted, but they can be one of the most important tools we have. I keep the notices divided into two groups—federal and state warrants."

Luke scanned the faces, relieved to see none that he recognized. The last thing he wanted was to be identified by a prisoner.

"Your office is in here."

"My office?"

"The marshal has his own private office," Tom opened the door and motioned for Luke to enter ahead of him. He did so hesitantly, glancing around the room while Tom raised the window shades. Light spilled into the room, gleaming off of a case holding at least a dozen Winchester rifles.

Tom grinned proudly, following Luke's gaze to the small armory. "That's more of my Pa's doing. Those are regulation rifles, just like the soldiers have."

Luke nodded in appreciation of the weapons. He could have guessed their purpose but let Tom elaborate on the importance of being able to quickly arm a posse in the event of a manhunt.

"When the time comes, we'll be ready," he declared, taking a rifle from the case.

Luke accepted the weapon, admiring the intricate carving

on the stock. "Your Pa thought of everything."

Tom beamed. "A judge in Abilene sent those as a . . . well, as a housewarming present for the new jail."

"Housewarming?" Luke chuckled. "Your Pa knew how to choose his friends."

"He never met a stranger," Tom said, his tone growing reverent. "Katherine always said she wouldn't be surprised if Pa wasn't the one who gave Grant directions to Richmond."

Luke smiled, easily imagining Katherine scolding her father for being too impetuous. He returned the rifle to Tom, who carefully replaced the weapon and locked the case. The young man's face was solemn, and he turned thoughtfully toward the marshal's desk.

Opening one of the desk drawers, Tom retrieved a small object and held it out to Luke. "I almost forgot this."

"What is it?"

"Your badge, of course." Tom grinned, letting the tin star fall into Luke's reluctant palm. "Go ahead, pin it on."

Luke closed his hand around the cool bit of tin, wincing as the points of the star dug into his palm. Reality settled around him slowly. This was real: he was officially the town marshal of Belle Plain, Texas—or at least Caleb Johnson was. Luke, however, was the one who would wear the badge.

Tom looked at him expectantly, and he quickly pinned the star to his vest in the same manner Tom wore his.

The deputy nodded. "It's something, isn't it? Pinning one of those on, I mean. I can tell you don't take it lightly."

Indeed, he didn't. Luke could feel the weight of the badge, slight as it was, tugging at his vest. He had only meant to hide out in Belle Plain until the word was out that Luke Cantrell's headstone now stood in the town cemetery and the reward had been paid.

Try as he might, he couldn't find the logic in hiding behind a badge. It was true that no one would come looking for him in Belle Plain, but what if someone came looking for Caleb Johnson? Well-known if not well-liked, the bounty hunter undoubtedly had acquaintances, even enemies, who would venture to town if word got out that he was now the marshal of Belle Plain.

"There's something else I need to talk to you about."

The deputy's voice drew his attention back to the matters at hand and he shrugged. "What is it?"

"My sister."

Luke tried not to react, but he couldn't quite look Tom McBride in the eye. Had Tom seen them kissing? Katherine was a decent woman, and her brother would be duty-bound to defend her honor if he thought she had been compromised by any man.

The deputy squared his shoulders. "Did she ask you to be marshal so you could look after me?"

Luke didn't miss the hesitant challenge in the youthful eyes. For all his inexperience, Tom McBride had his pride, and he was entitled to it.

Deciding to be honest when he could, Luke answered, "As a matter of fact, your sister didn't want me to be marshal."

Tom was surprised. "She didn't?"

"Not at all. She's afraid I'll be an evil influence on you." Luke propped one hip on the desk. "She was pretty shaken up the other night."

A guilty look came over the deputy's face. "Yeah," was all he said.

"You were pretty hard on her."

He nodded. "I shouldn't have yelled at her that way, but she treats me like I'm still a kid."

"The law is a dangerous profession, no matter what side you're on." Luke was amazed at the level of his hypocrisy. Who was he to lecture anyone? He coughed slightly. "I suppose she worries more about you because you're her brother. She said that you're her only kin."

More guilt. "Yeah, our mother died when we were kids, and we lost Pa just this year."

"I lost my folks young, too." Luke had never divulged that information to anyone; he never discussed his family. "At least you still have each other."

"We had it tough growing up," Tom admitted. "When our mother died, Katherine pretty much took over looking after me. But we're grown and, even now, she won't let me be the man of the house."

"What would you do if she did?"

The question surprised the young man, and he considered the matter seriously for what Luke knew was the first time.

"I don't guess I'd do much different than she does now." He crammed his hands in the pockets of his denims. "She should be thinking about getting married . . . having children, not running the house."

Luke decided to indulge a little of his own curiosity. "Or the town?"

"Isn't that something? Who ever heard of a woman mayor?" When Luke said nothing, Tom smiled, admitting, "She knows what she's doing, but . . . *I* should be the one seeing after *her*."

"By risking your neck to put drunks behind bars?"

Frustrated, Tom spread his arms wide. "I didn't risk my neck . . . not exactly. She overreacted, that's all."

Luke decided to drop the subject, for now. He couldn't erase Tom's dreams of being a lawman in one day, and trying too hard would only cause the deputy to distrust him.

By way of changing the subject, Luke glanced around the office and said, "Looks like I've got a lot to learn."

"I'm happy to show you." Tom accepted the truce. "In fact, we'd better get going."

"Where?"

"Rounds," he answered. "We have to make daily rounds. Besides, you need to meet as many folks as you can."

Luke nodded and followed Deputy McBride out of the office, pausing long enough to straighten his badge and imagine hell freezing over.

The town council of Belle Plain met promptly at ten o'clock on the second Tuesday morning of every month. Today marked only the second time in the existence of the council that a special meeting had been called. The first had been when Katherine's father had suddenly died; they had asked her to serve as mayor. Today they were gathered to discuss the appointment of Caleb Johnson as town marshal.

"I don't like it," Cecil Percy, president of the bank, declared before anyone had taken their seat. "I don't like it, not one bit."

"You haven't even heard what we have to say," Joe countered.

"'Pears to me, if you had anything to say to us, we should have heard it 'afore this fella was hired on." Silas Matthews owned the feed store and the livery, and he was generally opposed to everything. "Why bother having a council if Joe Perry is going to be calling the shots?"

Murmurs of agreement and discontent mingled with the sound of chairs scraping against the floor as the council members took their seats.

"It was as much my decision as Joe's." Katherine's soft voice silenced the protests. "There wasn't time to call a meeting, and there are no other candidates. Besides, this isn't permanent."

"That's right, gentlemen." Joe remained standing. "We needed a quick solution to our problem before the railroad men tour the town."

Dr. Sullivan leaned forward. "What do you know about this man, Katherine?"

She swallowed, keeping her eyes on the table before her. What did she know about Caleb Johnson? She suspected he knew something about losing people he loved, and he had promised to turn Tom away from being a lawman. Beyond that, she knew very little, except what Tom had told her. "He has a great deal of experience in apprehending criminals."

"He's fast with a gun, that's for certain," Silas Matthews informed the group. "Nearly killed a man in the saloon over a card game."

"He drew his weapon in defense of the deputy marshal," Joe corrected. "If anything, we are in his debt for saving Tom's life. That man was a drunken menace."

"The man works for me." All eyes turned toward Tyler Martin, a local rancher, at the end of the table. "He says he was cheated and then railroaded into jail."

"He was drunk and disorderly." Joe would not be dissuaded. "He attacked the deputy and nearly broke his nose. I'm not sure that's the sort of man I'd want working for me."

Martin's eyes narrowed. "All drovers get a little rowdy when they come into town. Just because they drink and scuffle is no call to lock them up. I resent it."

"You resent having to bail that feller out, is what you resent." Silas Matthews dealt as much in gossip as he did in sweet feed and alfalfa. He knew the comings and goings of everyone in town, and he had yet to tell a tale that could be proven wrong. "And you had to pay for the damages to the saloon. I reckon that was a pretty penny."

"It was either that or leave my best rider locked up during roundup." Martin sank back in his chair. "Hell, Zeke's always been a mean drunk, but I've never known him to be a liar."

"Mr. Johnson could have easily killed him with plenty of witnesses to verify it as self-defense." Joe continued to defend the new marshal. "I think he showed remarkable control by having him arrested. We need a man like that—someone who can remain calm in a crisis."

"We need someone who can make an impression on

those men from the railroad,'' Mr. Percy remarked. ''Need I remind everyone what we'll be faced with if they pass us up for another town?''

No, he certainly didn't, but he never missed an opportunity to do so. Most of the men on the council were businessmen, and their futures depended on Belle Plain being the next stop on the Texas & Pacific Railroad.

Silence fell over the room, and Joe and Katherine exchanged reassuring glances.

''I, for one, am willing to trust Katherine's judgment,'' Ty Martin finally said, relinquishing the argument. ''She's levelheaded, and I've never known her to spook easy. If she feels this man ought to be marshal, I'll stand by her decision. Time will tell.''

He favored Katherine with a rare smile, warm and inviting, as if she should be grateful that he agreed with her. She forced herself to smile back at him, much as one would smile at a preacher on Sunday morning. A year had passed since his wife had died, and he was rumored to be looking to marry again. Ty Martin had been smiling at her a lot lately, and she was careful not to encourage his friendliness. He was a nice man, but much older than she.

''When do we get to meet this fella?''

''Why don't you just get yourself arrested, Silas?''

Laughter erupted and even Silas Matthews managed a halfhearted smile.

''I imagine we'll all get a look at him on Saturday,'' Dr. Sullivan pointed out. ''He will be at the Founder's Day dance, won't he?''

''Of course, he will,'' Joe assured the men as they filed out of the room. ''Everyone for fifty miles will be there.''

He closed the door and gave Katherine a relieved smile. ''Well, we survived that. Now all you have to do is make sure Marshal Johnson puts in an impressive appearance at the dance.''

"Me?" she asked in surprise. "You're the one who promised he'd be there. You ask him."

"Oh, no." Joe only shook his head as he placed his derby on his head. He smiled slightly and said, "Not even to impress the city fathers will I escort a bounty hunter to a dance."

Luke's first official day on the job was off to a peaceful beginning. Tom had dutifully informed him of the latest outstanding warrants, apprised him of fines collected over the past week, and had promised to have the new wanted posters on the board by noon. Luke had then poured himself a cup of coffee, entered his office, and closed the door.

The chair behind the desk was comfortable and swiveled in every direction. The dark leather still smelled new, and sunlight gleamed along the row of brass tacks studded along the armrests. He leaned back slightly and propped his feet on the desk, taking advantage of the privacy to clear his mind of all the duties involved in running the marshal's office. Tom had memorized every statute in the book, and Luke had every intention of letting him run the office.

From what he could tell, the majority of those who occasionally occupied the cells were harmless cowpokes needing to sleep off a bender. Once they were sober and their fines were paid, they were released and a report was made. From time to time, a stranger in town might be arrested for vandalism or petty theft, but they were more likely homeless tramps looking for a dry bed and a hot meal. If caught, horse thieves and cattle rustlers rarely made it behind bars, and murderers and rapists usually answered to the victim's family before the law was ever involved. Frontier justice was swift, certain, and meted out by ropes and rifles rather than courts and judges.

Outside, Luke could hear someone enter the building, close the door, and speak softly to Tom. He didn't hear the deputy's reply, only the sudden knock at the door, and he swung his feet off the desk.

"Marshal?" Tom's head popped in the office. "Katherine's here to see you."

Luke grinned. "Does she have an appointment?"

Tom grinned as well. "I'll see."

The door closed and he strained to hear Tom's question. There was no mistaking Katherine's response.

"I most certainly do not have an appointment. Since when does anyone need an appointment to see the marshal?"

"The marshal only sees folks on official business, the deputy deals with the general public."

"I am here regarding an official matter," she countered. "Don't you forget my position in the town, *deputy*."

Tom peered inside the office. "She says it's an official matter."

Luke took a sip of coffee, replaced the cup on the desk and asked, "Could she be more exact?"

The door closed and Luke deliberately replaced his booted feet on the desk while Tom attempted to determine the nature of his sister's business.

"You stand aside, Thomas McBride," she warned. "I will not be toyed with."

The next time the office door opened, it was Katherine who stood in the open doorway. She stared at him with cool disdain, but the heightened color on her cheeks belied her indifference. "I see you've made yourself right at home." She glanced pointedly at his feet on the desk.

"It suits me . . . for now." His eyes were drawn to her mouth, full and pink, despite the pursed lips. "To what do I owe the pleasure of your visit?"

"Mr. Johnson, I am officially the mayor of Belle Plain," she reminded him as she stepped inside the office only far enough to close the door behind her. "I know you find that amusing, but I take my responsibility to this town very seriously."

"I admire your sense of duty."

She drew a deep breath, as if bolstering herself for an unpleasant task. Somehow he knew that he was the unpleasant part.

"There will be a Founder's Day dance on Saturday night." She reminded him of a judge handing down a sentence. "It is one of the most important social occasions of the year, second only to the Fourth of July picnic."

He made no reply, watching her struggle to come to her point. "The members of the town council are anxious to meet you, and this will be an excellent opportunity for you to do just that."

"I don't particularly care for such quaint activities. Tell the council members they're welcome to stop by here whenever they like."

"Oh, but you must be there." The defiance left her, and she approached his desk, her expression almost pleading. "They're expecting you."

"Expecting me? Why?"

She hesitated.

"So, you want me to show up at this dance like a trained dog and do tricks to impress your little council? Well, no thanks."

"It won't be like that."

"Will you be there?"

"As mayor, I have to be there."

Luke eased the chair back from the desk and rose to his feet. She swallowed as he crossed the room to stand before her. "Remember our bargain, kitten?"

"Katherine," she corrected. "I prefer Miss McBride."

"I prefer sweet manners." He grinned. "I'll go to your little dance, but not alone. I'll pick you up at your house, we'll arrive together, you'll dance with me—only me—and I'll escort you home."

"Everyone will think—"

"They'll think I must be one upstanding citizen if the mayor *herself* is allowing me to court her."

"But . . . that's not true."

"Things are seldom what they seem, Miss McBride." He took another step toward her until only a breath separated them. "I could kiss you right now, and you wouldn't think about stopping me. In fact, you might be wishing I would."

Her lips parted slightly, and he felt a swift tightening in his groin. It had been a long time since he had wanted any particular woman, and he didn't like the feeling. Whores were suitable enough for easing the desires of the flesh, but once a woman got under your skin, nothing would do but having her and only her.

He raised his hand to trace the line of her face, but she ducked away just before he touched her, skittering to the opposite side of the room. With distance and his desk between them, she favored him with a defiant smile.

"Don't ever think you can know what I wish for," she informed him. "There are more important things in a woman's life than whether she'll be kissed or not. We did make a bargain, Mr. Johnson, but that gives you no privileges with me."

"Privileges?" He laughed at that. Damn her high and mighty ideas. "That sounds like something that a man gets charged extra for in a brothel."

She backed away from him as if he were something dead she stumbled upon in the woods. When she spoke, her voice sounded strained, and he barely heard her. "The dance is at seven o'clock in the community building next to the church, and you're invited. That's all I came to tell you."

"Shall I pick you up at six-thirty?" he asked when she turned to leave. She only glared at him over her shoulder, prompting him to assure her, "Don't worry, Miss McBride, your privileges are safe from me."

❖ 6 ❖

Twilight had settled over the town, and Katherine stared out the front room window, watching as, one by one, her neighbors lit their front porch lights. She had just finished lighting her own, the bright light scattering the shadows that bore the night upon Belle Plain, and she lingered to appreciate the nightly ritual.

It really was a pretty town, she thought, considering how little promise it held in the beginning. Even now she could recall her crushing disappointment upon learning the wagons had reached their final destination. Mile after mile of empty grassland met them, and she feared her father had chased yet another empty dream, dragging her and Tom along with him.

The years of work and struggle had built the prosperous town he had envisioned, and she was thankful he had lived to see at least one of his dreams come true. Why hadn't that been enough for him?

He was never satisfied, always dreaming of something better than what he had. The promise of the railroad coming to Belle Plain had rooted dreams in his mind more grand than any he'd had before—dreams that would not be discouraged.

"Just look at Abilene and Dodge City!" he had exclaimed. "Nothing but wide spots in the road until the railroad came along. Now they're centers of commerce, and there is no reason Belle Plain can't do just as well, or even better."

This was his biggest dream. Now it was up to Katherine to see it through.

Had it not been for the twenty-five thousand-dollar bond hanging over their heads, Katherine might have hoped the railroad would choose another town. She liked Belle Plain the way it was, small and cozy, not burgeoning with businesses of every conceivable kind. For her, Belle Plain was already the realization of every childhood dream. It was home. She liked waking up in the same place every day, knowing everyone in town, and knowing where she would be tomorrow. She hadn't forgotten what it was like to be hungry or cold or worse, all because one of Father's hopes didn't "pan out." She had grown accustomed to prosperity and slept well knowing there was food in the pantry, money in the bank, and new clothes as she needed them.

The thought of losing that security terrified her, and she resolved herself to beat Caleb Johnson at his own game. She would have her impressive marshal when the railroad executives came to tour the town, even if she had to haul him to every church supper between now and doomsday.

Upstairs, she could hear Tom whistling as he dressed for the party. He had been whistling ever since he returned from work that afternoon. He and the new marshal were getting along fine, and he had been delighted to learn that Caleb would be going to the Founder's Day dance.

Outgoing and handsome, Tom loved social outings of every kind, and he always had fun. People liked Tom upon meeting him, and a person's faith was never wasted on him.

Charlotte, especially, had not been disappointed. Tom

had indeed issued his invitation to the dance well within the proper time frame, not so soon as to cause presumed intentions yet not so late that Charlotte's social standing was diminished.

Katherine had been dressed for almost half an hour. The dance was a special occasion, and she had taken pains with her appearance to the point that even Tom noticed when they met in the hallway.

"You look awfully pretty tonight," he'd observed. "Good looks just run in this family."

She studied her reflection in the front window. The dark blue of her dress accentuated her fair hair and pale skin, and she wondered if the marshal would also find her pretty. She shouldn't care, but she did. He was so confident and self-assured, and she found herself judging herself by his standards.

She thought of Caleb's dark eyes and hair, and his tanned skin. She felt her face warm with the thought. She couldn't forget the sight of his bare chest gleaming in the lamplight. More than color from the sun, his skin was naturally dark. The thought of those bare arms and the corded muscles of his back made her weak in the knees.

"Penny for your thoughts," Tom's voice cut through her musing.

She turned to find him standing at the foot of the front staircase. He was dressed in dark gray trousers with a white shirt and a black vest. His holster hung low on his waist, and the pistols shone as though newly polished.

"I believe you're right," she observed, hoping her blushing face wasn't too obvious. "Good looks definitely run in this family."

He smiled and studied his reflection in the hall mirror. "Indeed, they do."

"Do you really think you'll need your guns?"

His hands froze above his tie. "I'm the law, Katherine. I wear a gun."

"But it's a party," she pointed out. "Surely, you don't expect trouble."

She saw him stiffen, his eyes narrowing, and she wished she had not broached the subject. He had apologized for yelling at her the night he had come home bloodied, but she knew now that the subject was still a sore one for him.

"Trouble is always where you least expect it." He resumed straightening his tie and retrieved his hat from the coat tree. Satisfied with his appearance, he turned toward the front door. "I'll see you at the dance."

"Aren't you going to ride with me . . . and the marshal?"

"I promised Charlotte that I'd bring the buggy tonight." He gave her a knowing smile and opened the door. "Don't worry, he'll be right along."

The door closed, and Katherine could only stare after him. She hadn't considered the possibility that she would be alone with the marshal at any time this evening. Now she faced going to the dance and home again, just the two of them.

"It's just business," she assured her reflection. Caleb merely wanted the appearance of her friendship to gain the respect of the townsfolk. She didn't mind so much that he was using her prominence in town, for she was using him to save her brother and, in a way, the town itself.

Still, she was surprised to find that a man like Caleb Johnson put any value in the opinions of strangers. He possessed a ruthless and deadly reputation that made men fear him, if not respect him. He would leave Belle Plain, never to return, so why did he want to be well-thought-of while he was here?

Katherine turned toward the kitchen, shaking off her thoughts of the bounty hunter. She had baked a double batch of gingerbread that afternoon, and when it had cooled she sliced the cake into squares, dusted them with powdered sugar, and placed them in a basket covered with a checkered napkin.

She placed the basket on the table, savoring the heady aroma that still hung in the kitchen. Tom always bragged about her cooking, and she now wondered who she would cook for when he was gone. Charlotte didn't shy away from stating her plans for Tom, and Katherine had given little thought as to what would happen when he did marry.

Unexpected, troubling thoughts besieged her. One way or another, her life would soon change. Belle Plain would either get the railroad and become a boomtown or lose out and go bust. Tom might not marry Charlotte, but he would marry someday.

Only older by two years, she couldn't remember a time when Tom wasn't there. It had always been the two of them, facing life together. Once he married and had a wife and family, they would be his main concern.

The house was really all either of them had, and tradition dictated that Tom, as the only male heir, should inherit the home for himself and his family. Could she accept the bride Tom chose and gracefully adapt to the position of old maid sister-in-law?

A sudden knock at the back door startled her, and she reached for the knob, catching sight of the marshal smiling at her through the lace curtains. Dressed all in black, he looked wicked peering in at her.

"Good evening," she managed when she opened the door. Cool night air tugged at her skirts, sending a chill up her spine. "Tom went on ahead with the buggy. We'll have to walk."

He stepped inside, openly appraising her dress. He smiled appreciatively. "No need for that. I borrowed a buggy from the livery."

"Borrowed?" she repeated with doubt. "Silas doesn't loan anything . . . to anyone."

"Well, I explained that I was in need of transportation for a special lady, and he seemed to understand exactly what I wanted.'' He eased the door closed. ''Very special indeed.''

She managed to stifle the flattered smile that threatened at his compliment. He was a charmer, always knowing just what to say, and she reminded herself of the countless women he had no doubt showered with compliments. By *special*, he was surely referring to her being the mayor and nothing else.

He closed the distance between them and took gentle hold of her hands. She forced a placid facade while inside she was quaking at the prospect of their sharing another kiss. If he sensed her apprehension, she couldn't tell, but he made no move to draw her close. Instead, he raised her arms and twirled her about the kitchen.

She followed his lead, making three turns about the kitchen. One, two, three, she counted silently; one, two, three—dodge the table. One, two, three, keeping her back poker straight and a proper distance between them. The brief dance ended and he took a deep bow.

''I wanted to assure you that you will have a suitable partner for the evening.''

She smiled and couldn't resist applauding his elegance. ''I am impressed, sir.''

Again, he clasped her hands, this time raising her knuckles to his lips. ''That was my intention.''

His lips pressed against her hand and the warmth of his mouth ran up her arm like a bolt of lightening. She ignored the warning in her mind that clamored for her to snatch her hand away. Instead, she merely watched as he raised her palm to his mouth and shuddered at the feel of his mouth against the sensitive flesh.

Still holding her hand, he raised dark eyes to study her face, and she felt his fingers tighten around hers, as if to draw her nearer. This time she obeyed the silent alarm and made her escape.

''All I need to do is get my wrap and we can go,'' she

said by way of excuse and ducked out of the room, leaning against the wall. She drew a deep breath and willed her heart to slow its pounding. She gathered her black cloak from the coat rack and returned to the kitchen.

She found Caleb peering into the basket of gingerbread, the spicy scent filling the kitchen as he folded the napkin back from the contents. Unaware of her presence, he filched a small piece of cake from the basket and half of it disappeared in one bite.

"How is it?"

Startled at first, he glanced up and smiled. "Very good. My mother used to make this. I couldn't resist."

She nodded. "It's all right. Tom had three before he left. I'm sure it doesn't hold a candle to your mother's."

A shadow passed over his eyes, sobering them for a second. "She used to tell the story of a little girl in the woods carrying such a basket. The girl came upon a lobo who tricked her and devoured her for her trouble."

"Lobo?" Katherine neared the table, drawn by the deep timbre of his voice that had gone strangely husky and laced with an accent she couldn't place.

"The wolf," he explained. He took another bite of cake and she couldn't look away from the fullness of his lips. He held the last bite to her mouth, and she accepted. "Do you know the story?"

The spicy sweetness filled her senses, but the warmth and the feel of his fingers on her lips was all she could focus on. Behind his dark eyes, something lingered that she was seeing for the first time.

She swallowed the cake, but his fingers didn't leave her mouth. "Little Red Riding Hood," she said at last.

He traced her parted lips, grazing her teeth with his fingers, and she couldn't stifle the sudden intake of breath.

The mocking gleam returned, as quickly as it had disappeared. "It's been a long time since I was caught with my hand in a cookie jar."

"No better compliment to the cook." She slipped her cloak over her shoulders before he could move to assist her and turned toward the door. "We'd better get going."

"What's your hurry?" He opened the door, ushering her into the cool darkness. "The night is young, Miss Mc-Bride."

The community building was strategically located at the far end of town, backing up to a grassy field. Already, that field was filled with buggies and wagons with restless teams of horses intent on munching as much of the grass as they could. Music spilled from the open windows and doorways, rising with the scent of clover and becoming part of the night.

Luke reined the borrowed rig to a halt, grateful he had not had to park too far away from the building. He glanced at Katherine and smiled. She looked prettier than ever tonight, and he was tempted to say so. He decided not to, reminding himself that they were both here under false pretenses: hers to ensure the town a marshal, and his to pretend this was a place to call home.

He made his way around the buggy and graciously offered his hand to her. She smiled and handed him the basket of gingerbread.

"Are you always so cagey?" he asked as she nimbly made her way down from the buggy.

"Are you always so surprised to be outmaneuvered?"

He laughed and followed her toward the building. Laughter and chatter rose above the instruments along with the mingled aromas of a potluck supper.

As they entered the open doorway, Luke came to a halt and pinned her with a look that was more of a warning than a challenge. She merely smiled and, with a tilt of her chin, tucked her hand in the crook of his arm.

Several heads turned to survey the newcomers, and Luke felt conspicuous for the first time in fifteen years. They gaped in silence as others around them turned to look as well. Katherine discreetly urged him inside the room, seemingly unaffected by the reactions.

They made their way to the back table, already loaded with cakes, pies, and other delicacies. Couples on the dance floor turned to look, losing their step and causing other dancers to falter, and even the lively tune from the fiddle didn't drown their whispers.

"Isn't that the new marshal?"

"With Katherine McBride, of all people."

"You know what they say about still waters."

To his relief, Luke caught sight of Tom McBride waving to them from a nearby corner. Once Katherine had placed the basket of gingerbread on the table, he steered her in the direction of her brother.

"Well, good evening, Katherine." The young woman at Tom's side smiled as the two men shook hands. "Aren't you going to introduce me to the marshal?"

"Charlotte, this is Caleb Johnson." She glanced up at him. "This is my friend Charlotte Alston."

Luke smiled and gave a short nod. "Very good to meet you, ma'am."

"How are you liking Belle Plain?" She eyed him openly, like a trader sizing up good horseflesh. She glanced up at Tom and tightened her hold on his arm.

"It suits me fine," he replied, amused at being found lacking.

"Well, you're all Tom talks about these days," she assured him. "To hear him tell it, you can outshoot the Daltons themselves."

"Charlotte." The young deputy cringed at having his hero worship exposed. "I only mentioned a few things in passing."

"I've had worse said about me," Luke said, dismissing the remark. Everyone laughed except for Katherine who only smiled, looking guilty.

"Good evening all," a voice called. Luke glanced up to see Joe Perry approaching them. "Marshal Johnson, how nice to see you."

They shook hands, and Luke noted the exchange of smiles between Katherine and Perry. A pang of jealousy stabbed through his gut, and he realized how little he really knew about Katherine. He had wondered before why such a beautiful woman had no beau, but dismissed the situation, attributing it to his own good fortune.

Perry wasted no time in getting to his point. "I'm sure Katherine has told you how anxious many of the townsfolk are to meet you."

Luke had learned a long time ago to judge a man by the way he smiled, and he decided he didn't much like Joe Perry. The man smiled like he had two aces in his pocket and another in his sock. Of course, that was common to all lawyers, but he had learned not to doubt his instinct.

"She mentioned it," was the only reply he offered.

"Well, then why don't you come with me, and I can introduce you to a few members of the council."

"Bring them over later, and I'll be glad to introduce myself." The smaller man paled, but Luke merely glanced at Katherine, explaining, "I didn't ask Katherine to a dance just to leave her in the corner all night."

"I wouldn't mind."

"I would," he countered in a voice more harsh than he meant. He smiled and offered his arm. "They're playing a waltz if I'm not mistaken. Shall we?"

Worry knitted her brow, but she took his arm and followed him onto the dance floor, leaving the others behind.

Caleb Johnson was a constant source of amazement. Katherine was hard-pressed to keep up with him on the dance floor, his steps were so fluid and flawless. "Where did you learn to dance so well?"

He grinned down at her as they whirled past other less graceful dancers. "In Santa Fe."

Santa Fe. She put that tidbit with the unguarded accent he'd let slip earlier in the kitchen. "Johnson doesn't sound very Spanish."

"It's not."

She didn't miss the censure in his voice, and her curiosity was piqued more by his reluctance to talk than on what she had deduced already.

"Joe didn't mean any harm," she assured him, changing the subject. The feel of his palm against the small of her back was unsettling, but she was determined to keep the conversation going. "He's only anxious to make a good impression on the people of this town."

"He's anxious for *me* to make a good impression," he corrected. "I told him when I agreed to stay that I would answer to no one. Besides, you're the only one I want to impress tonight."

He smiled slightly, and she felt her heart turn over. She could scarcely recall the stranger who'd barged into her kitchen, covered in trail dust, and lectured her on manners. How quickly she'd grown accustomed to his arrogance, tempered by glimpses of a sentimental nature.

The dance came to an end and a second tune began, and he held her in place. Two dances in a row would definitely cause a buzz among the ladies, but Katherine didn't care. Her steps were more confident, and she felt light on her feet, allowing him to guide her movements.

The song concluded, earning applause for the trio of two fiddlers and a guitarist, and she experienced a twinge of regret when he escorted her from the dance floor.

When they returned to the sidelines, Joe stood waiting for them. He had dutifully rounded up several members of the council to meet the new marshal. The men wore eager smiles, and Katherine prayed that Caleb would be polite.

"Good evening, Marshal," Mr. Percy spoke right up, not

waiting for Joe to make the introductions. "I'm Cecil Percy, president of the Farmer's and Merchant's Bank. Mighty good to meet you."

The other men quickly offered their hands and welcome, and Joe looked on with obvious delight.

"Marshal," Ty Martin extended his hand with no smile or words of welcome. "Your reputation precedes you."

Caleb's expression darkened. "How is that?"

"Had to bail one of my men out of your jail this week," he explained. "I come to find out, he was arrested for fighting with *you*. Doesn't seem right, a lawman starting fights and then arresting his opponents."

Silence fell over the surrounding crowd, and Katherine felt a cold wave of apprehension pass over her. *Not tonight, please, not tonight.*

"I arrested that man." Tom rushed to the marshal's defense. "And it was for a lot more than fighting."

"The man says he was cheated at poker." Martin wasn't going to let it go. "I reckon that would rile me enough to fight . . . even the law."

"I wasn't the law then," Caleb finally spoke, his voice level with no trace of malice. "Just one hell of a poker player."

"Maybe too good."

"Give it a rest, Ty." Exasperated, Cecil Percy was quick to remind him, "Everyone knows Zeke is a mean drunk. You said so yourself at the meeting the other day. Why rehash all of that now?" The banker glanced at Katherine. "I've been thinking a few things over, but I'm still willing to stand by Katherine's decision."

"And mine as well," Joe piped up at last. "There's no need for any unpleasantness."

"I only meant the marshal shouldn't be gambling and brawling." Ty Martin backed down with little dignity.

"Besides this is a party. We should all be having a good time."

"That's right," Caleb replied.

"Katherine, I'd like to have the next dance with you." Reluctantly, Ty turned toward Caleb. "If you don't mind."

Katherine flinched. Asking Caleb's permission to dance with her was more than a concession of the moment's disagreement. It was a recognition of the assumption that they were a couple, something she had hoped to avoid. If everyone assumed the marshal was courting her, what would they think when he left town without a backward glance?

The marshal nodded and said, "I'll be waiting for her."

Ty Martin led her onto the dance floor, his steps stiff and awkward compared with Caleb's grace. "I got a bad feeling about that man. What do you know about him?"

"As much as he's told me," she answered. "Tom is quite pleased with him as a marshal."

"Your brother follows after anyone with reputation and a badge." He studied her intently and when she made no reply, he continued, "Katherine, there's something I should have spoken to you about sooner."

She groaned inwardly, knowing he was finally going to raise the subject she'd tried to discourage.

"Time has come for me to get on with my life, and I had every intention of courting you. I'm afraid my dallying may have let your interest fall to this . . . lawman."

"You seem rather certain of yourself, Mr. Martin." She came to halt along with the music. "Don't assume you had only to make your intentions known and I would be yours for the asking."

She stepped away from him and politely thanked him for the dance. His expression was somewhat crestfallen, and she felt a pang of guilt. He had been terribly hurt when his wife died suddenly, and he didn't deserve her curt rebuff. Still, she had her own pride to think of, and the only thing worse than being thought an old maid was being an eager old maid.

She turned from the dance floor, not waiting for him to escort her. A tingle passed over her as she caught sight of Caleb Johnson waiting for her near the buffet table, and she hurried to join him.

"Enjoy your dance?" he asked as she accepted a glass of punch from Charlotte.

She smiled at him over the punch glass, taking a sip before answering, "I believe you're the better partner."

He smiled. "I intend to prove it."

The late night air held an unexpected chill, and Luke wished Katherine had not thought to bring her cloak. He would love nothing more than to slip off his jacket, tuck it around her delicate shoulders, and let the warmth from his body be absorbed by hers.

Possessiveness was new to him. As a gambler, he'd learned not to become attached to anything, because the turn of a card could claim all that you own. Tonight, he'd enjoyed the rituals of courtship—pulling out her chair, getting her punch glass refilled, and she had saved the last dance for him. Yes, he'd missed these little exchanges and feared he could get used to them much too easily.

He reined the team of horses to a halt and faced her. "I hope your reputation will survive this evening."

"It will," she assured him. The filmy light of the moon lent an almost spectral glow to her countenance, and he felt a sudden pang of guilt. Katherine was a beautiful woman, and she shouldn't be wasting her time on a two-bit drifter like himself. He'd been only too aware of the way men were watching her this evening, as if they had never seen her before. Her coolness had disappeared, and watching her dance with him had given the men of Belle Plain cause to think again about the woman they knew only as mayor and spinster. He had no right, no claim on her, but he resented knowing they would all come calling when he left town.

"I'm indebted to you for the way you handled Tyler Martin." She glanced down at her hands, clasped in her lap. "He can be difficult, but he's not a bad man."

He shrugged, not feeling so noble. He would have liked nothing more than to punch the arrogant bastard right in the face, and the real Caleb Johnson probably would have done much worse. "He was just testing me."

She nodded, and he wondered if she realized she had been the reason for the man's ill manners. Martin had kept close watch on them all evening, and he had no doubt the man knew exactly how many dances they shared. He had not asked Katherine to dance a second time, but neither had he danced with anyone else.

Luke stepped down and rounded the carriage, offering her his hand. This time she accepted. The walkway leading to the front of the house was lined with tiny blue flowers, their heady fragrance blending with the night air.

Katherine released his arm the moment she set foot on the front porch, her shoulders regaining their stiff posture. "Well, good night."

"No kiss?" he couldn't resist asking.

With a tone of dismissal she said, "I hadn't considered it." He wasn't about to let her get away with that. He closed the distance between them and assured her, "Oh, yes you have."

Her eyes widened and the evening breeze rushed between them, dousing the flickering porch light. He didn't waste the opportunity, leaning forward with his palms braced against the door on either side of her head.

Her mouth was as sweet as he remembered, and even more hesitant. He didn't risk caution and deepened his touch, his tongue teasing the corner of her mouth. She trembled beneath him, and he dared not move his hands from their place.

Her own arms found their way around his shoulders, and

he could control himself no longer when he felt her fingers in his hair. He gathered her in his arms and groaned aloud at the way she felt against him. Her lips parted easily this time, and he savored the taste of her, warm and sweet. Her head lolled against the front door, and he traced the line of her throat with his mouth, her pulse throbbing against his tongue.

Though the porch was darkened, the moon was nearly full, and he thought better of risking the prying eyes of neighbors. He took her by the arm and led her to a corner of the porch not visible from the street. She had no time to protest as he quickly took her in his embrace and kissed her with the ardor he'd kept in check earlier.

Once again, her hands clung to his shoulders. He let his hands travel the length of her back, loving the feel of the warmth beneath the fabric of her dress. Carefully, he cupped the weight of her breast in his palm, teasing her nipple beneath his thumb. She whimpered slightly, and he deepened the kiss, shifting his body closer to hers.

Her fingers traced the muscles of his back, and he groaned when her tongue met his, hesitant but eager. He savored her innocent response, encouraging but not dictating her movements. How a woman so desirable had gone untouched was beyond him, but he was selfish enough to be glad for it.

She would never be his, but he could pretend just a little while longer. The taste, scent, and feel of her would haunt him, he knew, but for now he could only take what she would allow and hope this night would trouble her sleep as it would his.

Guilt suddenly assailed him. He shouldn't be doing this, not after the way he had deceived her—deceived everyone. He ended the kiss only to hold her in a comforting embrace, as if he could somehow make amends for what would eventually cause her embarrassment.

Her arms went slack and she asked, "Is anything wrong?"

He forced himself to look into her face and smile. "What could be wrong? Half the men in this town would kill to be standing in my boots."

She grew flustered and looked away. In a way, he hoped she would become angry and slap his face for taking *privileges* with her. Instead, she smiled up at him. "I'd say we're both rather lucky."

Before he could answer, the clatter of shod hooves announced the arrival of a wagon nearing the house. The hoofbeats grew louder and a horse nickered.

"It's Tom!" Katherine gasped, pulling away from him. She raised her hands to her tousled hair. "He mustn't see me like this."

"Go inside," he ordered. "I'll stall him long enough for you to get upstairs."

With a nod, she jerked the back door open, causing the windowpanes to rattle loudly. Before ducking inside the house, she raised a quick kiss to his cheek and hurried inside without a word.

The simple affection touched him deeply, more than any exchange they had shared so far. A week ago she had barely tolerated his presence, now they were exchanging good-night kisses in the moonlight. He turned and scaled the back steps, catching sight of Tom coming up the walkway.

"Evenin', marshal." The moonlight glinted off the badge pinned to his vest. "Have you ever seen a better night for a dance?"

"No, indeed," he answered honestly. "Not in my lifetime."

❖ 7 ❖

Sunday morning dawned cool, but the bright sun-light promised a beautiful day. Pastor Meeks' disapproval was obvious as he scanned his sleepy congregation, and Katherine didn't doubt that whatever subject he had chosen for today's sermon would prick more than a few consciences.

He could preach on hell itself, however, and not make her feel one bit guilty about last night. The evening she had dreaded had been the most wonderful in her life. She had fallen asleep dreaming of dancing with Caleb and awakened from dreams of kissing him.

She shifted slightly in the pew and tried not to think of such things in church, wincing when the hard edge of the seat bit into her thigh. She had visited churches in Austin that had upholstered seats, but the pastor had been scandalized when she mentioned the idea of having them placed in their church.

"Comfort for the soul is what we're about," he had haughtily informed her. "Not the backside."

"Fine for him," she thought. "He gets to stand during most of the service."

She scanned the small sanctuary, smiling at her neighbors. Patsy and Justin made their way into the church, claiming the space beside Katherine.

"Good morning," her friend said, leaning over to whisper. "How was the dance?"

"Wonderful," Katherine replied, unable to censor a smile of delight. "The best we've ever had."

Patsy exchanged a knowing smile with her husband before saying, "Sounds like you had a good time."

"Everyone had a good time," she said in her own defense.

"Everyone? Or just you and the marshal?"

She was spared having to elaborate when the pastor's wife stopped alongside their pew. "Good morning, ladies," she said in a cheery voice. "Don't forget that next Saturday we'll have to be here extra early to get all those eggs hidden for the children."

"I'll try," Patsy promised. "If Dr. Sullivan sees me out this morning, he'll scold me."

"Well, you take care of yourself," Mrs. Meeks warned. "We don't need you putting that baby at risk."

"Charlotte already promised to help me," Katherine added. "And there's always more food than we need, Patsy. You just come and have a good time."

"Only if the doctor approves."

When the pastor's wife was safely out of ear shot, Pasty resumed her questioning. "Well, is he a good dancer?"

Exasperated, Katherine answered, "Very good. Next time come for yourself, and I'll see that you have a front-row seat."

"It killed me to stay home." Patsy placed a hand on her swollen belly. "But my feet and ankles are already so puffy, I would never have survived."

Justin leaned over and asked, "Where's Tom?"

Before she could answer, Tom entered the church with Charlotte on his arm. Patsy and Justin shared yet another knowing look as the couple took seats on the opposite side of the sanctuary.

"Tom doesn't have a chance," Patsy whispered with a smile. "They do make a handsome couple."

Leola Nelson took her seat at the piano and struck a resounding chord for the first hymn. Everyone rose and joined in the familiar verse.

From the corner of her eye, Katherine caught sight of Tyler Martin. Dressed all in dark brown, he sang without looking at the hymn book, without so much as a glance in her direction. She thought about his declaration the night before and finally understood her reluctance to welcome his intentions. He was a great deal older than she, but he was dependable and well established in the community. His ranch was one of the largest in the county, and he was considered by everyone to be a wonderful catch. She might have been flattered once, but not since she had kissed Caleb Johnson.

In his arms she learned the meaning of passion, and she wanted more from a husband than just a suitable companion. She wanted to feel the way she had felt last night, and despite his good qualities, Tyler Martin left her cold.

Patsy nudged her, drawing her back to the present. She had not sung a note of the second verse, and the hymn book hung loose in her hand. She straightened and scanned the page, but it was useless; her thoughts remained on Caleb Johnson.

A second hymn was sung and then a third. The offering was collected and prayers were offered for the sick in the community. Finally Pastor Meeks took his place behind the pulpit, his displeasure for his wayward flock tempered with understanding. The Founders' Day ball was one of the few occasions for celebration in Belle Plain

Still his expression was solemn and Katherine felt her

face grow hot when he instructed, "Turn in your bibles to the second chapter of Ephesians in which Paul warns the church at Ephesus against the lusts of the flesh."

The tolling of the church bells drew Luke from the first decent sleep he'd had. He'd lain awake staring at the ceiling all night, finally dozing off at dawn. The bright morning sun streamed through the window, poking around the edges of the shade. He groaned and turned away from the glaring of a new day.

He cursed his own foolishness, knowing he should have left town and taken his chances despite the huge reward. There were dozens of towns he could have taken refuge in. Staying on the move would have been the smart thing to do, but knowing the reward had been paid would assure him that no one was looking for Luke Cantrell.

Or so he had told himself. Once he'd kissed Katherine McBride, he would have been grateful for a cholera quarantine if it kept him town. He was too old to be smitten, but that was the only way to describe what was happening to him. His body hardened at the thought of Katherine and the way she had responded to him, hesitant yet trusting. He was no seducer of innocent women, but last night had been different. The taste of her mouth, the feel of her breast against his palm, all had left their mark on him, making him want her in a way that scared the hell out of him.

He'd bedded more than his share of women, all willing and eager, but they were all hurried, carnal encounters meant only to ease the flesh. He wanted much more with Katherine. He wanted to make her his, to know that no other man would ever have her—a claim he had no right to make.

Not only would it be unfair to her, but impossible to even consider. He would be leaving Belle Plain the minute he felt the coast was clear, and there might not even be an opportunity to say good-bye to her.

He opened his eyes and considered the word. The last person he'd said good-bye to was his mother, on her death-bed. She'd made him promise to remember all that she had taught him and to become a man she would be proud to call her son. Then she'd held his hand to her dry lips and said farewell to her family.

Since that day, no one had given a damn whether he left or not, and there had been no need to bid anyone good-bye.

He thought of the promise he'd made to Katherine to persuade Tom to quit the law and to provide the town with a marshal. He thought of Tom's admiration of him, and what might happen to the inexperienced deputy if he was left behind to be marshal.

Tom's greatest weakness wasn't his lack of experience as much as it was his idealistic faith in the law. Luke knew full well how the system could be manipulated by those sworn to uphold justice, and he wasn't about to risk his neck to find out otherwise. Tom would learn soon enough on his own that there was no justice in a system that produced men like Caleb Johnson. Still, Luke knew he was playing them all for fools, and he resented the budding guilt he felt. Was this worse than drawing an ace and winning a man's money? He'd never cheated, but he knew how to bluff until a man would ante everything he had, certain that he would win.

Belle Plain needed a marshal and he needed a place to hide. They assumed he was Johnson, and revealing his true identity would have sent him to the gallows. It wasn't his fault Katherine had thrown her brother's life into the pot.

The sooner he left town, the better. Tomorrow he would have Tom send a second wire to Abilene to find out if the reward was on its way. Knowing that he was officially presumed dead, he would feel safe to travel.

Damn, he was making excuses again. He needed to leave: to hell with telegrams and rewards. He wasn't the only wanted man in Texas, and he could be in Mexico in three days if he rode hard. Luke Cantrell's grave marker was all he needed to leave behind, taunting those who would track a dead man.

Draping an arm across his eyes, he began weaving a feasible reason for leaving town. He was accustomed to stealing away in the dead of night, but that would arouse immediate suspicion. Why would the marshal suddenly disappear? Hell, Tom would probably organize a search party.

He chuckled at that, in spite of himself.

No, he would have to let them believe he would be coming back soon to collect the reward money, leaving his final good-byes unsaid. The money would arrive, lie in the bank, and by the time it was clear that he wouldn't be back, he would have had time to vanish. To Mexico, or even South America. His Spanish was rusty, but he knew enough to get by.

Would Katherine watch for his return? Would she wait? He didn't want to think about her kissing another man the way she had kissed him last night, but only a bastard would leave her to pine for a man she didn't really know and would never see again.

He could let a little time pass and have a letter sent telling them Caleb Johnson had been killed in the line of duty. It was only right, seeing as how Johnson *was* dead. He could even leave the reward money to Katherine.

A sudden knock at the door drew his attention. "Marshal?" It was Tom McBride. "You awake?"

"Yeah," he called out in a husky voice. "Anything wrong?"

"No, sir," was the reply. "Just wanted to tell you you're invited to Sunday dinner with Charlotte's family."

"I just woke up," he explained as his refusal. "I'm not even dressed."

"You've got time," he insisted. "We won't eat for half an hour."

When he didn't respond, Tom added, "Katherine will be there."

Luke damned himself and answered, "Give me time to shave and dress."

"Marshal Johnson, how delightful to meet you."

Charlotte's mother was completely charmed by Caleb's good looks and elegant manners. He had removed his hat before stepping onto the porch, thanked her politely for the invitation, and had not worn spurs to scratch her polished floors,

"Thank you, ma'am," he said, taking her extended hand. "The pleasure is mine."

He smiled and she was done for, a blush rising over her aging features. Ruby Alston was always composed and proper, and Katherine swore this was the first time she had ever seen the woman flustered. And flustered she was, so much so that she completely forgot about inviting him into the parlor. Instead, she merely stood gaping up at him, her veined hand hanging in his.

"Miss Alston, it's a pleasure to see you again so soon." He glanced toward Katherine and Charlotte. "And Miss McBride, it's always a pleasure to see you."

She couldn't keep from smiling back at him, fearing that she was as easily charmed as Mrs. Alston.

When the silence became awkward, Charlotte prompted, "Mother, why don't you have the gentlemen join us."

Somewhat embarrassed, the older lady belatedly remembered her manners and led the marshal and deputy to a settee facing the fireplace. "We can have a nice visit while Masie finishes putting dinner on the table."

Tom plopped down on the delicate furniture without ceremony, while Caleb waited until their hostess was seated before joining Tom.

Seating herself in a chair nearest to Caleb's end of the settee, Ruby Alston beamed at her company. "My, my, if

this won't be the safest home in town with all these lawmen.''

"You are more than safe with us," Caleb assured her,
and she blushed like a schoolgirl.

Katherine didn't miss the subtle show of finery through-
out the Alston household. The long table in the dining room
was set with the good silver and china, and the furnishings
gleamed from a liberal amount of beeswax.

Charlotte's mother prided herself on being self-sufficient
despite being a widow. "I want for nothing," she assured
her friends, and Katherine admired the way she maintained
her home and fortune.

She had joined the Alstons for many a Sunday meal, but
today was different. She and Tom were being shown what
a good family they could marry into. This, however, was
completely lost on Tom, who listened politely to Mrs. Alston's accounts of her family history dating back to the
early settlers of Virginia, but failed to be as impressed as
was expected.

"Where are your people from, Marshal Johnson?" Charlotte deftly turned the conversation away from her bewildered beau.

"Missouri, mostly," he finally replied after a moment's
hesitation.

Missouri? That couldn't be right. He held no trace of a
Missouri accent, and he had mentioned Santa Fe last night.

Mrs. Alston wasn't satisfied with that answer. "And your
parents? Are they still in Missouri?"

"My parents are no longer living, ma'am," he answered.

"Oh, dear, I am sorry." An awkward silence fell over
the parlor, but their hostess's curiosity would not be denied.
"In the war?"

"No, ma'am." His reply was again polite yet reluctant.
"They died before the war."

"My father died in the war," Charlotte offered as an

explanation for her mother's curiosity. "We came to Texas with my uncle."

The conversation lulled again, and Mrs. Alston smiled gratefully when Masie announced that dinner was on the table. Everyone rose, and Katherine didn't miss the hurt that flickered in the older woman's eyes when the marshal offered his arm to her instead.

Dinner proved to be a pleasant affair, and Mrs. Alston relished every compliment, especially those from the marshal. As coffee and dessert were being served, he again praised the meal. "If I'm not careful, I'll get used to this good cooking, and not even the hotels in Denver serve such fine meals."

"Surely, you're not leaving Belle Plain?" Charlotte's mother was stunned. "Why, you've only just arrived, and you *are* the marshal now."

"That's only temporary," he explained.

Everyone glanced at Katherine, as if she would deny his statement, but she kept her eyes on her dessert plate, unable to speak. Her throat grew tight, and she blinked her burning eyes, not daring to look at any of them.

"Caleb is only staying until we hire a permanent marshal." It was Tom who finally spoke. "Or until there's an election."

"Well, you will certainly have my vote." Mrs. Alston squeezed Caleb's hand and called for Masie to bring more coffee and a second slice of pie for the marshal.

When she was satisfied that they were all well-fed, she suggested, "Why don't you young people take advantage of the fine weather and take the buggy down to the creek after dinner?" Without waiting for a response, Mrs. Alston rose from her seat and headed toward the kitchen. "I'll just have Masie pack some lemonade and tea cakes for you."

At last, Katherine lifted her eyes to find Caleb watching

her. His eyes were as solemn as she felt, and she wondered how soon he planned to start missing Belle Plain.

A gentle breeze stirred the tall grass along the bank of the creek, causing the heads of the wildflowers to sway to and fro. Gaining strength, the wind began to tug at Katherine's hair, pulling tendrils free from the thick braid coiled loosely at the base of her neck.

Luke longed to run his fingers through her golden tresses and feel the softness against his palm. He could easily imagine the flaxen length unbound and tumbling over her bare shoulders, falling against his naked chest. Easy, that is, until he remembered the consequences she would face when he left her behind.

Katherine turned to find him watching her and gave him a slight smile. Tom and Charlotte had walked on ahead, claiming to know a spot where strawberries were growing wild.

"I don't know what they plan to do with those berries," she said hesitantly. "We have no bucket to carry them home."

He scanned the shallow stream that ran south of town, trying to gauge the distance from the livery. The creek would provide the best route in the event that a sudden escape was needed. He would have to trade Johnson's two horses for a faster animal, and he had no provisions packed, not even a can of beans.

Forcing his attention away from the creek, he managed a reply. "Most people eat more than they ever get home."

"That's for certain, especially Tom." She tugged absently at a length of the tall grass growing along the bank. "When we were children, he never filled his pail."

"Did you?"

Shadows fell across her face, as if the talk of berries had reminded her of something sinister, and her hand fell away from the grass.

"Katherine?" he said softly. "What is it?"

She tossed her head, as if shaking off the thought, and answered, "Oh, I'd sneak a few, but I knew that Mama needed the berries for jelly."

"You liked jelly that much?"

"Not really." The shadows returned. "She would sell the jelly to trappers and hunters. They lived on jerky and beans and were willing to pay good money for homemade preserves and jellies. Once, she made enough money to buy new coats for Tom and me both."

She seated herself on a grassy spot near the creek and resumed plucking at the long stems, twirling them between her fingers. "Mine was blue and his was brown. I'll never forget those coats."

He lay down beside her in the cool grass, balancing his weight on his elbows, and hoped nothing would dispel her rare talkative mood.

Katherine gazed across the creek bank, her eyes misty. "One time, when we lived in Kansas, a regiment of soldiers camped just beyond our dugout. She convinced the sergeant to let her offer to do sewing for his men, and they lined up with their torn britches and shirts."

"That's a lot of work."

She nodded. "She worked until late that night. When it grew dark, she hung a lantern from the wagon and kept right on sewing."

"Where was you father?" he couldn't help but ask.

"Traveling," she said in a tone that implied "where else would he be?" "We went to Kansas so Papa could start a threshing business. He was convinced that wheat farmers would pay a good price to have their wheat threshed, and he traveled from farm to farm, hoping to hire out."

"What happened?"

She shrugged. "That year marked one of the worst wheat crops ever. Farmers threshed what little they made themselves, and Papa had to sell his equipment at a loss. He did everything at a loss."

She smoothed the length of her skirt, brushing away bits of grass. She kept her eyes on her lap and said with a sly grin, "Perhaps, things would have been better in Santa Fe."

He grinned as well. "You caught that, did you?"

"Your secret is safe with me," she assured him in a conspiratorial whisper. "I am a little curious, though. Is Santa Fe your home?"

"Not anymore." He found himself willing to tell her things he rarely allowed himself to think about. "My father was killed breaking a horse when I was less than a year old. He was the Anglo: my mother was Spanish."

"Then Johnson is your father's name," she concluded.

"I go by my father's last name," he replied, as always telling her the truth when he could. "My mother remarried when I was three and had two more children."

"So, you still have family in Santa Fe?"

"I left Santa Fe a long time ago." He wished now that he'd kept quiet and decided to put an end to the discussion. "I'm sure they gave me up for dead a long time ago."

"But—"

Touching a finger to her lips, he silenced her reply. "Let's talk about something else."

"Like what?" she murmured against his hand.

"Like this."

He leaned forward and pressed his lips against hers, a little shocked by the way she leaned forward to meet him. Her mouth clung to his, warm and without hesitation, and he eased her back on the sweet new grass.

A tremble passed between them, but he couldn't be sure which of them it began with. For the first time in his life, he felt awkward and clumsy, and he hovered over her as if she were a delicate piece of crystal that would break if handled without care. Her arms found their way around his neck, and she was the one to deepen the kiss.

He raised his head and studied her face, open and trusting. She smiled, her lips slightly swollen, and raised her palm to his cheek. A warm, welcoming expression blossomed on her face like a rose opening to the sun, and he trembled at the feel of her fingers trembling against his throat.

"Oh, Caleb," she whispered. "I *am* glad you came to Belle Plain."

The name slammed into his gut, and he lowered his lips to her throat to prevent her from seeing the disgust on his face. He wanted to hear his name on her lips, her memories to be of him, not his face attached to a name and a life that were those of a stranger to them both.

She smoothed his hair with the flat of her palm, a warm, comforting gesture. "I hope you won't have to leave too soon."

He inhaled the scent of her flesh in a resolving breath and pulled himself from her embrace before he was tempted to make promises he couldn't keep.

Her expression was puzzled as he rose to his feet and held a hand out to her. "We'd better get back," he advised. "Your reputation will never survive if we don't."

"Good morning, marshal."

"Good morning, ladies," he answered, politely tipping his hat to the matronly pair of women coming out of the mercantile.

They smiled and exchanged nods of approval. Indeed, everywhere he went in town, folks knew who he was and were glad to see him. By now, everyone knew that he had escorted Katherine to the Founder's Day dance and had taken Sunday dinner at the Alston home, and they were duly impressed. Gone were the stolen glances of apprehension and hushed whispers behind his back. He could easily get used to the simple pleasure of walking through town with no thought to watching his back or avoiding trouble.

He ducked inside the general store, savoring the clean smell of new wood and leather. The shelves were teeming with an impressive array of merchandise, and he mentally listed supplies he might need.

"Well, well, Marshal Johnson." The storekeeper rounded the end of the counter and extended his hand. "Good morning, sir, I'm Eldon Sneed. I was hoping you'd stop by before too much longer."

Sir. He hadn't heard that in a while. He grinned and shook the man's hand. "I'm still getting settled in."

"Anything you need, we've got it." The storekeeper gestured broadly toward the row of shelves. "Just let me know if you can't find something."

Luke perused the shelves. He had decided to stock up on a few necessities in the event that he might need to leave town quickly. Cartridges and coffee topped the list, and he picked up two cans of peaches but put them back. He would add to his stockpile bit by bit and not arouse suspicion. The last thing he wanted was for the good folks of Belle Plain to fear that their marshal might vanish.

He rounded the corner and found himself in an aisle containing sundries and notions. Sunbonnets and wide-brimmed straw hats were piled high alongside jars of cream guaranteed to fade freckles. Children's toys were neatly stacked, boys' on one side, girls' on the other.

The decision to select a present for Katherine came on a whim. He wanted to buy her something completely impractical. Dime novels and puzzles would not be right, and he couldn't begin to know what sort of sewing notions she would like. Just when he was ready to abandon the impulse, he caught sight of a china doll on the top shelf, obviously placed there out of the reach of younger shoppers.

He studied the doll's blonde curls, dark eyelashes, and ruffled dress, remembering Tom's words. *We had things tough when we were growing up.*

He thought of Katherine's mother sewing and selling jelly to keep her children fed and clothed, and of her father's dreams that never worked out. He knew instinctively that Katherine had never had such a fancy doll as a little girl, just as he knew that she had probably always wanted one.

Carefully, he lifted the beribboned doll down from her place on the shelf and and studied the rosy cheeks. Katherine would no doubt find such a gift foolish and wonder at Luke's intentions. He couldn't very well tell her he pitied her poor childhood, but he didn't want to mislead her with noble gestures.

He glanced up to find the storekeeper at the end of the aisle, watching him. Sneed grinned sheepishly and said, "Pretty little doll."

"Yes, it is." Luke replaced the doll on the shelf without an explanation. "I'm surprised someone hasn't already bought it."

"Don't sell too many toys, but every now and then—"

The storekeeper's words were cut off by a sudden eruption of gunfire in the street. A woman screamed and more shots were fired.

"The bank!" someone shouted. "They're robbing the bank!"

Luke was outside the general store before stopping to think, an unexplainable instinct guiding him toward the danger. He swore under his breath and drew his pistol just as three armed men rushed out of the bank. One turned to fire back inside the bank while another began firing randomly in every direction.

The street was clogged with panic-stricken citizens scrambling toward safety, and the acrid stench of gunpowder filled the air along with the terrified screams of innocent bystanders.

"All right, marshal," Luke breathed and quickly stationed himself where he could fire but not be seen. "This is what you get for playing Good Samaritan.''

He aimed his pistol and fired with precision, striking one bandit in the shoulder and barely grazing the other in the leg.

"Get the horses!" shouted the one wounded in the shoulder.

The robber who had escaped the bullets made a quick survey of his situation and demanded of his cohort, "Give me the money!"

"Hell, no!" was the groaning reply as the man gripped the money bag with bloody fingers. "You get the horses. I can still ride!"

Dissension in the ranks—his best chance for stopping them. Luke glanced toward the alley and spotted a young boy, wide-eyed with panic, clutching the reins of four dusty horses. He was just a boy, no more than fifteen. Luke knew he would have to be taken down and the horses scattered.

Spooked by the gunfire, the horses reared against their leads, and it took all of the boy's efforts to hold them steady. He had yet to realize anyone had seen him, and he presented the surest and easiest way to prevent an escape.

Could he do it? Could he murder a youngster for the sake of the Belle Plain Merchant's Bank? The wounded bandits lumbered toward their only means of a quick getaway. They began to shout for the boy to bring the horses to them, one heedlessly shoving an elderly woman out of his way.

Before Luke could decide what to do, Tom McBride emerged from the nearby seamstress shop and waylaid the kid from behind. Startled and unarmed, the boy offered no resistance, and Tom wasted no time in relieving him of the leads to the panicky horses. He tossed the reins to the ground, and the horses needed no more encouragement to flee.

The lookout was handcuffed and lowered to the ground, and the deputy fired twice at the approaching outlaws, wounding the one Luke had missed.

Hit in the shoulder and thigh, the man slumped to the dusty street. Luke sprinted across the street, and he and Tom easily overtook the wounded trio.

Luke retrieved his own set of handcuffs from his belt and snapped them around the wrists of the least injured man. The other two were breathing hard, desperation draining from their expressions.

"We did it!" Tom's exuberance was not lost on Luke, who also felt an unexpected sense of elation.

The alley quickly filled with spectators now that the danger had been eliminated.

"Let's get them to the jail," Tom suggested. He turned toward one of the onlookers. "Go tell Dr. Sullivan I need him at the sheriff's office."

Luke hefted one of the captives to his feet, turning him in the direction of the jail. A few staggering steps were all he managed before Luke was forced to offer assistance. Taking hold of his prisoner's collar, he warned, "Take it easy and get your balance. The jail's not far at all."

Dazed, the man glanced back over his shoulder. "Say, mister, don't I know you from somewhere?"

❖ 8 ❖

DEAR MISS McBRIDE,

I was pleased to receive your letter. I was quite surprised to learn that Belle Plain is still in need of a marshal, and I am very interested in the job. My former captain was killed in the line of duty, but I will ask one of his superiors for a letter of recommendation. If all is satisfactory with you, I can be in Belle Plain within a week of your response. Thank you once again for—

Katherine let the letter fall to her father's desk without reading more. A week! She had completely forgotten about sending the letter to the former Cavalry soldier, and now he was ready to come at a moment's notice.

All along, she knew Caleb Johnson was only serving as a temporary marshal, but she never dreamed a replacement would be so readily available. Propping her forehead on four fingers, Katherine weighed obligation against sentiment.

As acting mayor, she was required to present every suitable candidate to the town council for consideration, but she knew Caleb Johnson would take his leave the moment he learned a permanent marshal was on the way.

"Well, don't be so surprised," she whispered to herself, knuckling her hands against her lips. "Isn't this what you wanted?"

It was, until the dance.

She no longer thought of Caleb Johnson as a ruthless killer hiring out for money, and she couldn't bear the thought of him returning to that sort of life. It was only a matter of time before he ended up on the trail of someone faster or deadlier.

Perhaps he'd never had the chance to do anything other than track outlaws. She wondered once again about his family in Santa Fe, and why he refused to discuss his life there. No one knew better than she about starting over in new places, but would he believe that a new beginning was his for the asking?

He certainly seemed to be settling in as marshal, and Tom had nothing but praise for him. If given the chance, he might even come to prefer living in a decent town like Belle Plain to drifting from place to place.

He probably hadn't even considered it, and she doubted the wisdom of approaching him with the idea.

Katherine leaned back in the chair and closed her eyes. It would be better if he decided on his own, but she should at least let him know he had the option. How tragic it would be to let him leave, never knowing that he would have been welcome to remain.

Tragic for whom? For Tom, left to wear a badge and face danger alone or with a marshal less qualified than Caleb? For herself, faced with a lifetime of regret for all that might have been? Mostly, for Caleb, never knowing the peace of mind and heart that comes with knowing where home is.

Before she could decide on the best way to suggest that

he stay on as marshal, the crack of gunfire startled her to her feet.

"The bank!" someone shouted just outside the courthouse building. "They're robbing the bank!"

Twice more, shots rang out, and she dared not go to the window. Outside, in the street, she could hear angry shouts rising above cries of panic.

"Give me the money!"

"Hell, no! You get the horses. I can still ride!"

Katherine stood motionless against the wall, listening as horses thundered past the building. In the wake of pounding hooves, she heard two more shots and then silence. She wanted to run to the window and dash out the door all at the same time, but fear kept her rooted in place.

"The deputy needs the doctor! Somebody go get Sullivan, and hurry!"

At that, Katherine tore out the door, her fear for herself forgotten.

Katherine could only stare at the chaos within the marshal's office. Slipping in unnoticed, she leaned against the door and breathed a prayer of relief at the sight of her unharmed brother. Panic had knifed through her, and she was near tears when she reached the jail.

Near the stove, Tom stood with his back to her, filling the kettle with fresh water. The stove was hot enough that she could feel the heat from across the room, and the kettle hissed even as he added another piece of firewood. Without glancing in her direction, he gathered a bundle of clean towels and hurried toward the jail cells.

"Hurry up with those towels, deputy! I can't do anything until we stop the bleeding."

"Here you are, doc. What else do you need?"

"Go see what's keeping Sneed with that whiskey. He should have been here by now."

Dr. Sullivan was bustling back and forth between the two cells, his sleeves rolled up past his elbows. Telltale stains of blood revealed that he had thought to roll them up too late.

Tom emerged from the cell, his own shirt now stained with blood. He dropped an armful of soiled towels into a waiting pail of water, his expression grim as be bent to cram them deeper into the water. He straightened, shaking water from his hand, and caught sight of her.

"Katherine, what are you doing here?" He rushed toward her, his voice held an unexpected note of authority. "This is no place for a lady."

"What in the world happened?" She scanned Tom's form from head to toe, grateful to see no bandages or other sign of injury. "I heard shots and there's a crowd gathering outside. Someone said the bank had been robbed."

"Everything is all right now." At her dubious expression, he elaborated. "Three men held up the bank and almost got away."

"Almost?"

A pleased, almost prideful, expression came over his face. "I apprehended their lookout and stopped their escape. They weren't going anywhere without horses."

"*You* stopped them? Where was the marshal?" With a hasty glance around the room, she asked, "Is he all right?"

"He's fine."

His reassurance was somewhat comforting, but her mind could not sort through the scenarios of what he was telling her and what panic had made her believe. "I heard gunshots," she repeated, certain that meant something ominous.

"They gave us no choice," he informed her. "We had to shoot or they would have escaped and probably killed someone in the process."

Her stomach rolled, and she realized too late the stench in the room was that of disinfectant and blood. Tom caught her by the arm just as a wave of nausea nearly overtook her.

"You'd better get on home," he advised. "Dr. Sullivan needs our help right now, and you'll just be in the way."

A shake of her head was the only protest she could manage. She had a responsibility to the town, and she didn't want it said that she couldn't handle herself in time of crisis. Squaring her shoulders, she shrugged her arm from his grip.

"I'll be fine," she insisted, hoping she would be.

Tom knew her well enough to relinquish the argument but led her toward his desk, putting a good amount of distance between her and the prisoners.

"My God, Tom, you could have been killed." She shuddered at the thought of him facing armed robbers and returning their fire. "Why didn't you let the marshal handle this?"

Before he could answer, she caught sight of Caleb inside one the cells, bending over a narrow cot. Dr. Sullivan knelt beside the prone figure, his thin hair plastered to his skull with sweat.

"You've got to hold him still," the doctor ordered. "If that bullet doesn't come out, he'll lose this leg."

Caleb nodded, and the doctor returned to his work. The man groaned and cursed as the lead was dug out of his flesh. The offending bullet made a hollow clink as Dr. Sullivan dispensed it into a waiting basin, and Katherine gagged at the sounds.

Tom turned her away from the sight and tried to steer her toward a nearby chair. "No one was seriously hurt, sis, and I wish you'd go on home."

Katherine leaned against him, as she feared her legs would not support her weight. His fingers left faint smears of blood on the sleeve of her white shirtwaist, and she sank into the chair, wishing she could go home and leave the town's welfare to someone else.

A knock sounded at the door, and she recognized the harried voice of the storekeeper. "Let me inside, someone," he called. "I brought everything Dr. Sullivan sent for."

Tom released her arm and rushed to open the door.

"Quite a crowd out there," Mr. Sneed observed, juggling an armload of supplies as he made his way inside. He paused long enough to push the door closed with his foot before handing the bundles to Tom. "Everybody's anxious to hear more about what happened. Just think, a bank robbery in broad open daylight."

Dr. Sullivan caught sight of Eldon Sneed and motioned for Tom to hurry with the items. "I need those bandages now, and they'll need that whiskey later."

"I brought laudanum, too," Sneed called out. "That'll be better."

"I had some in my bag, but they won't need anything that strong again." The doctor took the bundles from Tom and handed the whiskey bottle over to Caleb. "They won't be hurting too bad until the laudanum wears off. Just pour them a jigger of this if they holler very much."

He nodded and left the cell to place the bottle on the desk facing the door. Only then did he look in Katherine's direction, his dark eyes solemn and troubled. She wanted to run to him, throw her arms around his solid frame, and tell him how thankful she was that he was not harmed, but he turned away, and her nerve failed.

He crossed the room and filled a basin with water from the kettle and began methodically washing the blood from his hands and forearms with a sliver of lye soap. She was anxious to learn more details about the robbery, and why Tom had been in the middle of a shoot-out. But the tense set of Caleb's jaw and the grim expression on his face kept her questions at bay.

Cecil Percy was sprawled in a chair by Tom's desk, pale and visibly shaken but grateful to be alive. He held a folded cloth to his forehead, but Katherine could see a knot the size of a goose egg swelling above his temple.

"Mr. Percy." He looked up at the sound of her voice, and she asked, "What happened?"

"Oh, Katherine, I've never been through such an ordeal in my life!" He lifted the cloth from his forehead, and she could see the knot turning purple already. "They shot the place up, and made me open the safe. I just knew they would kill me once they had the money, but one of them just knocked me in the head with the butt of his pistol and out they went."

"Will you be all right?"

"Oh, I'll be fine. Dr. Sullivan had a good look at me and said this isn't serious." He replaced the compress, wincing as the cloth touched the bruise. "Hurts like the devil though. I'm just thankful no one was killed, and, thank God, the money has been recovered."

Caleb approached the desk holding a white cup. "Mr. Percy, the doctor said for you to drink a little whiskey to ease your nerves."

The older man shook his head. "I'm not much of a drinker."

"I cut it with some water and mixed in a little sugar. It'll make you feel better."

Nodding, Mr. Percy accepted the cup and drank deeply. "Marshal, I can't begin to thank you or Tom enough. If you hadn't been there—"

He couldn't finish the thought, and he gestured toward Katherine with his cup. "You were certainly right about this one, little lady. This man is just the kind of marshal we need."

She glanced back at Caleb and found his expression one of momentary surprise, but he made no comment. Mr. Percy babbled on about the robbery and the bravery of the two lawmen. Far from Tom's obvious revelry in the situation, the marshal appeared as rattled as she.

He turned toward his office, away from Mr. Percy's praise and shut the door, leaving Katherine to ponder his

reaction. Why would a bounty hunter with a deadly reputation be the least bit shaken by a mere shoot-out?

Luke closed the door behind him and sank into the waiting chair behind his desk. He felt sick—sick and angry.

When he'd decided to stay in Belle Plain, he had only
considered the obvious benefits to himself. It was a quiet
town where no one was looking for him, and all he needed
was a place to hide out until interest died down and word
got out that Luke Cantrell was dead and buried.

At this rate, that might end up being the truth. Luck, he
thought, had been on his side until now. No one heard the
outlaw's claim to recognize Luke, and the loss of blood
had rendered the man too weak to ask any more questions.
Dr. Sullivan had given each man a liberal dose of laudanum
before treating their wounds, and a new bottle from Sneed's
mercantile was safely in Luke's pocket.

He searched his memory but couldn't remember ever
seeing the man before. That, however, meant nothing.
There had been so many towns, countless saloons, and hun-
dreds of forgotten faces behind losing hands of cards. For
all he knew, the man might have lost everything he had to
one of Luke's lucky streaks, thus forcing him into a life of
crime.

For now, the laudanum would keep the man groggy
enough to dismiss anything he said, and Luke could only
hope that the recollections of the robbery and the aftermath
would be too hazy for serious consideration.

He swiveled the chair toward the window and stared out
at the back lot behind the jail. It was noon by now, and
things were slowly returning to normal. The bank would
not reopen today, but the general store and barber shop
were filling with customers whose curiosity kept them from
returning home.

From the cafe's back door, the cook emerged to empty
a bucket of mop water and waved to Luke. He raised a

hand in response and resisted the urge to draw the shade. Shutting himself away in the office wouldn't solve his problem, but he needed a chance to think, away from the grisly reminders of the day's events.

This little game was becoming all too real. Today he had *been* the marshal and had been faced with killing a kid in the name of upholding the law. The fact that he would never know what he would have done haunted him and would for the rest of his life. If Tom had not appeared when he did, could he have fired, even while looking into those eyes wide with panic? The boy was no older than he had been when he left Santa Fe, and in a perverse way he had seen himself standing there clutching the reins of those horses. The boy had not been hurt, but he would face jail time for his part in the robbery. Accessory to the fact—a lesser charge, Tom had said—but the state still would seek prosecution.

Luke resisted the guilt that tugged at his insides, knowing full well that a pardon would only send the youngster to find a tougher gang to ride with the next time, and he would know better than to be unarmed. Innocence, he knew, was a fleeting thing on either side of the law.

At the door, a soft knock drew his attention, and Katherine stepped into the room just as he looked up, not waiting for permission. She studied him for a moment, her expression one of cool reserve.

"Dr. Sullivan has gone home now." She held her hands primly before her, reminding him of a schoolmarm addressing a problem student. "He said that he will be back this evening to check on the . . . prisoners."

He nodded. "What about Tom?"

Her lips thinned. "Tom has gone home to gather a few things. He has decided to stay overnight here at the jail."

He didn't miss the disapproval in her voice. "I take it that does not suit you?"

"Nothing about this mess suits me. I can't believe you let this happen."

"What the hell are you talking about?"

"Mr. Percy is planning to write to the governor!" she cried. "He wants to have a citation awarded to Tom—for bravery!"

"What's wrong with that?"

"Mr. Johnson, we had a bargain," she reminded him in a voice thick with accusation. "You said you would convince Tom he shouldn't be a lawman."

Mr. Johnson. He sat back and studied her with what he knew was a blank expression. He had learned long ago to keep his feelings from his eyes, and didn't want her to see the sting he felt at her icy formality.

He rose from the desk and crossed the room. "I told you that Tom would have a chance to find out that the law doesn't suit him. Maybe it does."

"You know better than that." She didn't back away as he thought she might, instead she crossed her arms and faced him, cold and unflinching. "He's too young and he doesn't—"

Glancing down, he caught sight of dull brown smears on her sleeve that could only be blood and realized that her anger was a natural reaction to the horror she must have felt.

Forcing a soothing quality into his voice, Luke tried to reassure her. "He handled himself pretty well today."

Indeed, Tom had reacted more efficiently than he had, responding to the situation as a whole rather than focusing on the robbers alone.

"And what about the next time?" Her eyes narrowed. "He'll have just enough confidence to be dangerous. What will happen then?"

"What are you really afraid will happen?" he countered, losing patience. He understood her concern for her brother, but didn't she give a damn that he had been at risk as well?

"I think you're more concerned about his success than his failure."

She raised her chin in defiance. "Perhaps I just want more for Tom than a life spent behind a gun with nothing to show for it but a bad reputation."

"You pious little hypocrite." He didn't miss the comparison to himself, and he decided she wanted nothing from him but a human shield for her brother. "My reputation was good enough when you needed a marshal to wipe your brother's nose and send him safely home."

"All I wanted—"

"All you wanted was someone to discourage Tom," he cut in, refusing to listen to any more self-righteous sermons on her concern for her brother's safety. "Perhaps Tom wants more out of life than he can find in this two-bit town hiding behind your skirts. It's not your brother you're trying to protect, it's yourself."

"How dare you judge me?" she seethed, and he knew he'd hit a nerve. "You know nothing about me."

"I know more than you meant for me to know." He deliberately let his voice drop to a husky whisper. She swallowed hard and her lips parted with a sharp intake of breath. "I know much more about you than any man ever will."

The angry flush on her face quickly drained, leaving her pale and wide-eyed with hurt and confusion.

He was tempted to open his arms and offer her comfort, but he would not risk the pain of her rejection. He stood waiting for her to say just a word or make one move in his direction, but she remained stock-still.

At last, she turned away from him. She paused as she gripped the doorknob, forcing herself to look back. "I don't fool easily, *marshal*. You can brag about pulling the wool over my eyes this time, but mark my words, it won't happen again."

The only sound in the kitchen was the ticking of the clock, marking the passing of seconds, minutes, and hours.

Katherine had intended to use her time alone to finish revising the proposal for the town budget. Instead, she had sat staring at figures that suddenly made no sense.

Nothing made sense anymore. Her well-laid plans for turning Tom away from being a lawman were no more than chaff in the wind. Rather than displaying his shortcomings, her brother had somehow overcome them. Cecil Percy went on and on about how Tom had effectively diffused a potentially deadly situation. Even in the solitude of the empty house, the words rang loudly.

"That brother of yours is a hero."

The filmy sunlight grew stronger and brighter as the dawn gave way to morning, and she hurriedly stacked the papers and shoved them away. She could think of nothing except the foiled bank robbery and the consequences of Tom's heroics. He would surely be appointed as marshal when Caleb left town. Mr. Percy himself would see to it. And that day might even be today.

She shouldn't be surprised. Caleb Johnson was not the sort of man to keep his word, and she had been a fool to make bargains with him. She had been a greater fool to allow herself to believe there was more to him than met the eye.

She blinked back the tears that threatened, and clasped her hands over her trembling lips. She would not cry over the likes of Caleb Johnson—a bounty hunter. He had not made a fool of her; she had done that herself, and she should be glad to see him leave. Already a dull ache was settling inside her at the prospect of never seeing him again, and tears plopped onto her knuckles.

The sound of boots on the porch alerted her to someone approaching the back door, and she made a hasty attempt to dry her face with the back of her hand.

The door rattled, and Tom stepped inside the kitchen. "What are you doing up so early?"

"I couldn't sleep." She glanced over his shoulder, grateful that he was alone. "What about you? I didn't think you'd be home this morning."

"I came to check on you," he admitted. He closed the door behind him and joined her at the table. "You were so upset yesterday, sis, and Mr. Percy said you were almost in tears when you left."

"It was all that shooting," she lied, studying her brother's face. He looked older this morning, more mature. "I don't think I could stand it if you were hurt."

"I don't want you to worry, but things like that will happen from time to time. If they didn't, the town wouldn't need a marshal or a deputy." He grinned slightly, the growth of dark blond whiskers accentuating the strong line of his jaw. "We've got to earn our keep."

She stiffened at his teasing. "Is that what Caleb Johnson told you?"

"Of course not." Tom leaned forward and studied her. "Why can't you like the man?"

"Like him?" she repeated. "What in heaven's name is there to like about him?"

"Is that how you really feel about him? Sounds like you're trying to convince yourself, not me." When she said nothing, he pressed the subject. "I'm not the only one you could have lost yesterday, and you know it. That's what really upset you, isn't it?"

Katherine could feel bright color rising to her face, and she rose from the table in hopes of changing the subject. "I need to make you some breakfast. Have you had coffee?"

"Katherine, you're being so unfair," Tom wouldn't let it go. "He's as good a marshal as Stuart, maybe better. You're not giving him a chance."

"I wouldn't put so much faith in this marshal of yours," she advised, reaching to light the stove. "I suppose he'll be leaving town now that there's been some trouble."

"Caleb's not going anywhere," he assured her. "He

knows how badly the town needs two lawmen. He wouldn't leave us in a bind.''

''Oh, Tom, he's not the sort of man who'd worry over the welfare of a lot of strangers,'' she sighed, taking an iron skillet from the cabinet. ''I wouldn't be surprised if he's gone by dinnertime.''

''No, he won't.''

''How do you know?''

''He won't leave until he gets his money.''

Her hold on the skillet loosened, causing the cast iron to clang loudly against the stovetop. ''What money?''

''The reward for the man he brought in that first night.'' At her startled expression, Tom suddenly looked sheepish. ''He might not have wanted anyone to know.''

''Well, you've already let the cat out of the bag. What kind of reward?''

''There was a reward for that gambler, Luke Cantrell,'' he confided. ''Ten thousand dollars, and he's waiting on the money.''

Katherine closed her eyes, absorbing the impact of Tom's words. So that was it. He would have stayed in Belle Plain anyway, and being marshal offered a pleasant amusement—and so had she.

All her bargaining and pleading had been for naught, but what hurt was that she had let herself believe his feelings for her might be real.

Dr. Sullivan surveyed his patients once more, satisfied that they were all out of danger, and closed the cell door behind him. ''When will the Rangers be coming to claim them?''

''Not until tomorrow.'' Luke handed the doctor a freshly poured cup of coffee and motioned for the old man to be seated. He crossed the room and peered out of the window, hoping for a glimpse of Tom McBride on his way back to the jail. He had sent the deputy to check on Katherine almost an hour ago, and he wondered what was taking so long.

He had been tempted to go himself, but the last thing he wanted was a repeat of the argument they'd had the day before. In their own way, they were both right and neither would concede the position. In the beginning, his confidence in Tom's ability was as lacking as hers, but the deputy was proving himself to be able.

Katherine knew how capable Tom was becoming, and she blamed Luke for his honed abilities. Even if he were responsible, he would resent her anger. Tom had the drive and determination to be a lawman; age and experience were the only tutors he needed.

"I know you'll be glad to see them go." Dr. Sullivan's voice drew his attention. "Quite frankly, so will I, marshal. I've had more patients since you came to town than I usually have all year long."

Luke claimed his own cup of coffee and propped one hip against the desk. "Mr. Percy told me this was the first time the bank has ever been robbed."

The physician glanced back toward the jail cells. "They weren't counting on us having much law in this town. We made the mistake of giving our last marshal a big send-off and word spread quickly that he had left for California."

"Tom was still here as deputy."

"Tom didn't have a reputation . . . until now."

Katherine's words about false courage nagged at his resolve. "A reputation? No one was killed."

"A lawman builds a reputation on sending men to jail, not killing them."

Before he could reply, the door burst open and Joe Perry rushed inside. His gaze darted first to Dr. Sullivan, then to the cells, and finally back to Luke. "My God, it's true."

"You mean, the robbery?"

"It's all over the county." Joe sank to the chair beside

the doctor. "A bank robbery, right here in Belle Plain. What next?"

"I thought you were on your way to Baird." Dr. Sullivan finished his coffee and began returning his medical equipment to his bag.

"I had to probate Hattie Nelson's will. I left yesterday morning," Joe explained. "I heard about the robbery last night. It's all anyone at the hotel was talking about. Naturally, I set out for home at first light to find out for myself what happened."

He paused, glancing around the jail. "My God, where is Tom?"

"He's just fine," the doctor assured him. "Gone home to see about Katherine, right now."

"Katherine? She wasn't hurt, was she?"

The doctor relayed the events of the past twenty-four hours, stressing over and over how lucky the robbers had been and how well the marshal and his deputy had handled the entire situation.

"You should be commended," Joe declared. "I'm surprised Percy hasn't already suggested it."

"He has," Luke finally spoke up. "I want nothing to do with it."

"But why not?" Joe was incredulous. "You certainly deserve it."

He certainly did. Any man wanted by the law and stupid enough to pose as a bounty-hunter-turned-marshal deserved to be on the front page of every newspaper in the state.

Before he could answer, Dr. Sullivan turned to Joe and said, "If those railroaders aren't impressed by this, nothing will impress them."

"That's right." The concern melted from Joe's face. "I should have thought of that myself. Marshal, this robbery could turn out to be the best thing to happen for this town, and if you're to thank—"

Luke folded his arms across his chest. "Joe, I won't take

credit for this. Tom McBride is the one who saved the bank's money, and he probably kept me from getting killed.''

"What difference does it make who saved who?'' Joe insisted. "All that matters is this will make a good show for the railroad.''

"What kind of show?''

The two men exchanged furtive glances, and Joe finally asked, "You mean Katherine hasn't told you?''

Luke only shook his head and waited. He hadn't been bluffed in years, but had a feeling Katherine was the first person to do so with a hand he'd dealt for himself.

Katherine could only stare across her father's desk. "You had no reason to tell him any such thing.''

"Well, I naturally assumed that you had told him.'' Joe crossed the room and seated himself without waiting for an invitation. "Why wouldn't you?''

"The railroad matter has nothing to do with Caleb Johnson or anyone else we hire to be marshal. Besides, I hope he will be leaving soon enough.''

"Leaving? Why on earth would you want him to leave?''

She rolled her eyes. "We need law and order, not a 'wild West' show.''

"Have you stopped to consider the predicament we'd be in if that money had not been returned to the bank?''

Katherine knew only too well, but she said nothing.

"Those men had cleaned out the safe, and if the bank were to fold—''

"I know,'' she interrupted. "We'd never secure the railroad, and even if we did it wouldn't do any good.''

"By the time those railroad men get here, they will have heard all about our marshal apprehending three desperate outlaws and they'll be anxious to meet him.'' He paused, adding impact to his words. "You know these Eastern types. Once they hear Percy's exaggerated account of the crime, they'll want to see his gun, drink whiskey with him, and even take a souvenir home to their wives. A bullet, perhaps, or maybe even a lock of his hair.''

"I never heard such foolishness."

"Well, what's really going to sound foolish is when I have to tell these gentlemen that our marshal, the one they've heard so much about, the one they traveled out of their way to meet, has left town because our lady mayor feared he was just too uncouth. Imagine, shooting at armed robbers. What will the man do next?''

She glared at him for a full minute, both of them knowing he was right. Joe was shrewd, calculating, and better able to keep his emotions out of business matters. She didn't resent him nearly so much as the fact that Caleb Johnson had gotten under her skin, and she wasn't able to be objective.

Finally, she conceded. "When will they be here?"

"They have business in Fort Worth and will arrive there this week," he replied smoothly, too much of a gentleman to gloat. "Linus McGregor and four other men will be touring several towns in that area before coming here. They'll send a wire when they are on their way."

Anyone she hired as marshal now would barely have his badge pinned on before McGregor arrived. Once again, Katherine was forced to admit that Marshal Johnson was her only hope.

❖ *9* ❖

"I'VE NEVER SEEN so many eggs in my life." Tom surveyed the kitchen with amusement.

"Six dozen, to be exact." Katherine spooned the last of the hard-boiled eggs out of the kettle, taking care not to crack the shells. "I'm doing half in pink and the other half in green. The preacher's wife is dyeing just as many, only in yellow and blue."

"All these eggs and not a bite for dinner."

Katherine harrumphed, turning back to the stove. She had been boiling eggs for the last hour and had thought little of preparing a noon meal. She would be lucky to have the eggs dyed and delivered to the church by late afternoon, and she had no intention of cooking supper. If Tom wanted more than leftover biscuits and bacon from breakfast, he'd have to cook for himself.

"There's a fresh pitcher of lemonade, if you'd like some." Charlotte hurriedly wiped her hands on a clean dishrag, her cheeks flushed from the heat of the kitchen. "I could slice the cake Mama sent for you."

Tom grinned. He purely enjoyed the attention Charlotte

lavished on him every chance she got. "I'm just teasing. Besides, I don't have time. The marshal is expecting me to meet those Rangers at the jail this afternoon. We'll both be glad to see those prisoners gone."

"Why can't the marshal take care of such things?" Charlotte was clearly disappointed; the lemonade and cake had been no coincidence.

"The marshal stayed over last night so you and I could go for that buggy ride," he reminded her. "We've had two more prisoners, and the transfer papers for the bank robbers had to be in order this morning."

"I thought he left all the paperwork to you." Katherine poured herself a glass of lemonade, smoothing a damp strand of hair from her face.

"He offered this time," Tom replied. "Besides, it's good experience for me to deal with the Rangers."

He didn't have to say "since I'll be marshal someday"; the implication was clear enough. Claiming his hat and gunbelt, Tom made hurried good-byes and left.

"Not even a peck on the cheek." Charlotte stood in the center of the kitchen, hands on her hips. "All that brother of yours thinks about these days is that jail. I don't know whether to hope Marshal Johnson leaves or stays!"

Katherine sipped her lemonade, deliberately remaining quiet. Charlotte often rattled on about things she shouldn't reveal when she was upset, and Katherine knew the best way to learn what she knew about Caleb's plans was to listen without asking her any questions.

" 'Caleb Johnson. Caleb Johnson,' that's all I hear." Frazzled, Charlotte sank into a chair, propping her elbows on the table. "If I never get a ring on my finger, I'll blame that lawman for the rest of my life."

Pouring a second glass of lemonade for Charlotte, Katherine joined her friend at the table. They peered at each other over trays of bright pink and green eggs, Charlotte's unhappy expression in stark contrast with the cheery Easter colors.

Katherine had stayed away from the jail, using the presence of the prisoners as an excuse. Each day, she expected word that the marshal had packed up and left town, but none came. If there was anyone in town with whom Caleb would discuss his plans, it was Tom. And Tom would tell Charlotte, in confidence of course.

"I know he loves being the deputy," Charlotte continued when Katherine remained silent. "But I don't want to come second to my husband's work."

"What if Tom becomes marshal?" she posed the question, hoping for an ally. "When Caleb leaves, Tom will expect to be appointed his successor."

"Tom is determined to keep him from leaving." Charlotte toyed with her glass of lemonade, finally raising the glass to her lips. She swallowed hard and leaned forward, her expression intense. "Please don't tell Tom the things I confide to you. But he says having Caleb Johnson as marshal is the best thing to happen to this town, and that we just can't let him go."

"That's the same thing he said about Stuart Carey," Katherine scoffed. "Tom admires anyone wearing a badge."

"No, it's more than that. Tom has truly come to think of Marshal Johnson as a friend." She ducked her eyes. "Besides, we saw him kiss you Sunday by the creek, and Tom is counting on having him for a brother-in-law as well as a marshal."

The glass nearly slipped from Katherine's hand, her face flaming at the thought of her brother seeing her in the marshal's arms. Dear Lord, what if Tom actually approached Caleb about the matter?

"Don't be embarrassed." Charlotte laughed in spite of herself. "Everybody smooches a little now and then, and you're overdue."

"It was a mistake," she tried to explain, but nothing came to mind that made sense. "I won't let it happen again, and I'll be glad when he leaves."

Charlotte's expression was one of stunned confusion. "You mean you don't care anything about him?"

Katherine set her glass down and considered the question, remembering her paralyzing fear when she'd heard the gunshots and the overwhelming relief when she learned of Caleb's safety. She knew when he left Belle Plain, he would resume hunting men like animals. It was only a matter of time before the prey turned predator and he would be the one buried in a town where no one knew him.

"I know better than to care about a man like that." Rising from the table, she gathered several clean dishtowels and began lining the row of baskets. She considered her next words carefully, daring not to reveal the forsaken bargain she'd made with the marshal regarding Tom. "You know what they say about moss growing on a rolling stone. He'll be gone sooner or later."

Charlotte came to stand beside her. "Surely, he wouldn't leave knowing you have feelings for him."

"Like I said, I know better than to care about such a man," Katherine said in a stern voice, wanting the subject closed before she admitted anything. "We'd better get these eggs finished and over to the church. I don't know how we'll ever get them all hidden before tomorrow."

The grassy lot behind the church was swarming with children well before noon on Saturday. Hastily organized games of tag and "Red Rover" were in full swing even as more families arrived bearing food, blankets, and more children. What had begun three years ago as an Easter egg hunt for local children had mushroomed into a full-scale town social with dinner on the church grounds.

Families from miles around gathered for the celebration, and this year there were more faces Katherine did not recognize than ever. Preacher Meeks worked the crowd as if he were an elected official, making everyone feel welcome.

"Just look, they're coming in droves." Charlotte's mother scanned the growing crowd, dismayed by the number of those arriving empty-handed.

"You know the preacher invites every new family in the county to come and share." Katherine began spearing serving spoons into kettles of beans, corn, and potatoes. Platters of sliced ham and cold roast beef were paired with jars of cucumber and beet pickles. An entire table was needed for the desserts—cakes, pies, and cookies of every kind. "I just hope we have enough food."

"We always do," Charlotte assured her.

The breeze picked up, billowing their skirts and the tablecloths and tugging at Katherine's hair despite the pins. She glanced up to see Tom and the marshal enter the grounds, and her heart lurched upon seeing Caleb for the first time since the bank robbery.

"What a crowd," her brother observed, coming to stand beside Charlotte. He scanned the length of the heavily laden table appreciatively. "You ladies have outdone yourselves."

Charlotte tucked her hand in the crook of Tom's elbow and cooed, "I hope you two are hungry."

"Starved, aren't we, Marshal?"

Caleb nodded and glanced in Katherine's direction; his eyes revealed no emotion beneath the shadow of the brim of his hat. "Good day, Miss McBride."

"Marshal Johnson," she replied, hating the pang of regret that speared through her heart. "How nice of you to join us."

Before he could reply, Mrs. Alston made her way around the table and took his arm. "Marshal, you came after all. How delightful. I just know you'll have a wonderful time."

"I certainly appreciate the invitation." He favored her

with a smile the devil would have envied. "You are truly a gracious lady."

"Shame on you," she gushed. "You'll have me blushing like a schoolgirl."

Katherine rolled her eyes, tempted to tell Ruby Alston that the moment his blood money arrived, the good marshal wouldn't give a whit about her or whether she ever blushed again for the rest of her life.

"May I have everyone's attention?" Preacher Meeks called out in a loud voice. Silence fell over those nearby, spreading slowly to those gathering into the crowd. "I want to welcome all of you. We have a fine dinner, plenty for everyone."

Katherine and Charlotte exchanged hopeful glances.

"After everyone has eaten," the pastor continued, "the children will have their egg hunt. At this time, I ask that you join me in thanking our heavenly Father for this beautiful day."

Preacher Meeks asked the Lord's blessings on the food, on those who prepared it, and on those who would receive it. Katherine bowed her head but her eyes remained fixed on Caleb. He had removed his hat, and the breeze feathered his dark hair around his face. He glanced up and their eyes met, and for all her lectures to herself on courting sorrow, Katherine knew her heart would not be denied.

Feelings for Caleb Johnson had taken root in her very soul, and that realization frightened her. His focus remained on her face, and she knew her expression betrayed her anguish.

The prayer came to a close, and people thronged toward the long tables of food, dispelling the visual connection between Katherine and Luke. Her attention was forced to the quickly disappearing food, and she and Charlotte scrambled to refill platters and bowls. When she glanced back in Caleb's direction, he was nowhere to be seen.

The line of people was endless, and Katherine forced

herself to smile as she doled out extra napkins and second helpings. Charlotte rushed to oversee the dessert table, re-routing stray children.

"No dessert until you've eaten dinner," she admonished in a firm but gentle voice. When they grumbled, she assured them, "There will be plenty left when you've finished."

Mrs. Alston caught sight of new arrivals bearing much-needed contributions for the dinner and rushed to collect the food, leaving Katherine to manage alone. It didn't take long before she was overwhelmed by those waiting to be served. They dipped into bowls with dirty spoons, helped themselves to everything, and she barely managed to pre-vent the catastrophe of an overturned jar of pickled beets.

"Need some help?"

She could only stare as Caleb made his way around the table, not waiting for her answer. He took his place beside her and began spooning potatoes onto a little girl's plate.

"How about some gravy?" he offered.

The child giggled and nodded, fascinated to see a man serving food, and he doused her potatoes with rich brown gravy. He winked at Katherine as the little girl dipped her finger into the gravy, sampling it with an approving smile.

Katherine smiled as well and forked chicken drumsticks onto three outstretched plates. She couldn't resist asking, "Can I get you an apron?"

He laughed, glancing down at his shirtfront. "I promise to be careful."

The line was endless. Dozens of folks filed along the table, helping themselves as best they could, but the re-quests clamored continuously.

"Any more biscuits?"

"Just a little more gravy."

"Pickled what?"

They crossed arms and bumped elbows, but Katherine had to admit the marshal was more help than Charlotte, who worried too much about her clothes. The line finally

began to dwindle, and Caleb scanned the scant remains of
what had been a feast.

"A swarm of locusts would have left more." He gave
her a wry smile while wiping his hands on a clean napkin.

"They'll be back for seconds, just wait."

She busied herself covering dishes with napkins to keep
out the flies, but she could feel him watching her every
move. She focused her attention on the food that needed
tending, but her glance darted back to him again and again.
Each time, she found him watching her and grew so flustered she nearly knocked over a jar of corn relish.

"Careful there, Katherine."

She glanced up to find Polly Meeks, the preacher's wife,
approaching the table. "You know Mrs. Polk will want her
jars back unbroken."

Katherine nodded, wiping her hands on a napkin.

"You two have earned a break," Mrs. Meeks declared.
"Fix yourselves a plate and have something to eat while
the children have their egg hunt."

Katherine opened her mouth to protest, but Polly
wouldn't hear it, thrusting a plate into Caleb's hand. "You
and the marshal run along. After all, what good is a picnic
if you don't share with . . . a friend?"

Luke was quite impressed by his first church picnic. The
food was good and plentiful, and the atmosphere was quaint
and pleasant. His mother had often entertained guests out-
doors, serving dinner in the courtyard. Of course, the food
was prepared by a host of servants who then attended the
needs of every guest. The wealthy and affluent of Santa Fe
would never deign to carry fried chicken or peach pies in
wicker baskets to share with their neighbors.

Considering the chaos of the serving line, he couldn't
help but wonder if Katherine and the other ladies were only
making more work for themselves than necessary.

"Wouldn't it be easier for people to bring their own food rather than serving so many?"

Katherine thought for a moment. "It would be easier, but there are so many without much to bring."

Luke's glance followed hers toward the clumps of families savoring the communal fare. He and Katherine had taken refuge at the far edge of the clearing, away from the throng of picnic guests, but the din of laughter and light-hearted conversation feathered toward them like a breeze.

Balancing his weight on his elbows, Luke stretched his legs across the faded blanket and downed the last of the lemonade in his glass. Damn, if he wasn't becoming a regular teetotaler. He kept a bottle in his hotel room but hated to drink alone. The saloons might as well be off-limits to him. Every time he ventured through the bat-wing doors, he was called upon to break up a fight or settle an argument over the gaming tables. He'd tried to sit in on a friendly game of poker once or twice, but found few willing to sit across from a tin star. It wasn't until Katherine shut him out that he realized how dreary the town could be. Belle Plain was like a ghost town without her.

He glanced toward her just as she set her plate aside, the food mostly untouched. He didn't doubt for a minute that she was exhausted, and he wondered if anyone realized how much she had done in preparation for this day.

She looked up to find him watching her and grew slightly flustered. "There's still plenty of food," she offered with a sweeping gesture toward the tables. "If you'd like something else to eat."

He shook his head. "You didn't eat much."

She shrugged. "Too tired, I suppose. It was nice of you to help out the way you did."

"Anything for a lady."

"Or money." She looked down at her folded hands.

He shot her a quizzical look. "I won't deny that."

"You could have told me," she said in a matter-of-fact

tone. "I would have thought no less of you because of the reward. After all, it is your business."

"You *would* have thought less of me." He wouldn't let her deny it. "The only thing worse than a bounty hunter is a well-paid bounty hunter."

"So why bother playing marshal?"

He shrugged. "It's a nice town. One worth saving."

An uneasy expression came over her face. "I think so too."

He chuckled. "Looks like neither one of us was exactly honest about me being marshal."

"I did mean what I said about Tom," she countered. "The town's business with the railroad isn't your worry."

"It's yours," he concluded. "What will happen if they pass up Belle Plain?"

Before she could answer, a muffled scream filtered through the nearby stand of trees. Luke heard Katherine's startled gasp, but he was already on his feet. Not waiting for her, he took off toward the sound, and she had to run to keep up with his long strides, racing in the direction of the frightened cry.

The wooded lot behind the church was thick with dense undergrowth, and brambles clawed at Katherine's skirts as they hurried in the direction of the now faint cries.

"Over here!" Caleb called over his shoulder, rushing toward a gully.

Katherine reached his side and peered into the washed out ravine. To her horror, she caught sight of young Billy Masterson lying in a crumpled heap at the bottom of the drop. Near the child lay a battered basket, the brightly colored eggs spilled all around the tiny figure.

"Billy!" she called. The boy twitched but didn't answer, and she exchanged a worried glance with Caleb.

"He must have fallen," she said, realizing that the child must have slipped away from the others in search of hidden eggs. "They probably haven't even missed him yet. Do you think you can reach him?"

With a nod, he began climbing down the steep side of the wash, and Katherine held her breath until he reached the boy. She watched as he gently touched the child, turning him over to reveal a bloodstained face.

"Go get the doctor," he ordered.

The urgent tone of his voice sent her scurrying toward the main grounds where she found the old physician coaching the Morgan twins on the probable whereabouts of Easter eggs. One look at Katherine, and he met her halfway.

"What is it?" he demanded.

Katherine provided a hasty explanation, found Billy's mother, and led them both to the gully while half the town followed. Mrs. Masterson peered over the drop and nearly fainted.

"Should I move him?" the marshal called up. "His leg is broken, but his ribs feel fine."

Dr. Sullivan frowned. "Do you know how to make a splint?"

Caleb nodded and removed his belt. Not a sound was made as they watched the marshal fashion a splint with two sticks and his own belt. The boy began to cry, calling for his mother.

"I'm up here, Billy," she called out at Katherine's urging. "You be a good boy for the marshal and let him fix your leg."

When the splint was in place, Caleb lifted the tiny figure in his arms and raised his eyes to the top of the ravine. "I can't climb up holding him; I'll have to carry him the long way around."

"The road is just past those trees, less than a quarter mile." Dr. Sullivan pointed toward a narrow path. "We'll be waiting for you."

The crowd moved like a single body, quickly reaching the outskirts of town where the road widened. They waited in silence until the little boy's mewling cries reached their straining ears.

"Here they come." Dr. Sullivan and Mrs. Masterson rushed to gather the injured child, and the grateful mother sobbed as she thanked Caleb for his help. Dr. Sullivan inspected the splint and grinned. "You've given me another patient, but I'm mighty grateful for this one."

Doctor and patient hurried off toward his office with Billy's mother on his heels. The crowd thronged around the marshal, and Katherine looked on as her neighbors took turns shaking his hand or clapping him on the back.

Even Pastor Meeks proclaimed, "Marshal, this town is lucky to have a man like you. That child might have suffered for hours before anyone found him."

"You said it, preacher." Tom practically beamed. "I don't see how this town could get along without Caleb Johnson."

The late afternoon breeze held a trace of coolness, forewarning a chilly night. Luke watched Katherine climb up the back steps ahead of him, her shoulders slumped wearily. They were both heavily laden with baskets containing dirty dishes and utensils.

"Days like this are nice," she observed, juggling her load of pie tins and wooden bowls. "But I'm always exhausted and glad to see them over."

She grappled with the knob but the door stuck tight. She drew a deep breath and blew it out in exasperation. "Twice this week I asked Tom to see about this door."

"Here, let me." He closed the distance between them and clasped the doorknob. Easing his shoulder against the wooden door, he turned the knob and shoved with his weight. It gave easily and swung open, admitting them into the shadowed kitchen.

"Thank you," she said, entering the house. She placed her burden on the table and began sorting through the mess.

"Where do you want this?" he asked, holding up the stained tablecloth.

She took it from him and turned toward the sink. "I'll soak it overnight. It should come out, but it's no loss if it doesn't. I know better than to take anything new or costly."

She began working a steady stream of water from the pump, dousing the tablecloth. Stray droplets of cold water splashed against his shirtsleeve as he leaned against the counter, and he was struck by the pleasant homeyness of the moment.

Had it only been a few weeks since they'd first met in this room—he a trail-weary stranger and she a wary spinster? Even that first night, he had tried to imagine what it would be like coming home to her every night. Now he knew, and knowing only made the longing worse.

She kept her eyes on the tablecloth, furiously rubbing the soiled cloth beneath the water. Even now, she wouldn't let herself be at ease around him, and he was surprised at her attempt to make small talk. "It's a nice town, isn't it?"

He nodded, watching her. "You never did tell me what will happen if the railroad doesn't come."

She glanced over her shoulder, a troubled expression on her face. "It won't be good. What little commerce we have now will dry up, and the businessmen won't be able to stay."

"That's a lot to bet on one hand," he remarked, knowing she was holding back the worst of the story. Had she even come to terms with it herself? "No wonder you're keeping your cards close."

"My cards?" she asked.

"Not wanting anyone to know what you're betting on."

She turned back to the tablecloth. "That doesn't excuse me from telling you the complete truth."

He started to tell her that he was the last person to whom she owed explanations, but he kept quiet. She gave the tablecloth one final push, submerging it beneath the water.

She raised dripping hands and looked around for a dish-towel. He retrieved the one hanging near the stove and of-fered it to her.

"Thank you." She took the white cloth and began drying her hands. "You certainly have made your place in Belle Plain."

"You mean finding Billy?" He shrugged. "Anyone else would have done the same."

"I doubt the Mastersons feel that way," she countered, hanging the dishtowel back in its place. "Or anyone else. After today, you can call this town your second home."

He didn't miss the tiny hope that struggled in her blue eyes. "A man like me never calls anyplace home."

"That's rather sad, don't you think?" she pressed softly, taking a seat at the kitchen table. "When I was little, we were always setting out for somewhere new, and I swore someday I'd have a home and never leave."

He joined her, resting his arms against the tabletop. "I swore someday I'd leave and never look back, just keep on going."

She covered his hand with her own, and silently they shared a subtle exchange of past sorrows. In a unique way, he understood her hunger for stability and sensed that she accepted his need to stay on the move.

"Don't you think that you'll grow weary of traveling someday?" She lifted her face to his, and Luke was stunned by the emotions shimmering in her eyes. Warmth and af-fection that he had no right to claim radiated in the blue depths. "It's so dangerous, and you shouldn't—"

"Katherine, don't build your hopes on what might hap-pen someday." He threaded his fingers through hers, wish-ing with all his heart he could promise this woman something tangible, but he refused to lie to her. "The time will come for me to leave, perhaps sooner than we think. I can't even say where I'll be going, but—"

"Is that what you really want?"

He looked down at their clasped hands and asked himself the same thing. For the first time in his life, the answer wasn't ''something else'' or ''something better.'' What he wanted was right in front of him, but it might as well be at the other side of the world.

''I'm a man with few choices left anymore. I do what I have to do.''

Her fingers tightened around his. ''But if you *could* make the choice, if there was a way, wouldn't you rather stay where you have a future?''

He finally nodded in concession. ''Yes, if it were ever possible, Belle Plain would be the place.''

''That's the wonderful thing about having a home,'' she managed, her voice thick. She tried to smile, but he didn't miss the way her lips trembled. ''It's always there when you're ready to come back.''

''I'll remember that,'' he assured her, cupping her cheek with his hand. Loose tendrils of golden hair tickled his knuckles, and her flesh was like silk against his palm. ''Always.''

A warm, trusting expression came into her eyes and a warning sounded in his mind. She leaned forward, and he forgot the danger, taking her lips in a kiss meant to silence her pleas but instead sealing a bargain he couldn't keep.

Her mouth yielded to his, welcoming the gentle foray of his tongue. She tasted even sweeter than he remembered, and he slid his arms beneath hers, dragging her into his lap. Her arms went around his neck, and he deepened the kiss, dimly aware of the chair she'd been sitting on toppling over on the floor.

Katherine didn't flinch at the thunderous crash, and he let his hands trace the small of her back, finding the curve of her hips. When she made no protest, he gently shifted her weight until her bottom was firmly settled against the aching proof of his desire.

She whimpered slightly, and he broke the kiss, his mouth

seeking the tender flesh of her throat. She arched her neck, allowing him better access, and he slid one hand under the bulky weight of her skirt.

"*Querido,*" he whispered against her throat, the warmth of her flesh searing his palm through the thin muslin shift. She was limp in his arms, pliable with a desire she couldn't understand. Sweat broke out on his forehead as he resisted the urge to delve his fingers inside the folds of her under-clothes, knowing he would find her wet and swollen with need.

If he touched her, he would be unable to leave her in-nocence intact. As desperately as he wanted to take her then and there, he would not sate his lust and leave her behind, ruined and possibly pregnant. She deserved better than that—better than him.

"Kitten," he groaned as her fingers combed through his hair. "We have to stop."

She opened her eyes, looking at him with a dazed ex-pression. As if she hadn't heard him, she bent her mouth to his, and he allowed himself one chaste kiss before rising to his feet, gently pulling her along with him. She swayed against him, but before she could say anything, a shout came from just outside.

"Katherine!"

Startled, they both rushed out onto the back porch to find Dr. Sullivan reining his buggy to an abrupt halt just shy of the back walkway. The old physician's expression was anx-ious, and he shouted, "Katherine, Patsy Reynolds' baby is coming."

Katherine gasped, looking up at Luke in panic. "Patsy is a friend of mine," she explained before turning back to Dr. Sullivan. "But she isn't due for another three weeks."

"You try telling that to the baby," Dr. Sullivan barked. "Justin sent one of the ranch hands in to fetch me, and Patsy said you were to come with me."

"Yes, I promised I'd be with her."

Impatience drew the doctor's face into a tight scowl. "If you want to ride with me, you're welcome but I can't wait."

Katherine rushed down the steps, grasping the side of the buggy. "I'll have to gather a few things. Can you give me just a few minutes?"

"Katherine, I can't wait. First babies rarely come early without complications."

"You go on ahead, doctor." Luke came to stand beside her. "I'll take Katherine out there myself."

❖ *10* ❖

Luke knew as much about babies as he did about being marshal. He remembered very little about his brother being born and less about his sister, only his stepfather proudly referring to them as his *real* children. No opportunity was ever missed to make that distinction, and after his mother's death . . . Christ, life had been hell.

The moment he and Katherine arrived, the expectant father whisked her upstairs to his wife, and she had not been down since. Luke stationed himself on the front porch, not wanting to leave Katherine and not wanting to be inside the house with all the drama of childbirth going on.

He sat in the chill of the wee hours, listening to Justin Reynolds babble on about getting a herd ready for a drive to Kansas. Had he ever been to Kansas? Well, there was no better place to take Texas cattle. The Kansas railheads were the quickest way to transport the beeves to meat packers.

He nodded politely as Justin went on and on about new methods of treating various bovine diseases, all the while the father-to-be smoked one cigarette after another and nervously rolled more.

"Sure you don't smoke, marshal?" he asked, expertly tapping tobacco onto the thin rolling paper.

"I'm sure." He rose from the porch swing, his legs stiff. He glanced up toward the bedroom window, easily recognizing Katherine's shadow hurrying back and forth. Dr. Sullivan's shadow rushed toward hers and then they both disappeared.

"How long have you been in the cattle business?" Luke queried.

He'd made the mistake of letting the conversation lull an hour or so ago, prompting Justin to go into the house to check on his wife. Dr. Sullivan had run him back downstairs, assuring him that everything was fine. To Luke, he had growled a warning to keep Justin's mind off the baby and his nose out of that bedroom. "He'll faint dead away, and I haven't time to tend an expectant father."

"Ever since I was big enough to follow my pa out to the range on my own horse," Justin answered, crushing the remains of yet another cigarette beneath his boot. "Moved here about ten years back, riding herd for Tyler Martin. I've only had this place since winter before last."

"Tyler Martin?" Luke was mildly interested, remembering once again the way the man kept his eye on Katherine.

"He still has the biggest outfit in the county." Justin rose and stretched, pacing the length of the porch. "Year before last he drove one herd to Abilene and sent another to Wyoming. Made a fortune—every rancher up there wants longhorn stock to mix with their own."

Luke was treated to another lecture about the benefits of crossbreeding cattle. He listened, leaning back against the porch railing, halfway admiring the small house. Modest at best, the home was cheery and neat. Flowers bloomed along the walk and in various pots near the steps.

It was so different from the sprawling house of his youth.

He grinned, remembering the whitewashed adobe walls and the shady courtyard. Unbidden memories assailed him, and he wondered if the younger children still lived in Santa Fe. Were they married? Did he have nieces and nephews?

A few years back, word of his stepfather's death had reached him in San Antonio by way of a horse trader lamenting the loss of a faithful and wealthy customer. He had been tempted to write and even to visit, but resisted both. What would it have accomplished?

Shying away from forgotten memories that suddenly throbbed like a sore tooth, he forced himself to concentrate on Justin's recitation of the importance of castrating calves before a certain age.

"So why don't you run a herd to Wyoming?" he asked hoping to change the unpleasant subject.

Justin considered it. "If Martin decides to go this year, I might throw in with him."

"Why didn't he go last year?"

"His wife died." Justin struck a match on the porch railing and lit his smoke before elaborating. "Lost her third baby in a row, only that one took her with it."

Luke said nothing, and Justin glanced nervously toward the window. "Bad luck all around. Every man wants sons to leave his land to when he's gone, and Martin says he'll marry again. Says he wants a bride young enough to get babies, two at least."

Luke remembered the way the man studied Katherine and the seemingly odd comment about how healthy she looked. Fury knotted his gut at the thought of that bastard sizing her up like a brood mare. Any man with a brain in his head could see she was a smart, caring woman who deserved. . . .

Who deserved more than *he* could ever hope to give her. What right did he have to judge Martin? At best, Luke was no better than her father. Laughter and bright promises with no future or security. The successful rancher could at least provide a fine home and a comfortable life.

Damn, this was all Caleb Johnson's fault. Luke had never agonized over being a lacking suitor before. Hell, he'd never been a suitor! Women had never been more to him than a pleasant distraction, and he had never offered them more than a few laughs and good memories . . . and a few dollars.

He'd had his share of decent women—widows and neglected wives—but mostly he sought the company of saloon girls and outright whores who never expected anything from him. Life had been so uncomplicated before he came to Belle Plain.

The screen door creaked, and Katherine stepped onto the porch, a tired smile on her face. "Congratulations, Justin," she said, touching his arm. "You have a son."

The young man's jaw went slack, and Luke feared the man would faint after all.

"A boy," Justin whispered and glanced back toward Luke. "Did you hear that, marshal? A boy!"

He let out a whoop and embraced Katherine. "When can I . . . I mean is it all right if—"

"Dr. Sullivan said you may come up for a minute, but Patsy will need her rest."

Justin nearly tore the screen door from its hinges, leaving it to bounce open three times before finally staying shut. Katherine laughed and sounded weary, seating herself on the swing. "What an ordeal."

"Will she be all right?" Luke stepped on Justin's last cigarette, still glowing on the porch.

"Oh, she'll be fine." Katherine sank back against the swing and let her head fall forward. She raised her fingers and began kneading the base of her neck.

He was tempted to sit down beside her and massage her tired muscles, but he dared not touch her. If he touched her, he would hold her, and holding her would lead to kissing her. When he kissed Katherine, he longed to make promises a man like himself couldn't begin to keep.

She glanced up at him expectantly, letting her eyes drop when he made no move toward her, but he didn't miss the disappointment on her face. The passion that flared between them earlier was new to her and, in her innocence, she was more willing than she should be.

"I suppose you need to get back to town," she said, graciously making an excuse for him. "I left Tom a note."

I know you did. I watched you write it and almost kissed you then.

"Yeah, I need to get back." He paused. "What about you?"

"May I send a note with you to Charlotte?"

He nodded.

"Tom will bring her out to relieve me, and he can drive me home." When he made no offer to drive her back to town, she again provided a gracious excuse. "I should stay here with Patsy."

When he said nothing, she rose from the swing and went in search of paper on which to write the note. The screen door closed softly behind her, and he knew that her hand had lingered to keep the door from closing too quickly in the hope that he would follow.

Instead, he turned away from the house to stare at the eastern sky as it grew pink and gold with the rising sun. He had sealed his own fate years ago; he would not seal Katherine's.

Katherine stretched and yawned, tugging the sheet over her bare arms. She had been so exhausted by the time Tom brought her home that she had stepped out of her dress and collapsed onto her bed, falling asleep in her shift and stockings. At some point, she had grown cold and roused only long enough to pull the covers back and burrow under them.

She glanced toward the window, trying to judge the time. Late afternoon, she guessed by the shadows. Birds were still singing, so dusk was still a few hours away. This would be one Easter Sunday she wouldn't forget, and she knew by now that everyone in town had heard about Patsy's baby.

As tired as she was, she could only imagine how her friend must feel. Katherine had never helped deliver a baby, but Patsy had made her swear she would come, and now she was glad she did. Seeing Patsy suffer had been horrible, but when Dr. Sullivan had placed the squirming baby boy in the blanket she had waiting, Katherine understood why older women assure younger women that childbirth is worth the agony.

The baby was perfect—the most precious thing she'd ever seen. She'd bathed him and dressed him in a tiny nightgown, assuring Patsy that he had ten toes and ten fingers. Katherine would never forget the wonder on Patsy's face when she placed the tiny bundle, mewling pitifully, in his mother's arms. His cries ceased instantly, and she and Patsy were awed by the instinctive recognition between mother and child.

Katherine rolled on her stomach and thought about babies, a subject she had never given much consideration. Years ago, when her friends daydreamed about large families and picked names for their imagined children, she had vowed never to bring a child into this world unless it would be well provided for. Love was crucial, but children deserved more.

Patsy and Justin were delighted by the new arrival, but a drought or a deadly cattle disease could leave them bankrupt and the baby in want. Katherine doubted they had even considered the possibility.

Just before Tom and Charlotte arrived, Katherine had taken a tray upstairs for Patsy. The bedroom door had been left ajar, and she caught sight of Justin sitting on the bed watching his wife nurse their son. She should have turned away from such an intimate scene but had been struck by the loving expressions on the faces of the new parents.

They both studied the baby's tiny head, nestled against Patsy's breast, and then gazed at one another with the same joyous devotion. Katherine turned silently down the stairs, leaving the tray covered on the stove, besieged with emotions: envy for her friend's happiness, an unexpected longing for a child of her own, and anger at Caleb Johnson for refusing to believe that he could ever change.

Once again, tears sprung to her eyes, and she made no attempt to attribute them to exhaustion. She knew what kind of man Caleb had been before he came to Belle Plain, but she also knew the man he could become. That was the man for whom she cried. The man who couldn't start over, choosing instead to throw away happiness—his and hers.

Perhaps she was wrong to blame him. Heaven knows she'd handled the whole matter badly. Spurning him at every turn only to beg him to stay, and throw herself in his arms. She shrank from the thought of how wanton and eager she had been, arching beneath his touch like a cat.

A knock sounded downstairs, and she listened to hear if Tom was in the house to answer it. The knock sounded again, and she glanced in dismay at the dress crumpled on the floor. She forced herself to rise and headed downstairs, slipping into her faded dressing robe as she went.

She swiped at the dampness on her face, knowing her eyes were red and swollen from sleep and tears. She couldn't help it, and whoever was knocking insistently at the door would receive no explanation.

"Katherine!" She recognized Joe's voice. "Open the door!"

She did, forcing herself not to be angry. Her voice was deep and scratchy when she asked, "What is it?"

"I'm sorry to disturb you," he said, somewhat taken

aback to find her in a dressing gown at that time of the day.

"It's all right." She motioned for him to come inside the house, ignoring his obvious concern. "I was out at the Reynolds' place last night. They have a little boy, and he took all night to get here."

"Well, this is a monumental day." He waived a folded slip of yellow paper. "Look what I have."

"A telegram?" she said, doubtfully. "On Sunday?"

"When the president of the railroad wants a wire sent, it doesn't matter what day it is."

"What does it say?"

She followed him into the parlor, and he handed her the telegram. "Read for yourself."

She scanned the telegram and glanced up at him in astonishment. "They're coming here? Now? Before Baird and before Rock Falls?"

She couldn't believe it, quickly rereading the wire. It was from the President of the Texas & Pacific Railroad advising them that the survey committee would be in Belle Plain within a week to tour the town before the final selections were made for the stops along the new tracks being laid between Fort Worth and Abilene.

"Even before Tate," he gloated as she handed the telegram back to him. "Oh, Katherine, do you know what this means?"

"They must truly be interested in Belle Plain," she concluded. For the first time, she felt excited by the prospect of being a railway stop. Before it was all just talk, but now the possibility was very real. "This could really happen."

"Of course, it's going to happen," Joe insisted, all doubt swept from his voice. "We're going to make sure it does."

She glanced up at him. "We are?"

"We are," he assured her. He sat down on the sofa and withdrew a sheaf of papers from his leather case. "I've called in every favor owed to me, and we're going to put on a show these men won't soon forget.''

Katherine accepted the papers he held out to her and scanned them quickly, smiling up at her friend. ''Joe, this is wonderful!''

''You're not still unhappy about Tom being awarded a medal for bravery?'' he asked, a note of reserve in his voice. ''That will surely make a lasting impression.''

Her smiled broadened as she reread the papers, the words giving her the first real hope she'd had in days. ''I won't mind, not if we'll be swearing Caleb in as permanent marshal at the same time.''

Luke knew Belle Plain was a quiet little town, but today it seemed deserted. All the families were gathered in their respective homes, sharing Easter dinner. Katherine had made a halfhearted offer to prepare a late supper, but he had suggested she take the day to rest and not worry about cooking.

Surely, she was back in town by now, but he had seen no sign of her or Tom. He fought the urge to go to her house under the pretense of seeing if she had arrived home safely or to ask about Patsy Reynolds. All he really wanted to do was hold her and swear never to leave. It was a lie he meant with all his heart.

Luke had returned to the marshal's office after sending Tom and Charlotte off to the Reynolds' place. He couldn't bear the drab little room at the hotel, though the jail offered little cheer. At least there were no prisoners and no one had need of the marshal's services on the holy day.

He sat for the longest time, boots propped on the desk, and tried to think about anything but Katherine. But there was nothing. In a few short weeks, he had accumulated more memories of one woman and one town than he had of all the places he'd been in a lifetime.

The vague promises he'd made to Katherine and the hope

in her eyes ate away at his conscience. It wasn't a question of whether he wanted to stay in Belle Plain. There simply was no way that could ever happen. He let his mind spin wild plans in search of a means to start over as Katherine had begged him to consider, but nothing could erase the fact that all his lies would never let him rest.

Finally, he abandoned the hope of coming to any solution. There was none: the die was cast for his life.

He left the jail, trudging back to the dreariness of his rented room. The hotel was all but deserted, eerily quiet, and no lamps were lit in the lobby. He closed the door behind him and turned toward the stairs.

"Marshal, hold up there." From his private living quarters, the innkeeper rushed toward him. "You have a visitor."

A tingle of apprehension feathered up Luke's spine. "A visitor?"

"He came in this afternoon asking for you," Mr. Parvin explained. "I told him you were out at the Reynolds', but he said he'd wait as long as it took."

The apprehension flared, making the hair on his neck stand on end. Obviously, this visitor had asked for Caleb Johnson by name, and the fact that he had waited signified that the visit was not by chance.

"Who is it?" was all he could think to ask.

"I didn't ask," the innkeeper replied. "He's not the sort of man you question."

Luke nodded and the innkeeper turned toward his quarters, stopping mid-stride. "Mother and I have already had dinner, and the other boarders ate earlier. There's plenty left, if you and your friend are hungry."

"I'll ask him."

Satisfied with the answer, Teddy Parvin resumed his steps and disappeared through the heavy curtain that separated him and his aged mother from the rest of the hotel. Luke stood in the center of the sparsely furnished front room, contemplating what to do: run or pack his things and run?

Just as he turned toward the stairs, a voice stopped him dead in his tracks. "I been waiting for you all day, you old dog."

Luke's legs were like lead as he turned, expecting to find a pistol aimed at his heart, but no one was there. He scanned the room but still found himself alone.

"Come on in here and set a spell," the voice called a little louder, coming from inside the shadowed parlor.

Cautiously, Luke approached the double doors that led into the tiny parlor set aside for boarders to relax and visit. In the center of the room, Luke could make out the figure of a man perched on the edge of the worn sofa. Despite the shadows, Luke could tell the man was relaxed and at ease, not poised to draw a weapon. Still, he proceeded with caution, well aware that Caleb Johnson's enemies were now his as well.

"Well, I reckon it's true," the man embarked on the conversation, confident that Luke would join him. "Caleb Johnson turned lawman. I guess all the folks you've sent to hell are enjoying the freeze."

In spite of himself, Luke chuckled at the wry humor, all the while letting his hand linger near his holster. Whoever this man was, he could mean nothing but harm to Luke. One look and the man would expose him as an imposter and a wanted man. "Well, what have you got to say for yourself?" The man maintained his expectant posture, never looking in Luke's direction, only leaning forward slightly, listening for a reply.

Luke coughed slightly, forcing a hoarse quality to his voice. "I'm afraid you have the better of me, mister. Can't say as I recognize you."

Laughter was not what he expected, but the visitor slapped his knee and let out a loud guffaw. "Damn, but you ain't changed a bit. Light one of them lamps and see if you don't know me then.''

Luke hesitated but knew that his ruse couldn't go on forever. Without turning his back on the visitor, he struck a match and lit the lamp on the table near the doorway. He adjusted the wick and the room filled with light, and he watched the stranger's face come into view, waiting for some sign that the man realized he wasn't Johnson.

The bright light flooded the room, chasing shadows into the farthest corners, but the expression on his guest's face did not change. In fact, he barely blinked as he slowly turned his face toward Luke.

The face was older than Luke would have anticipated, heavily lined and weathered by the sun. A battered Stetson sat atop a mop of gray hair, but it was the man's eyes that held Luke's attention.

Unfocused and half closed, the eyes turned toward him but saw nothing.

"My, God, you're blind," he breathed and the old man cocked his head at the sound his voice. Stunned and relieved, Luke leaned against the doorjamb not sure what to say or do next. He certainly wasn't prepared for the older man's laughter.

"You're the last person I figured would feel sorry for old Hank Malone going blind." The laughter faded. "Well, don't be. I get along just fine."

Luke slipped inside the room and seated himself across from the sofa. Out of his own curiosity, he asked, "What happened?"

Hank turned his head, revealing a nasty scar at his left temple. "A bullet, what else? Hell, I'm lucky to be alive, they tell me."

Luke didn't miss the regret that flashed across the older man's face, quickly disguised by a proud grin. "The bastard who shot me wasn't so lucky. I got him in the gut before he could fire at me, and his aim was off. Another inch and I'd have been dead before him.''

"How long ago was that?" Luke noticed that Hank still wore a holster. Did he really think he could defend himself or was the presence of a gun merely a throwback to the habit of a lifetime?

"About fifteen years," Hank answered after a little calculation. "Right after you left Fort Smith. I heard you went to the Indian Territory."

"For a while," Luke answered, having not an inkling of an idea about Caleb Johnson's past. He was beginning to believe Hank and Johnson had been friends, but he couldn't picture the bounty hunter as a friend to anyone. "What about you?"

A shadow passed over Hank's face. "Well, I took up scouting for the army. What with the war and all, the soldiers out west were pretty much on their own fighting the Indians. I wasn't at it six months before a buck private got me with a Cavalry pistol. Can you believe it?"

Luke nodded and realized Hank was still waiting for a reply.

"You said he died?"

"He sure did. The snot-nosed brat challenged me to a damn duel over a woman. I laughed it off, but he was waiting for me that night when I took watch."

Luke couldn't help but be curious about the unexpected turn of the story. "A woman?"

"Yeah, the captain's daughter. Prettiest little thing you ever saw." An almost wistful expression came over Hank's weathered face, his useless eyes growing bright with threatening tears. "I still can't believe she gave a polecat like me a second look."

"I know what you mean," Luke replied honestly.

Hank nodded. "She sat by my bed for three whole days, praying and holding my hand. I made it through, but when they took them bandages off . . . well, what good is a blind man to any woman?''

"She ran out on you because you were blind," Luke concluded, not surprised but a little disgusted. He'd known such shallow women in his day. "You're better off."

"You got it all wrong, Caleb," Hank quickly corrected him, his voice sharp with reproach. "That little gal loved me. Don't ask me why, but she did. *I* sent *her* away."

At that, Luke was surprised.

"It wasn't easy to do, but she needed a man to take care of her, not one that would be a burden."

"If she cared about you—"

Hank raised a hand in censure. "She did. And just knowing that kept me going all these years. I've had a good life, took up being a wheelwright."

"A wheelwright?"

"My ma always did want me to learn a trade." He laughed, extending his calloused palms for inspection. "I learned to carve the wood just by feel. I've got a little shop in Amarillo, a nice little town. You ought to get up there some time, unless being marshal keeps you too busy."

Luke had to ask. "What brings you to Belle Plain?"

"Just stopped for the night," he said with a shrug. "The stage pulled in yesterday evening, and the next one won't leave until daybreak. I'm on my way to visit my brother down around San Antonio."

"How did you know I was in town?"

"Pure damn luck," he answered with a grin. "Came in here for a room and heard that innkeeper tell his ma not to expect Caleb Johnson for dinner. Well, I'm nosy enough to ask and sure enough . . . I knew it had to be you. A bounty hunter turned lawman."

Hank laughed at the irony, and Luke was forced to smile, all the while praying the old man would continue to be content talking about himself and not ask questions about Caleb's past.

Hank leaned forward and lowered his voice. "They told me you took your woman out to visit a sick friend, and I knew right away what had turned your life around. Tell me, is she pretty?"

Luke drew a deep breath, telling himself that deluding Hank was as much out of kindness to a lonely old man as it was to save his own neck. "Prettiest thing I ever saw."

Hank smiled and nodded. "I'm glad for you, Caleb. There ain't too many of us old timers left anymore. Most of 'em are dead, or in jail, or worse. Old Jake Mathis is a town drunk in Saltio, sweeps out the saloon for drinks and a place to flop. You and I are the only ones that made it. I'm just glad you didn't have to take a bullet in the head to wise up."

Luke sank back in the overstuffed chair, and tried to think of a reply. Caleb Johnson had not made it. He had ended up dead, buried in a another man's grave. Telling Hank the truth would do neither one of them any good. He promised himself that someday he would send word of Caleb's death to Amarillo, but for now he had to think of something besides the truth.

Just then, Teddy Parvin stuck his head into the parlor. "Marshal? I thought I'd see if you and your friend would care for a bite of supper. I can put a pot of coffee on if you like."

The hopeful look on Hank's face was almost childlike, and Luke couldn't have refused if the man had two good eyes and a bloodhound. "That sounds fine, Teddy."

"Y'all go right on to the dining room," the innkeeper directed. "Nothing fancy, but good food just the same."

Luke and Hank stood at the same time, and the older man groped for Luke's vest, his skilled fingers finding the tin star.

"I still can't believe it," he said more to himself. "All these years, I figured you for dead, and here you are as strong and able as you were all those years ago. I reckon you owe it all to the little lady.''

Luke nodded and led the way to the dining room. ''I owe her my life.''

❖ 11 ❖

LUKE PAINSTAKINGLY PLACED the last of his things in the bulging saddlebag. He had enough food and ammunition to last at least three days, and a deck of cards to get him that much more ahead if the need arose. He breathed a curse and tightened the cinch, glancing around the tiny room he'd grown far too familiar with over the past few weeks.

Everything was packed and ready to go whenever he wanted, and that was the trouble. He didn't want to go. He kept making excuses to stay one more day and then another and another. He told himself over and over that Tom needed him to stay or that Katherine was depending on him, but he knew the real reason. He had let himself care.

He tried to remember the last time he'd stayed anywhere this long, and could only recall a time in an Arizona mining town when he'd been badly cut in a fight over a straight flush. A deep gash above his navel had rendered him unable to ride, and he was tended by a whore whose name he couldn't recall.

There had been so many towns and faces, none standing

out in his memory, but Belle Plain would remain with him like a phantom pain reminding an old soldier of a missing limb. He would wonder what became of Justin Reynolds' dreams of driving cattle to Wyoming and whether the baby would grow up to follow in his father's footsteps. Would Tom remain a lawman and marry his pouty sweetheart? And most of all, what would Katherine do when he'd left for good?

"Take good care of that little lady," Hank had admonished him early that morning as he boarded the stage. "You don't find many like her in this world."

The words still rang in his ears, though the stage had been gone over an hour, and he refused to contemplate what might have happened if Hank had asked pointed questions or brought up specific incidents from the past. In the end, the old man had been content just to have someone listen to him for a few hours. Luke wondered if he would end up the same way someday, pouring his heart out to anyone who would listen, telling them about the good times in his life.

There was this woman once. . . .

He forbade the thought from forming. He wasn't running out on Katherine; he wanted her to be happy. She deserved every happiness this world had to offer, but could he bear not being the man to give her those things? There was no point in even wishing he could.

The coming months would be spent slinking from one hideout to another, always looking over his shoulder. Even when he reached Mexico, his safety would not be guaranteed, and it would be years before such a large reward was forgotten.

The time had come to quit making excuses and leave Belle Plain. He would devise a plausible story about needing to file a claim on a wanted man or learning of a recent escape. Anything, as long as it didn't arouse suspicion.

A knock sounded at his door. "Who is it?"

"Message for you, mister." He recognized the small voice belonging to the innkeeper's young son. The boy always made sure he was the one to bring news or towels to Luke's room, knowing the marshal would give him a penny, enough to buy licorice at Sneed's store.

He opened the door, unable to resist smiling down at the freckled face. He accepted the folded note and slipped two pennies in the boy's palm, just in case he wasn't around much longer.

The youngster's eyes widened beneath bangs that always needed trimming. "Thanks!"

Luke watched him race down the hall toward the stairs and closed the door as the sound of miniature boots pounding on the wooden stairs began to fade. Something else to remember and care about—would the boy have a source of candy money when he was gone?

He unfolded the note, not recognizing the sprawling script. He was being summoned to a meeting of the town council set to begin in half an hour. No explanation was given and no reply was requested. He refolded the note and pondered what the summons might mean.

He glanced back toward the overstuffed saddlebag and wondered if the time had come to leave. He dismissed the idea that he had been discovered, confident that no one would send for a wanted man by means of a note. Still, he couldn't shake the feeling that the meeting and the call for his presence meant something ominous.

The midmorning sun was dazzling as he stepped out of the hotel, falling in step with the throng of bustling townsfolk. He no longer felt the need to avoid curious glances or listen for whispered accusations. The persona of town marshal still prevailed, and it worried him that he had so easily shaken off his true identity.

"Morning, marshal," a voice called out.

"Morning," he replied, avoiding a man balancing a ladder on one shoulder.

Two older men stopped him long enough to shake hands and convey their admiration for the way he had saved the Masterson boy. "We're proud of ya, marshal," they assured him.

As he neared the town hall, Luke was already dreading the return to his real life: keeping company with cardsharps and con men in smoky saloons where the turn of a card dictated wealth or poverty and sometimes life or death.

He'd grown accustomed to the simple pleasures of church picnics, town socials, and walking down the street with his head held high—things that only a month ago he knew nothing about and would have scoffed at the idea.

Entering the spacious town hall building, his senses were assailed with odor of new wood and fresh varnish. The building was painfully new, erected by faith in the dreams of a dead man. He reached the entrance of the council chambers realizing that if Belle Plain went bust, Katherine's worst fears would come true.

God, how he wished he could be there for her, offering some sort of refuge. He drew a deep breath, putting such foolish thoughts behind him, and rapped soundly on the heavy oak door.

"Come in," a voice called.

Every man in the room stood as he entered the meeting, and Joe Perry wasted no time in voicing a welcome.

"Marshal, thank you so much for you promptness," he said in a rush to shake his hand and usher him to a seat at the foot of the table. "I apologize for the short notice, but this was not a scheduled meeting."

The other men took their seats once he was seated, and Joe sauntered back toward his end of the table. Luke glanced after Joe to find Katherine seated at the head of the table, her hands folded before her.

She smiled at him ever so slightly, before ducking her eyes and resuming a dignified pose, and turned at the sound of Joe's voice.

"Marshal Johnson," Joe began, reveling in the formality and importance of the situation. "Big things are taking place in Belle Plain. As you know, there has been serious consideration by the Texas & Pacific railroad to make our town a stop on the new route. We have made every feasible effort to promote the town as a center of commerce and stability."

Murmurs of agreement rose from the members of the council, and Katherine nodded in concurrence.

"The recent robbery of the bank could have been a disaster that would have eliminated every hope of securing the rail stop." Cecil Percy rose from his seat, as if on cue. "However, thanks to you and the deputy, tragedy was averted. I still feel you were largely responsible, but I have respected your wishes that no attention be placed on you."

He paused dramatically. "I did write a letter to the governor," he continued. "And, being a man of astute judgement, he agreed with my position that your actions are deserving of tribute.

"The governor's office will bestow a medal of valor for Tom." Joe would not have his thunder stolen completely. "And thanks to strategic scheduling, the medal will be presented in a special ceremony when the railroad executives come for their final tour of the town."

Caleb glanced from face to face, finally settling his gaze on Katherine. "I'm not sure how this involves me. I want no recognition; Tom is the one who deserves all of the glory. He acted out of bravery; I just did what comes naturally."

Katherine at last spoke, unable to keep a smile from her face. "Caleb, we understand and appreciate your sense of modesty, but the council feels you deserve some recognition for your efforts. We will respect your wishes and not ask that you participate in the ceremony, but we want to make a gesture of our own for your bravery."

"It's not just your efforts in the robbery," Joe elaborated. "Even before Saturday's picnic, the citizens of Belle Plain have come to regard you as marshal, and they feel even stronger about that now. They haven't been shy in expressing their feelings on the matter, and the council wants to extend the same contract that was offered to Stuart Carey to you, with all of its benefits."

"Except, we want to increase the salary," Mr. Percy cut in. "We've also added a housing allowance, enough to rent one of the nicest cottages in town. We want you to stay, marshal, and we'll make it worth your while."

Luke felt as if he had just been dealt five aces—a winning hand that would get him killed if he played it. As best he could, he managed not to react, although he wasn't sure what to do. He glanced from one expectant face to another. Obviously, they were waiting for what they believed would be an acceptance speech, but he remained silent.

"I have the papers right here, if you'd like to look them over," Joe offered, breaking the silence. He gave the assembly an assuring glance as he slid the contract across the table. "Everything is in order, and I'm sure we can work out any concerns you may have."

At last, Luke forced himself to look at Katherine, remembering the talk they'd had at her kitchen table. What would he do if there was a place he could call home? Now he knew the answer; there could never be such a place.

He didn't reach for the papers Joe slid toward him, afraid the mere act of touching them would tempt him beyond his ability to refuse. Instead, he removed his hat, remembering his manners a tad too late.

"That's quite an offer, gentlemen," he paused, forcing himself to meet the hopeful expression in Katherine's eyes. "Ma'am. But I'm afraid I just can't consider such a thing."

The members of the council were taken aback, each shocked at having their offer so quickly refused, and Katherine's expression went flat. Joe Perry found his voice first.

"I'm sure you'll feel differently after you've read over the contract," he insisted. "We have been very generous."

"You've already been generous to me," Luke assured him, grateful for a reason to look away from the stifled hurt in Katherine's eyes. "More so than I deserve, but I simply cannot commit to any town for that length of time."

"So this is the thanks we get," Tyler Martin remarked to those sitting around him. "I told you he was just a lot of fast talk. Well, maybe we'll be better off with another marshal."

Luke rose to his feet, not the least bit tempted to react to Martin's taunts. The man would love nothing more than to lure him into a fight in front of the council and Katherine.

He forced himself to look at her. Her eyes were downcast when he said, "You will be better off, Martin; the whole town will be."

He turned and left the council chambers, resisting the urge to look over his shoulder to see if Katherine watched him leave.

May was proving to be dry and dusty, and Katherine dreaded the summer already. She watched as Joe tossed his valise up to the stage driver, secretly glad that she wasn't the one going to meet the men from the railroad. Travel by stage was at best uncomfortable and a misery in the summer heat.

The railroad party was on their way from Fort Worth, and Joe would travel two days to meet them at a comfort station a little less than halfway. Under normal circumstances, the mayor would be expected to greet such important visitors, but propriety would not allow Katherine to travel so far alone to meet a group of men. So, Joe was going in her stead, leaving her behind to get everything in order for their arrival.

"Mind you secure that case," he called after the driver.

"Last time, my things were so jostled around that I had to have everything re-pressed at the hotel."

"Well, ain't that a turd-bustin' shame," the driver sneered. "Why don't you ride up there yourself and keep it safe."

Incensed, Joe merely glared at the man before turning back to Katherine. "If for no other reason, I hope we get the railroad so that I won't have to ride this stage every time I have a deed to file or a will to probate."

She shrugged. "Baird is the county seat."

"I still say that privilege should belong to Belle Plain," he insisted. "We'll see when the railroad ties are laid; there may be a different attitude in this county."

Katherine looked on as two other men boarded the stage ahead of Joe, followed by a lady whining about the heat. He turned to her and smiled again.

"Well, wish me luck."

She handed him the box of sandwiches and cookies she'd packed for his trip. "You'll need it."

"Oh, Katherine, don't be so glum." He accepted the box without a word, knowing she wouldn't hear his thanks for the gesture she never failed to make. "We still have a wonderful town, and there are many reasons the railroad should settle here."

"But we have no permanent marshal," she reminded him, knowing it was unnecessary. "All we have is a bounty hunter and an inexperienced deputy."

"Well, Tom has something to brag about," he tried to make her see the bright side.

"He apprehended an unarmed man."

"All aboard that's gettin' aboard!" The stage driver glared down at Joe, and spit a stream of tobacco juice on the ground, missing their shoes by mere inches. "That means you, fancy pants."

"We'll have the railroad," he assured her with newfound vengeance. "If I have to lay the ties myself."

Joe climbed up into the stage and leaned out the window. "Katherine, please don't worry. We've found two marshals. We'll find another."

"How?"

Glancing down at the stage seat, Joe produced a folded newspaper. "We'll advertise, just like before. In fact, you look through here—"

He paused to read the headlines. "This one is from Denver. Men always advertise for employment. Perhaps you'll find a marshal looking for a town."

The driver called out several vulgar commands to the team of horses and the stage lurched forward. Joe tossed down the paper to Katherine, and waved good-bye while she simply looked at him with doubt.

"I'll send a wire when they arrive!" he called out.   The rest of his words were lost in the thunder of hooves against the street. A cloud of dust forced Joe inside the stage, but she was certain he had shouted something meant to encourage her.

"Advertise," she muttered, not at all happy at the prospect. She flipped through a few pages, noting the growth and prosperity Denver was enjoying. There were several articles describing a new theater, four taverns, and a restaurant boasting clams and oysters.

She wondered if Caleb had ever been to Denver. No doubt his travels were extensive. She tried not to think about where he would go next or whether he would meet another lonely woman, loathing being thought of herself in such terms. With effort, she returned her thoughts to the newspaper.

Not all the headlines were boastful. One detailed the arrest of a local minister on charges of fraud, another proclaimed the need for improved public sanitation. She turned to the editorial page and her eyes locked on one boldly printed line that took up much of one page.

FUGITIVE GUNNED DOWN LIKE MAD DOG!
BOUNTY HUNTER JOHNSON COLLECTS LARGE
REWARD!

She crushed the newspaper in a frantic attempt to fold the section before anyone standing nearby caught sight of the bold lettering. Thankfully, no one noticed her startled reaction, as they were too intent on unloading cargo from the newly arrived stage and finding the hotel.

Tucking the paper under her arm, Katherine turned away from those milling about on the sidewalk and turned toward home. She managed to smile and speak politely to several friends, but she didn't stop, anxious to get home and read the article.

She slipped inside the back door, listening for any sound of her brother. Only silence greeted her, and she wasted no time in getting upstairs. Once the door to her bedroom was closed and locked, she sank to her bed and began smoothing the crumpled paper.

The bold print leapt out at her, and she read in astonishment the sinister account of the bounty hunter apprehending a wanted man in a town just forty miles outside of Denver. Caleb Johnson, the writer declared, was a name synonymous with cruelty and injustice and no fugitive, regardless of his alleged crime, deserved to be hunted down like a mad dog.

The outlaw, wanted for robbing a stage, had been hiding out in his mother's home. Johnson had ransacked the humble abode in search of the man, finally setting fire to the barn in an attempt to force a surrender. Katherine shuddered at the vivid account of horses and cows burning to death, as Johnson refused the mother's pleas to open the barn door and spare the livestock. The fugitive, hiding in the hayloft, finally leapt to the ground before being overtaken by smoke. His mother rushed to his side only to be pushed aside by Johnson, who loomed over the injured man.

Katherine could read no more, letting the paper fall to the floor, and sank back on her bed. Huddled against the soft pillows, she refused to believe the man she had grown so fond of was capable of such callous disregard for life, human or otherwise. She herself had assumed the worst of him, but was soon forced to admit the man and his reputation were like night and day.

Why would a man so heartless ride into their town seeking medical attention for a prisoner? Would it not have served his purpose just as well to let the man die? Rewards were paid for capture, alive or dead.

There were many things about the marshal that had surprised her, pleasantly so, and she began to tally the conflicting traits. He had proven to be levelheaded, shrewd, and refined. Obviously he was from an affluent family, possessing a preference for the finer things. No ruffian could have charmed Ruby Alston in her own parlor the way he had.

Something was not right.

Sitting up, Katherine retrieved the fallen newspaper and forced herself to read the entire article. The bounty hunter was described as a once masterful tracker who was losing his edge to age and liquor. With graying hair and growing paunch, he was prone to shooting men in the back rather than bringing fugitives into custody, even more so since losing his trigger finger in a knife fight in Kansas City.

A cold dread began to settle in her belly as she thought of the marshal's lean build and dark hair. He had touched her often enough that she knew his hands had not been maimed.

She resumed reading the paper. The writer went on, pleading for an end to the system of rewards paid for delivering fugitives, dead or alive, without benefit of trial. How many wrongly accused suspects would be gunned down for merely having their name on an arrest warrant?

In America, he declared, every man is entitled to trial by jury, not condemnation by wanted poster. If there was to be true justice in America, he concluded, men like Caleb Johnson must be put out of business.

Perhaps he already has been.

Katherine thought back to the stormy day in the cemetery when they had buried Caleb Johnson's prisoner, a man named Cantrell. When she had arrived with Preacher Meeks, Tom and Caleb Johnson were waiting near the sealed casket. Dr. Sullivan had been the last person to see the deceased, as Belle Plain had no undertaker, and Tom had only seen the man slumped over a horse in the dark.

No one had asked for proof of the bounty hunter's identity, certainly not Tom, who was swept away by the man's reputation and the opportunity to actually be associated with burying an outlaw. Katherine had simply accepted him as the man her brother claimed him to be.

Inconsistencies began to mount, and she reminded herself that newspaper reporters often exaggerate the facts to entice readers. Still she could not deny her own thoughts. Why had he lied to Mrs. Alston about being from Missouri? Why had he insisted that Tom be the one to deliver the would-be bank robbers to the Texas Rangers? And most of all, why would a man who lived by his reputation refuse recognition for foiling a robbery and apprehending the bandits?

With great care, she folded the newspaper, smoothing the creases razor-sharp. She glanced at the front-page headlines and realized the paper was over three months old, and she wondered who had left it behind on the stage.

She stole down the stairs, listening for any sign of her brother, but she was alone with her suspicions. With the paper clutched in her hands, she stood in the center of the kitchen where she had first danced with the marshal, where she had first met him.

Uncertainty began to mingle with doubt. What should

she hope for? If he was Caleb Johnson, he was monster, but if he wasn't the infamous bounty hunter, then who was he?

Had she fallen in love with the murderous bounty hunter or an outlaw who had fooled the whole town? Either way, she stood to lose him, for neither man could remain in Belle Plain.

She had to know, that was all there was to it. She couldn't go on pretending she had no doubts, but she dared not approach him with her suspicions.

The only other person who might help her was Dr. Sullivan. He had seen the dead man last and surely would have remembered what he looked like. She didn't need a detailed description of the corpse, only whether the deceased had nine fingers or ten.

The clock ticked, keeping time with her pulse, as she tried to decide on the best possible way to approach the old doctor. No one must know of her suspicions. She crossed the kitchen and crammed the newspaper into the stove, stirring the ashes with the poker.

The crumpled paper writhed as the flames consumed the newsprint, leaving only blackened wisps remaining. She stirred the fire again, and the charred remains collapsed beneath the end of the poker. She wished she could do the same with her own misgivings, but only fools ignored their instincts. Slamming the stove shut, she replaced the poker and turned toward the back door.

Despite his lack of familiarity with jails, Luke was certain the one in Belle Plain was the best-run in the country. Not one sheet of paper ever lay out of place waiting to be filed, and no job that needed doing was ever put aside for later. Today, however, Tom had taken on the task of culling the wanted posters with a vengeance.

With hardly a good morning, he had gone to the task, ignoring Luke's suggestion of going for breakfast as they always did.

"I ate at home," was the curt reply when Luke pressed the matter.

Luke continued sipping his coffee and watched the deputy, tempted to advise the younger man never to pursue a living at poker. The deputy's mood read like a billboard Luke had once seen on a whorehouse in Montana—loud, and leaving no doubt as to what was going on inside.

So, Tom was peeved that he wouldn't be staying on as marshal, and he wondered if Katherine had been the one to tell him. Perhaps he should be flattered. Hell, no one had ever cared whether he stayed or left, let alone enough to get angry. Despite all the lies he'd told, he wanted Tom to know that if things were different he honestly believed he would stay in Belle Plain.

Clearing his throat, he chose another tactic. "Say, Tom, what do you hear from that telegram about the Cantrell reward."

Tom's shoulders stiffened and he went still. A second passed, and he resumed spearing a tack into a wanted poster before answering. "Haven't heard back yet."

"Think you ought to send a second wire?"

This time he whirled around, anger darkening his fair complexion. "Why don't you do it, if you're so damned anxious to get your money and leave?"

Luke placed his half-empty cup of coffee on the desk. "Maybe I should. You don't seem very concerned, but ten thousand dollars is a lot to be anxious about, don't you think?"

"I guess it would be, if I were a bounty hunter instead of a lawman."

Silence hung in the room.

"You knew I was a bounty hunter the first time we met," Luke countered, the packed bags and waiting horse weighing on his conscience. "I never said I'd stay."

"I thought you would . . . oh, hell never mind."

"You thought I would what? Change? Change and do what?"

Tom only glared at him, as if counting to ten before he spoke. "I thought you'd do right by this town. We took you in and trusted you, and then offered you the job with all the benefits. And you turned it all down like it was nothing."

"I thought you'd be pleased," Luke pressed. "With me leaving town and you the big hero, you're a shoo-in to be the next marshal."

Tom looked like a child whose mama had slapped him, and the anger left him. "That's what you thought?"

"Well, you want to be marshal, don't you?"

"Not enough to give up my best friend." Forsaking his wanted posters, Tom turned and left the office.

The door slammed behind him, and Luke flinched, wondering if this was how Judas felt before hanging himself. No, at least the fallen apostle had enough sense to end it all. Luke would just leave, taking his misery with him.

"Say ah."

"Aaah." Katherine winced as Dr. Sullivan pressed the dry tongue depressor against the back of her throat.

"Again," he instructed, peering into her gaping mouth.

He felt her throat and shook his head. "You don't have a bit of swelling, and your throat is not inflamed. Have you been coughing?"

"No, sir. I just woke up feeling poorly." She fidgeted in the chair as he reached for yet another queer looking scope, this time he peered into her left ear then her right.

"Well, I don't *see* anything wrong with you." He stroked his drooping white mustache. "I know you've been under a lot of strain here lately."

"Yes, sir," she answered, peering down at her folded hands. "I suppose I have."

"You've been eating right? Sleeping alright?"

She nodded. "It's just a headache. I suppose it will pass."

"Hmmm . . . could be." He continued studying her until she felt like a specimen in one of the glass jars he kept on his windowsill. "Katherine, how old are you now?"

Her head snapped up. "Twenty-five. Why?"

"Twenty-five," he repeated gravely. "I've known you since you were a shirttail kid, and this is the first time you've been in my office with any kind of a complaint."

When she said nothing, he asked, "When did these headaches start?"

She shrugged, wishing she hadn't come. Her intention had been to question Dr. Sullivan about the night he had attended the dying man brought to town by Caleb Johnson, but her nerve had failed. The doctor naturally assumed she had come to see him because she wasn't feeling well and ushered her into the examining room.

"About the time the new marshal showed up, I'll bet." Dragging a chair close to hers, the old physician sat down and patted her shoulder. "Katherine, I'm afraid there's nothing I can do about being lovesick."

Mortified, Katherine started to deny it, but his knowing look censured her argument. "You must think I'm a fool."

"Not at all. You're a beautiful young woman, and thank God you were smart enough to wait for the right man."

"The right man?" she scoffed. "He's leaving town as soon as he can.

"He hasn't left yet, and I saw how he looked at you when he turned that job down." Dr. Sullivan crossed his arms and nodded at the wisdom of his observation. "No, ma'am, don't start planning his going-away party just yet."

"But he's a bounty hunter," she reminded him. "He'll never give that up. There's too much money in it."

"Money isn't everything, Katherine. I suspect being marshal and living in a decent town has shown Caleb Johnson another side of life." Dr. Sullivan's eyes twinkled as he added, "And taking a shine to a pretty lady makes a man stop and consider his future."

Katherine decided to take advantage of the doctor's willingness to advise her, and she asked, "Do you remember very much about the night Caleb came to town?"

Nodding, he leaned back in the chair. "Indeed, I do. It's not every night a lawman shows up at my door with a dying prisoner."

"Did Caleb tell you very much about the man?"

"Tom did most of the talking. The marshal only said enough to let me know he wasn't overly concerned with the man's welfare."

"Do you think the marshal had anything to do with the man's death?"

"Oh, Katherine, is that what's worrying you?" Dr. Sullivan's eyes were full of reassurance and understanding. "The prisoner had obviously lived a hard life, and his vices simply caught up with him. He was old and fat and reeking of cheap booze, and I doubt he gave the marshal much of a fight. My Aunt Essie could have brought in that one."

The old doctor chuckled at the idea, but Katherine felt the dread return. "I'm sure he was a dangerous man at one time."

He nodded. "He definitely had the scars to prove it."

"Scars?"

"Old bullet wounds and the like," he explained. "He'd been knifed a few times."

"Stabbed?"

"Not stabbed," Dr. Sullivan mused, thinking of a more accurate description. "More like he'd been slashed in a knife fight . . . even one of his fingers had been whacked off. Guess that's how he got captured. Don't see how a man could shoot straight without a trigger finger."

She swayed forward, a great roaring in her ears, and the room swam before her eyes. It had to be true; the dead man was no prisoner, and the marshal was no bounty hunter.

Dr. Sullivan caught her around the shoulders. "Katherine, my God, what is it?"

"Nothing," she murmured, letting her forehead fall against her palm. "Just dizzy."

"I suspect you've been working too hard," he declared, "and worrying too much. Why don't you take a break? I was just fixin' to ride out to the Reynolds' place to check on that new baby. Ride out there with me. The fresh air will do you good."

She nodded, grateful for any excuse to get out of town, even if just for the afternoon. "I'd like that."

The fresh air and pleasant company did little to ease her worries. She listened attentively to the doctor's stories of his early years in the medical practice. He rattled on about rural Kentucky, and Katherine knew he meant to distract her from thoughts of Caleb Johnson.

"I remember one family, their name was Johnstone." He smiled wistfully, as if he had found a forgotten treasure. "The woman was younger than you are now, but she had a houseful of youngsters. That youngest boy of hers was always into something. One time he swallowed a penny to hide it from his sister, and he wanted me to cut it out when it was time to spend it."

Katherine smiled, but her thoughts remained troubled. There was no doubt now that the man buried in Belle Plain fit the description of the notorious bounty hunter, leaving her to speculate on the marshal's identity. Caleb Johnson had sent word that he was coming to town with a prisoner. Somehow they had switched places on the way.

"Katherine, have you heard a word I've said?"

Startled, she glanced toward the doctor just as they neared the Reynolds' ranch. "I'm sorry, my mind wanders."

"Not far, I'm sure." He smiled and reined the rig to a stop. Before Katherine could reply, Patsy rushed onto the porch, her face beaming with delight.

"Katherine, what a wonderful surprise," she called.

"Don't you come down those steps," Dr. Sullivan ordered. "You're still weak as a kitten."

Rolling her eyes, Patsy motioned for Katherine to hurry. They embraced, and Katherine clung to her friend.

"You simply must see my precious angel." Patsy's happiness was almost contagious, and Katherine wished just a little of the joy would rub off on her. "He's just perfect."

"Where is the little sweetheart?" she managed, forcing herself to return Patsy's smile.

"Upstairs, in his crib. I put him down about an hour ago and he went right to sleep."

"Well, you show him to me and let me get on with my business," Dr. Sullivan interrupted. "You two can chat later."

Katherine watched them disappear inside the house and sank to the wooden swing. She braced the toes of her shoes against the porch and set the swing in motion, the predicament with the marshal pushing to the forefront of her thoughts.

What on earth would she do now? She couldn't blithely pretend she knew nothing of his deception and allow the charade to continue. If she had figured out the situation, it was only a matter of time before someone else did.

Tom had said the prisoner was wanted for murder, and Katherine shivered despite the afternoon sun. If the marshal really was Luke Cantrell, then he was still a wanted man. My God, if anyone found him out, they would turn him in for the reward and a hanging.

Katherine knew she should warn him, but a sudden departure would only arouse suspicion. Everyone would want to know why the marshal had left without explanation, and she would have no answers for them.

She fought back the panic, rationalizing that others might not be so quick to suspect the town marshal, but sending him off in a panic would set tongues to wagging. The best thing for her to do would be to remain quiet, and let him leave in his own time.

The barn door swung open and Katherine recognized Justin Reynolds and, to her dismay, Tyler Martin. The two men stood in the open doorway engrossed in conversation. At last Justin closed the door and the two men turned toward the house.

Tyler noticed her first, his expression growing pleased. "Miss McBride, what a pleasant surprise."

"Where's Patsy?" Justin asked, glancing toward the doctor's buggy. "Nothing wrong, is there?"

She smiled at his immediate concern. "Not a thing, Justin. Dr. Sullivan wanted to check on Patsy and the baby, and I tagged along to see your little one again."

"He's a fine baby," Justin boasted. "Strong as a bull, already."

Katherine smiled at his exuberance. "A bull? Now why do I find that hard to believe?"

Justin grinned sheepishly. "I'd better get upstairs, and make sure Doc Sullivan doesn't do too much poking around."

Once the new father had disappeared inside the house, Katherine was acutely aware of being alone with Tyler Martin. She glanced in his direction knowing she would find him watching her intently.

"Good afternoon," she offered with a weak smile.

"So, your marshal is leaving town," Martin got right to the point. "I say the sooner the better. I'm sorry you wasted a minute on that—"

"It's none of your concern," Katherine cut him off, deeply resenting his condescending attitude. Despite her suspicions regarding the marshal, she didn't want to hear talk against him. "I don't wish to discuss it."

"Well, I do." Tyler scaled the steps and stood before her, his booted feet spread wide. "You've always been a level-headed woman, and I've always believed in straight talk—not a lot of flowery words and empty promises. I'm looking to marry again, Katherine, and you're the woman I have in mind.''

Katherine felt her face flame at his blunt talk. ''I've told you before, you have no right to assume I would accept any proposal from you.''

As if she hadn't said a word, he sat down beside her on the swing, his voice dropping. ''Everyone in town is speculating on what's been going on between you and that drifter you picked for a marshal.''

Dumbfounded, Katherine could only stare at him. She wasn't certain which was more insulting: the fact that she was the subject of small-minded talk or that Tyler thought she had reason to be concerned.

''I don't hold with idle gossip,'' he quickly said in his own defense. ''But you've got a reputation to think of. Marrying me will snuff out any speculation that you've been . . . well, spoiled.''

''How very noble of you.'' Katherine rose to her feet, seeking escape into the house. ''But my reputation is no concern of yours, and you shouldn't listen to idle gossip if you don't hold with it.''

''He's going to leave you behind.'' Catching her gently by the arm, Tyler forced her to face him. ''No matter what's happened between you, he'll leave the minute he gets that money.''

''How did you know about that?''

''You can't hide big news like that in a little town.'' A look akin to pity flashed in his pale eyes. ''You've played the fool long enough. Let him go, Katherine.''

From inside the house, she heard the baby cry and Patsy called for her to come in and see the child. Satisfied he'd made his point, Tyler let go of her arm, and she stumbled inside. *Let him go.*

She made her way up the stairs, wishing that she could.

❖ *12* ❖

ARRIVING IN TWO DAYS WITH RAILROAD EXECUTIVES
-STOP- ALL ANXIOUS TO MEET OUR MARSHAL -STOP-
PUT ON A GOOD SHOW -STOP-

Katherine folded the telegram from Joe and laid it aside.
Two days wasn't much time, and the telegram was a day
late in arriving, but she'd make it be enough. She had already alerted the hotel, and the council members awaited
her instructions. All she needed now was a marshal, and
there wasn't time for coyness. He would be leaving Belle
Plain soon, but he owed her one last favor before he left.

She had managed to avoid seeing him since reading the
Denver newspaper, and she had been grateful for the time
to sort out her feelings. Every time Tom came home, she
expected him to bring news that the marshal had left town,
but nothing out of the ordinary was mentioned.

She dared not discuss her suspicions with anyone, even
Tom. What if she was wrong? The story in the newspaper
could have been a fabrication woven with a few strands of
truth. And even if he wasn't Caleb Johnson, he might not

be Luke Cantrell. Still, her greatest fear was that she was right and confirmation of her conclusions would send him to the gallows.

There was also the matter of the town's honor. Belle Plain would be a laughingstock if word got out that they had hired a wanted man to run their jail, and the railroad wouldn't begin to consider a town with such a reputation.

By now, Joe had most likely bragged to the railroad committee about the exploits of the marshal, playing up the bank robbery for all it was worth. They would arrive expecting to be impressed, and she would not have them disappointed. He had played bounty hunter/marshal this long; he could keep it up long enough to do her some good.

With renewed determination, Katherine left her office to find him and invite him to the party for the railroad committee. His presence was essential, and she didn't intend to be refused.

It didn't take long to locate the marshal. She couldn't think of him as Caleb Johnson, and she found not knowing his true identity strangely comforting. Halfway down the main street, she caught sight of him at the foot of the church steps, his hat doffed and dangling from his long fingers.

"Marshal, you are such a dear to take time away from your work to spend with us," Ruby Alston gushed, never taking her eyes from his handsome face. "I simply cannot thank you enough."

"I should be thanking you," he corrected, "for such a lovely afternoon."

The other ladies quickly chimed in how happy they were that he had joined them, and he favored each of them with a smile. Katherine could only look on in disbelief. The man she feared was either a murderous bounty hunter or a wanted killer had been invited to and attended the monthly luncheon for the Ladies' Auxiliary at the church.

An unexpected rush of anger passed through her at the idea of him being fussed over like a favorite son while she had been agonizing over keeping him from the gallows.

He caught sight of her and excused himself from the covey of admirers. "Pardon me, ladies, I believe I am needed for official business."

Longing glances followed him as he turned and made his way toward Katherine, and the women quickly huddled into a whispering knot of speculation. She had dismissed Ty Martin's warning about being the brunt of gossip, but she could now see for herself that there was more than a passing interest regarding her relationship with the marshal.

"I didn't mean to interrupt something so important." She couldn't keep the sarcasm from her voice.

He raised an eyebrow, but smiled, saying, "One can never have too favorable of a public image."

She managed a tight smile at his return jibe, and couldn't keep from saying, "Mrs. Alston might just butter your paws if she finds out you're leaving."

He placed his hat on his head, the dark brim shadowing his face, but she didn't miss the censure in his eyes. He was the one who'd made it clear he had no intentions of remaining and be damned if she would apologize for mentioning it.

"Maybe she'll just avoid me, the way you have."

His accusation hit home, and she didn't bother to deny the fact that she had gone out of her way to keep from seeing him, but not for the reasons he believed. She dared not look at him for fear her suspicions were plainly revealed in her face.

"I'm sorry about that," she managed, but she wasn't. She was deliberately preparing herself for the day he left town, hoping her heart would break one piece at a time. She decided against making excuses and came right to the point. "I've come to invite you to a dinner tomorrow night."

Fully expecting his mocking grin, she was unprepared for the wariness in his eyes. "A dinner?"

"The railroad commission will be arriving tomorrow and the town council will hold a dinner party for them at the hotel," she explained in a rush of practiced words. "You and Tom are invited."

He nodded. "I'll be there."

"Good," she breathed, managing a weak smile. Her eyes began to burn and she blinked furiously. "I'll see you there."

"Katherine." His voice brought her to a halt as she turned to leave. He waited until she faced him again. "Look, I never meant for things—"

"Good afternoon, marshal." A man Katherine recognized from the feed store paused long enough to shake hands with the lawman, and she took the opportunity to escape.

The sidewalk was teeming with midday shoppers making their way to the mercantile, the dressmaker, and the bank. Luke caught up with her and took her by the arm to lead her from the middle of the busy walkway.

Once out of the flow of traffic, he released her, but she could still feel the warm imprint of his fingers. She pressed her back against the wall of the general store, needing to put distance between them. The group of ladies from the church had scattered, but several passersby turned curious glances toward her and the marshal.

"This really isn't a good place to discuss this," he began.

"No it isn't," she agreed. "But you owe me no explanation."

His eyes narrowed slightly, but she didn't care what he thought. Anything he told her would most certainly be a lie, and she certainly didn't want to hear the truth now.

"I didn't think I'd be here even this long," he began, his voice holding no note of apology. "I suppose staying at all was a mistake."

She nodded, feeling a lump swell in her throat. "We all make mistakes."

"You should have asked me about staying before getting the council involved."

She took a deep steadying breath. "It was as much Joe's idea as mine."

"But I told you I couldn't stay."

"You said if there was a way, you would stay," she reminded him, her voice barely above a whisper. "Well, we gave you a way, so there must be another reason."

His eyes narrowed, and she felt her heart lurch. God, why did she say that? The reasons didn't matter now, and she needed to put on a good front for the railroad. The last thing she needed was for him to leave angry.

"I do have a reason," he answered, his voice had gone soft and husky. "I wish to God I didn't, but I do."

She nodded. "I understand, really I do. Will you still come to the dinner tomorrow night?"

"What time?"

"Seven o'clock."

Silence followed as they both stood waiting for the other to turn and leave. Katherine pressed her back even harder against the rough-hewn boards of the store, not daring to take a step in his direction, and there was no way around him without brushing against him. Finally, he raised a finger to the brim of his hat and turned away. She watched him disappear into the crowded sidewalk and only then did she let herself breathe easy.

"Your little town is quite impressive."

Katherine smiled. "Thank you so much, Mr. McGregor. My father worked very hard to make Belle Plain what it is."

"He sounds like the kind of man I am." McGregor paused to light a fat cigar, his jowls puffing until the end glowed orange and the room filled with the sickeningly sweet scent of aromatic tobacco. "Thing weren't easy when I first started out, let me tell you."

Pushing his dessert plate aside, the rich confection of apples and raisins hardly touched, Luke could only imagine trying to stop him. A waiter appeared to collect the dish and refill his coffee cup, but he'd had enough and waved the steaming pot away. Indeed, he feared his patience and tolerance had been pushed to the limit.

For two hours, he had sat through a dinner consisting of overdone vegetables and chicken nearly as dry as the conversation. Linus McGregor, chief surveyor for the Texas & Pacific Railroad, had favored them with one boring anecdote after another. The man had one favorite subject—himself, and no attempt to divert the conversation had yet to succeed. Even Joe Perry, a lawyer schooled in debate, had long since given up and sat nodding occasionally in response.

Luke glanced across the table where Tom sat absorbed in something on the table before him. Luke craned his neck to peer around the large centerpiece, and found, to his amusement, that the deputy was engrossed in constructing a tower of sugar cubes. Further survey of the glazed expressions on the surrounding faces assured Luke that he wasn't the only one who found McGregor to be an intolerable bore.

Only Katherine sat captivated by the man's boasting, the enchanting smile never leaving her face. She laughed at his stale jokes, beamed at his contrived compliments, and worst of all, asked him more questions about himself.

"You have much to be proud of," she said reverently, and Luke couldn't keep from rolling his eyes.

McGregor puffed deeply on his cigar and tossed the match into a water glass, turning his attention to Luke. "Marshal, Perry here tells me you've brought a little excitement to town."

Joe cleared his throat, looking sheepish, but Luke only

grinned, toying with his coffee cup. "Nothing to write home about."

McGregor's eyes narrowed. "Is it true your skills at the poker table nearly cost one man his life?"

"My skill at poker cost him a week's wages," Luke countered. "His own foolishness nearly cost him his life."

Everyone laughed, and McGregor chuckled before puffing away on the cigar. "Think you could do as well against me?"

The laughter faded, and Luke glanced toward Katherine, her brow knitted with concern. Still, he couldn't ignore the first interesting thing the man had said all night. "You play poker?"

"Of course, of course." McGregor gestured with the cigar toward his entourage. "My men are always up for a game, isn't that right?"

Chimes of agreement rose quickly if not enthusiastically. McGregor said, "We play amongst ourselves all the time, but I always like a fresh hand in the game."

"Gentlemen, I fear gambling would be inappropriate here at the hotel." Katherine's tactful discouragement was easily brushed aside.

"Nonsense." McGregor never took his eyes off of Luke. "Here is just fine. Besides, I promised my wife I'd stay out of saloons."

Katherine's eyes widened and shot a meaningful look in Luke's direction. "The marshal feels he should set an example for the town by not—"

McGregor slammed his fist on the table and glared at her. "Good God, woman, let the man speak for himself!"

Luke didn't miss the anger that flashed in Tom McBride's young face nor the disdain in Joe Perry's eyes. Katherine sat in stunned silence, and Luke knew his was the only face remaining impassive. Someone needed to teach the puffed up toad a lesson, and he was just the man to do it.

"I don't mind a friendly game," he replied in an even tone. "If you don't mind taking a friendly beating."

McGregor smiled widely at a challenge that would have infuriated most men. From his pocket, he produced an unopened pack of cards and barked at the waiter, "Look sharp, there! Get these dishes out of my way."

As the waiter hurried to clear the dishes, Katherine sent one last imploring look in Luke's direction, clearly disheartened when he ignored her. One of McGregor's flunkies appeared with a money belt and full bottle of whiskey.

McGregor tossed the pack of cards toward Joe. "You there, break the seal and shuffle them up for us."

Joe did so, placing the new deck in the center of the table.

McGregor gestured toward the cards with his cigar. "Well, marshal, it's your deal."

Luke gingerly gathered the cards, his fingers tingling at the sensation. He had almost forgotten the intoxication of an opening deal, rich with possibilities. The cards were stiff, sailing into neat piles before each man in the game.

He set the remaining cards aside and sized up the hand he'd dealt himself—a pair of jacks, a ten, a three, and a seven. Nothing much, but he never folded on the first hand.

He anted after McGregor, who said, "Cards, gentlemen?"

The men tossed out the unwanted cards, and Luke dealt the number of cards each man requested. He waited to be last, gauging each man's expression as they tucked the new cards into their hands.

McGregor tossed a pair of cards aside. "I'll take two."

Luke dealt two cards and took two for himself.

"I'm in," one man announced.

"Me, too," another chimed.

McGregor studied the hand, rolling the cigar between his fingers. "I'm in and I raise ten."

Luke matched the ten as did all but one man in the game.

McGregor studied his hand, the cigar steadily twirling between his fingers. He glanced around the table. "Well, gentleman?"

He had to have a good hand, Luke decided, otherwise McGregor wouldn't call so soon. Novice gamblers always play their winning cards too quickly. Luke noticed the way the other men quickly displayed their cards, and he went along with the precedent. His golden rule for poker was to always bet low and hold your cards close until you figure out the strategy of the other players.

This game would be easy to figure, with McGregor setting the pace and his flunkies quickly following suit. Sure enough, the next two hands proved no different from the first, and McGregor won both hands.

The fourth deal was not to McGregor's liking. He studied the hand intently, puffing on the cigar. "I'll take three."

The cards were dealt, and he puffed even harder, smoke billowing from his lips. Luke suspected that McGregor's luck at cards was always poor, and even the greenest of gamblers would soon realize the obvious handling of the cigar. A good hand set the cigar twirling and a bad one caused him to puff smoke like one of his own locomotives.

The pile of money in the center of the table grew, and McGregor passed cigars around the table. Luke glanced up as Katherine rose from the table, her eyes troubled.

"Goodnight, gentlemen," she said, forcing a bright smile as she rose from her seat. "I wish you luck in your game."

Those not holding cards rose from their seats, and Tom insisted on walking her home. As Katherine left the dining room, Luke didn't miss the concern on her face as she glanced back at him over her shoulder. He had sensed it the day before and now he was certain.

Katherine was worried for him, almost frightened. A warning sounded in his mind, but he dismissed the idea that she had any reason to suspect his true reason for leaving town.

"I'll raise twenty."

McGregor's voice drew him back to the game, and he noticed that two men had already folded. He glanced back at his hand, three sevens and a pair of tens, the best he'd had all night.

"Twenty it is." Luke tossed his money into the center of the table with a nonchalance he had perfected years ago. "And why not twenty more to make things interesting?"

Several pairs of eyebrows lifted around the table, and Joe hid a smile against a coffee cup. McGregor straightened, unprepared for the sudden increase in the stakes.

McGregor fingered his money, mentally calculating what he'd already wagered. The pressure to remain in the game increased, and a third man folded, his cards abandoned.

At last, it was Luke and McGregor alone in the game. The burly man had removed his jacket and loosened his collar. He sat hunkered over his cards, his grip on them tight enough to bend the edges, and the cigar was reduced to a glowing stub clenched between his teeth.

Luke remained cool as before, his reactions nonexistent as the stakes mounted. He had won and lost many a fortune over the past ten years, and knew how to prevent even the slightest reaction to either. McGregor gulped the whiskey remaining in his glass and barely resisted refilling the tumbler. Instead, he glared once more at his cards and tossed the remaining cash into the center of the table, much as a knight of old would throw down a gauntlet.

"I call," he ground out. "What have you got?"

Luke could feel the collective intake of breath as everyone in the room waited for his response. McGregor was a piss-poor gambler, and he would no doubt be an even worse loser. If Luke cleaned him out, McGregor would gather his things and leave town, dooming Belle Plain to a pauper's fate. He had no use for men who gambled with their pride.

Luke covertly eyed the pile of money in the center of the table, taking a moment to consider his hand. McGregor's brow glistened with a fine sheen of perspiration, and Luke wouldn't have been surprised if the man swallowed the lit cigar.

Finally, Luke shook his head and laid the cards face down on the table, satisfied that he had made his opponent squirm enough. "Too rich for me. I fold."

"Ha!" McGregor tossed the bit of cigar onto the floor, gloating as he scraped the winnings across the table. "Marshal, you have a lot to learn about playing cards."

"Indeed, I do," he conceded as the railroad flunkies rushed to clap their boss on the back and refill his whiskey. "I'll think twice before tangling with someone as skillful as you."

"No hard feelings?" the man extended his hand.

"None at all." Luke accepted the handshake and the consolation glass of bourbon.

From the corner of his eye, Luke saw Joe Perry scoop up the cards he'd cast aside and discreetly slip them into his pocket. Luke made no comment, tossing a good deal of the bourbon down his throat. He caught sight of Tom rushing back inside the dining room, and the deputy had no trouble assessing the scene.

"So he won," Tom said in a low tone when he sat down beside Luke. He was clearly disappointed. "I thought you had him."

"That's why they call it gambling," Luke reminded him. "Did you see your sister home?"

The deputy nodded. "She's been in an odd mood lately."

Luke downed the bourbon remaining in his glass. "Maybe she's angry because I can't stay on as marshal. I seem to be losing a lot of friends over that."

Tom looked away. "I'm still your friend."

"Are you?" Luke didn't want trite assurances. "Then

you understand that not everything a man chooses is what he wants?''

The deputy only nodded sadly. ''You will be at the ceremony tomorrow?''

''Do you think I'd miss seeing you as the town hero?''

Tom smiled at that. ''Good, and I'm sorry if I've been acting like a horse's ass.''

''No harm done.'' Luke wanted to find out what had Katherine so worried, and he didn't want Tom following him back to their house. ''I'm calling it a night. Why don't you stay and help Joe keep everyone entertained?''

''I'll be glad to,'' Tom answered, rising from his chair as Luke did the same. ''See you tomorrow.''

Luke ducked out of the hotel before McGregor could suggest another game. The cool night air was welcome after so many hours inside breathing cigar smoke. He glanced down the street and debated the wisdom of going to see Katherine so late. Perhaps he had only imagined the worry in her eyes.

''Marshal?'' Luke turned to find Joe hurrying down the hotel steps. ''A word, please.''

''What is it?''

''I believe a full house beats three of a kind.'' He withdrew Luke's cards from his pocket and studied them in the moonlight. ''Although I've never been one for cards.''

''A full house? Are you sure?''

Perry grinned, slipping the cards back into his pocket. ''That was quite a gesture back there. I'm sure McGregor would not have been a gracious loser.''

''The pot was small,'' Luke said by way of excuse. ''Not enough to risk the town's future over.''

''I wonder, marshal, why you feel so strongly regarding the future of Belle Plain if you have no plans to be a part of it?''

Luke glanced down the street and then back at Joe. ''Whatever future I have, I owe to Belle Plain.''

* * *

What further proof did she need?

Katherine groped for the tiniest thread of doubt, but knew in her heart that the marshal was not who he claimed to be. Tonight he had shuffled and dealt cards with the precision of a well-oiled machine. Tom had referred to the bounty hunter's prisoner as a highly reputed gambler wanted for murder.

She knew nothing about poker, but even she could spot the cool manner in which he bet and lost money, manipulating the odds to suit the cards he held.

With her hands folded as if in prayer, she tried to sort out her twisted emotions. Elation warred with despair. She was relieved to know that he was not the despicable bounty hunter who maimed and killed for sport and money, yet her heart broke knowing he would be doomed for the gallows the moment his identity was discovered.

She didn't believe for a minute that he had deliberately killed anyone. He was too intelligent, never letting a situation get the better of him, and she had yet to see him exhibit a bad temper. Even when Tyler Martin insulted him, the marshal had been able to keep his anger in check and walk away, leaving Martin to look like the smaller man.

No, if he had killed a man, it would have been to save his own life, but what would that matter to a bounty hunter or an angry mob? A shudder passed through her as she recalled the nasty bruises he'd had when he first came to town. How close had he come to being killed then?

She would have to send him away, make whatever excuse she could, and end the campaign to keep him as marshal. Sooner or later someone would recognize and point him out for arrest. She wondered where he might go that was safe, but couldn't think of anywhere. Anywhere but Belle Plain.

A soft knock sounded at the back door and she knew it was him. Tom wouldn't knock and no else would come to the back door this late. Drawing a deep breath as she rose from the chair, she steadied herself and blinked back any traitorous tears.

He stood on the porch, looking in at her, and she felt as if she were seeing him for the first time.

Luke Cantrell. The name fit him, as did the persona of gambler.

"You left early," was all he said.

"I couldn't stand the cigar smoke another minute," she lied. He only nodded, and she finally stepped back, opening the door wide. "Would you like to come in?"

"I didn't want you to be worried about McGregor."

"McGregor?" She couldn't take her eyes away from him, burning his image into her mind. Would this be the last time she saw him? Or would it be tomorrow? "Oh, yes, Mr. McGregor."

"He's no gambler but fancies himself one." He closed the door as he stepped inside. "I gave him a good scare and let him win a pot full of money."

Let him win. The words rung in the silent kitchen. Only a gambler by trade would see the outcome of a game as a controlled result, subject to his manipulation.

Katherine felt her pulse begin to race. She knew nothing about him, and he was leaving. Suddenly, she felt cheated. Her memories would be of Caleb Johnson, not the man standing in her kitchen, a stranger with whom she had fallen in love.

"Why don't—"

"I'd like—"

They both let their words fade away, finally saying in unison, "Coffee?"

She nodded and turned toward the stove. He had come to tell her good-bye. She had seen it in his eyes when she opened the door, and now she could only put it off with coffee and leftover cake. Stealing a few memories of someone she would never know.

*   *   *

Coffee had just been an excuse, an excuse to keep from leaving when he knew he should. He had made up his mind once and for all that he would leave tomorrow. The moment Tom's medal was pinned on his chest and McGregor and his little gang toddled out of town, he would be gone.

No good-byes. No explanations. Just get the hell out of town and leave no trace of who he was.

Easy enough until he tried coming to grips with never seeing Katherine again. He watched her fill the coffeepot with water and nervously wipe her hands on a dishtowel.

She withdrew two cups from an overhead shelf and then reached for a pair of saucers. A cup slipped from her grasp and shattered on the kitchen floor.

"Oh, God," she whispered and dropped to her knees. Tears sprang to her eyes as she tried to gather the tiny pieces of the cup. "Those dishes belonged to my mother. I'll never be able to glue so many tiny pieces together."

Luke knelt beside her, watching mutely as he let the shards of china fall from her hands. She drew a deep breath, biting her lip, but her eyes shimmered with unshed tears when she looked at him.

He wasn't sure who moved first, but suddenly she was in his arms. He crushed her against him, and she clung to him as if for her very life. He inhaled the sweet scent rising from her hair, burying his face against her throat.

The kiss was just as sudden, raw with passion, and he wasn't sure whose desire set the pace. Her teeth grazed his lips, and he tangled his fingers in her hair.

Her arms found their way about his shoulders, and he let his hands cup the firmness of her bottom, causing her to whimper into his mouth. God, he wanted her and by some miracle she wanted him. But why now, when it was too late?

Luke let his hands fall away from her hips, placing them on her shoulders. He withdrew his tongue from her mouth and tried to set her away from him. She fought to maintain the embrace, tightening her arms around his neck and kissing him deeply. As gently as he could, he pulled her arms from around his neck. The last thing he wanted to do was reject her, but he couldn't take her knowing he would be gone tomorrow.

"Katherine," he whispered, holding her loosely. "I don't want to hurt you."

The heated rush of desire ebbed around them, and their embrace grew more intimate and less desperate. He rose to his feet, gently pulling her up with him.

With their hands still joined, he said, "I have to leave."

She nodded, looking up at him. "Kiss me good-bye."

The request was so pure and sincere, he couldn't spoil the moment by offering explanations about why he was leaving or, worse, the truth. Instead, he lowered his lips to hers.

The sweetness of her mouth grew salty and he looked down to see tears streaming down her face. She covered her trembling mouth with her hand, but he drew her close before she could turn away.

He expected her to sob against his shoulder, but she grew quiet instead. A shudder passed through her, and he hooked his finger under her chin, forcing her to look at him.

He wiped a gleaming tear from her face. "What is it, kitten?"

Her voice was broken. "I . . . I'm afraid I love you."

If she had said, "I have a dire illness and will die before morning," the words would not have caused him more agony. How could she love him? She didn't even know who he was. And why now, when he had to leave?

Drawing her even closer, he pressed his lips against her forehead and whispered, "I'm so sorry."

"So am I," she breathed. "So am I."

❖ *13* ❖

THE LIVERY STABLE was mobbed with dozens of those arriving for the festivities, all seeking to stable their horses for the day and possibly overnight. Word had quickly spread that Belle Plain was hosting dignitaries from the governor's office, and that a local citizen was being recognized for bravery.

Little more explanation than that was needed to draw a crowd, anxious to take part in any celebration, and the promise of a parade followed by an old-fashioned Texas barbecue were added incentives. They had flocked from miles around and tempers were already flaring over the shortage of available rooms at the hotel and provisions at the livery.

Luke, however, was thankful for the chaos, as it allowed him to slip in unnoticed and stash his gear in the far corner of his horse's stall. The bay gelding nickered softly in hopes Luke was bearing a bucket of oats. The twin saddle-bags containing all that he needed to make a quick getaway were quickly covered with clean straw, but all he had time to offer the powerful animal was an assurance that the stable boy was coming with breakfast.

As it was, Luke barely had to time to escape the confines of the stall before the youngster appeared with a generous portion of grain. Stepping out into the brilliant sunshine, Luke felt nothing but gloom. He felt his pocket for the hundredth time, assuring himself that the letter he'd written to Katherine was still there.

His plan was to slip away from the ceremony unnoticed and slide the letter under her door on his way out of town. The letter made no apology for his actions, only his regret for any hurt he had caused her. He wished to tell her in person but he didn't dare—all it would take was the sight of a tear on her face or one kiss and he would make more excuses to stay.

He was taking the coward's way out, but perhaps that was best. He wanted to give Katherine as much reason to hate him as possible. The last thing he deserved was to be a hero in her eyes. At best, he was an imposter; at worst, an outlaw doomed to the gallows.

"Morning, marshal," a man called out and Luke returned his wave.

Thronging with people, the narrow sidewalks of Belle Plain could barely accommodate the stream of visitors filing into town. It wasn't every day a representative of the governor of Texas came to town to decorate a local citizen for bravery, and area merchants were taking advantage of the influx of people.

The seamstress had set up a table in front of her shop stacked with sunbonnets and parasols for ladies wishing to avoid getting freckles while standing in the bright sunshine. Eldon Sneed stood in the open doorway of his mercantile, beckoning shoppers to browse before the ceremony got underway.

"Soda crackers! Dried apples! Hoop cheese!" he called out. "Pack a lunch for the parade!"

Luke was surprised to find the jail empty when he ducked inside the building, expecting to find Tom waiting for him. He scanned the neat layout for the last time, silently reciting many details Tom never failed to point out to a visitor.

Reluctantly, he went inside the office he'd come to think of as his own, closing the door behind him. The chair squeaked unexpectedly when he sat down, and he knew that Tom would see that it was oiled properly. He leaned back and scanned the ceiling, savoring the feel of the leather upholstery against his back.

Glancing down, he caught sight of a note on the desk. He bent to read Tom's sprawling script. "Gone on to the courthouse," it said. "See you there."

Luke knew the smart thing to do was leave as soon as everyone was assembled for the ceremony. But Tom had reminded him twice of the time and the need to be prompt, and Luke just couldn't let Tom down more than what was inevitable. Besides, he rationalized, the deputy would insist on keeping the proceedings on hold until the marshal arrived.

With great effort, Luke rose from the chair he'd grown far too accustomed to and made his way around the highly polished desk. As an afterthought, he unpinned the tin star from his vest and held it in his palm, remembering the pride in Tom's face when he'd first pinned it to his chest. Pushing the regret from his mind, he tossed the badge into an open drawer and shut his false identity away for good.

Katherine studied her reflection in the hall mirror and forced herself to smile. She had to appear cheerful and proud today, without a care in the world, but she feared the circles under her eyes would betray her misery.

She had promised him she wouldn't cry anymore as they said good-night rather than good-bye, but that had been a lie. She had seen the flicker of panic in his eyes in response to her tearful confession that she loved him. He probably left town during the night, and she, for his sake, hoped he had. Katherine could no longer feign ignorance of who he was and what he had done, and she vowed to send him away if he had not already disappeared.

Just as she reached for her gloves, Tom bounded down the stairs, his freshly shined boots ringing against the polished floor. "Are you ready?"

"Yes, I am," she managed to answer. Tom was dressed in his best jacket of cream-colored broadcloth, a brocade vest, and dark blue trousers. "Don't you look nice!"

"I do my best." He stood still while she straightened his tie. "Being a hero is demanding work."

She smiled, giving the black string tie an extra tug. "Don't let this hero business go to your head. You might not be around for the next ceremony."

His confident expression never wavered. "Don't sell me short, sis. I might just surprise you."

"I don't like surprises." Her fingers gripped his lapels and she made no pretense of smoothing the fabric. "Tom, promise me you'll be careful."

Concern drew his brows together and his hand covered hers. "What's the matter?"

She hesitated. Should she share her suspicions now or wait until she was certain the marshal was out of town? The last thing she wanted to do was spoil her brother's special day. "I just don't want anything to happen to you."

"I'll be careful," he promised, squeezing her hands.

She nodded.

"We'd best be on our way," he brushed aside the solemn turn of the conversation. "I told Charlotte we'd meet her at the courthouse along with the marshal."

"The marshal?" she repeated, following him out the front door.

"Of course," he replied without looking back. "I left him a note at the jail."

Katherine paused to close the front door. "So, you didn't see him this morning?"

"It was early when I went by the jail," Tom explained, taking the two front steps in one leap. "Before breakfast, even."

Katherine drew a deep breath, steeling herself against the questions that would be raised by the marshal's sudden disappearance. Tom would be devastated. The council would demand an explanation, and they would all look to her for answers she couldn't give.

Her steps slowed as she considered the possible explanations she might give, and she found herself lagging behind Tom's long strides. She tried to hurry in order to catch up with him, but she finally had to call out to him to wait for her.

The festive atmosphere of the town was unmistakable. Mr. Percy had declared today a holiday, and the shades were drawn at the bank. Local merchants propped their doors open in welcome to the crowds, and vendors selling lemonade and popcorn were already doing a brisk business. The walk to the town square took twice the normal time due to the numerous people stopping Tom to congratulate him and extend their best wishes.

Katherine was grateful when at last they arrived at the courthouse. Joe was waiting for them at the top of the stairs, a big smile on his face.

"Everything has come together beautifully," he informed them as they made their way inside the building. "It's just like the Fourth of July."

Inside, several people were gathered around a punch bowl, filling their cups and munching on ladyfingers and sponge cake. Katherine recognized Linus McGregor and members of his committee surrounded by men from the town council. Each man doffed his hat as she approached.

"Good morning, Miss McBride." McGregor took her hand. "Lovely to see you again."

"Thank you."

"I want to introduce you to Carlton Russell."

A red haired man with spectacles offered his hand. "Miss McBride, I'm from the governor's office, and it is an honor to be in your fair city."

"Thank you," she managed once again, hating politics more than ever. "We are so pleased you could be with us today."

"The governor regrets that he could not bestow the honor on your brother himself, but urgent business kept him in the capital," Russell recited the practiced words with clarity and just enough sincerity. "It is my good fortune to act in his stead."

Gently catching Tom by the elbow, Katherine drew him toward her for a word of introduction. "Tom, this is Mr. Russell, from the governor's office."

The two men shook hands and Katherine felt an unexpected pang of regret. Oh, if only Father could be here! He would be so proud of Tom, and he dearly loved all the pomp and circumstance that went along with politics. Gatherings such as this were his delight, and he would befriend everyone in attendance. There were a few faces she did not recognize, but most everyone was from Belle Plain. She couldn't help but search for the marshal among them, but he was not to be found.

In the corner, Joe was engaged in conversation with a pair of strangers, and Katherine couldn't begin to guess who they were or why Joe was so interested in them. She glanced at the timepiece pinned to her blouse, noting the time for the ceremony to commence was at hand.

The marshal still had not come.

She drew a deep, steadying breath and blinked away the tears that stung her eyes. She knew his leaving was for the best, but the knowledge that she would never see him again or know what became of him was like a knife in her heart.

"Katherine, did you hear a word I said?"

She glanced up at Tom, his face marred with concern. "No, I'm sorry. What did you say?"

"I was just telling Mr. Russell how lucky we were that Caleb had been in town when we needed a marshal."

"Lucky, indeed." Ruby and Charlotte Alston wasted no time in claiming Tom upon arriving. The older lady smiled approvingly when Tom offered his arm to her daughter. "Few towns can boast such honorable lawmen. Isn't that right, Katherine?"

"Oh, yes, of course." From the corner of her eye, she caught sight of Joe approaching from across the room, and she was thankful for the distraction.

"Katherine, I want you to meet someone," he said. The two strangers stood behind him. "This is Will Hagan from Colorado."

Katherine nodded at the man. "Mr. Hagan."

"Sheriff Hagan, ma'am," he corrected politely. "And this is my deputy, Beau Conner."

A chill feathered up Katherine's spine as the deputy tipped his hat. "*Sheriff* Hagan, what brings you to Belle Plain?"

Joe smiled. "He's here on official business, and I told him that his timing couldn't be better."

"I'm here to pay a reward," he stated. "A man was buried in your town cemetery a while back. He was wanted for a killing, and there was a sizeable amount on his head."

Katherine's heart was slamming so hard against her chest she feared everyone in the room could hear it. Any grief she felt for the marshal's disappearance vanished, and she steeled herself against any reaction that might betray him. Feigning only mild interest, she said, "A reward?"

With a boastful smile, he said, "Yes ma'am. We wanted that varmint caught and hung."

Katherine swallowed hard, barely squelching a gasp of horror. "And now you find him in our cemetery. I hope you're not disappointed."

"I reckon not. Dead is dead," the sheriff conceded, draining the punch from his glass. The dainty cup looked odd cradled in his meaty hand. "Still, I hate to pay such a hefty amount without the satisfaction of a hanging. You could usually count on Johnson for a live prisoner."

"Well, things don't always work out as we hope," she said by way of sounding sympathetic. She turned back to Joe. "Shouldn't we be getting started with the ceremony?"

"We have to wait for the marshal," Tom insisted.

"Yeah, I want to see Caleb Johnson wearing a badge." Sheriff Hagan gave a coarse laugh. "That'll be worth the trip all this way."

"Do you know . . . Mr. Johnson?"

"Bloodhound Johnson? I've known him since Conner here was in diapers." The deputy blushed, and Hagan laughed. "How he ever sobered up enough to wear a badge is anybody's guess."

Katherine knew her anxiety showed when she glanced back at Joe. "We shouldn't keep Mr. Russell waiting."

Carlton Russell unwittingly came to her rescue. "Yes, unfortunately, I must leave soon after the ceremony."

With a crestfallen look, Tom looked around the room. "The marshal should have been here by now. I left him a note."

"He's probably sleeping off a bottle of tequila," Hagan said with a sneer. "I bet he owes most of this reward to the saloon by now."

"Perhaps he was only delayed," Joe suggested diplomatically. "Surely, he will be here before the ceremony concludes."

Katherine took Tom's arm and tried to sound reassuring. "He'll be here if he can. Let's go on. Everyone is waiting."

The ceremony was to be held on the front steps of the courthouse. A podium had been placed at the top of the first step and chairs were waiting for those participating in the ceremony. Katherine led Tom to the center seat and a rousing cheer rose from the crowd.

"Very impressive, Miss McBride." Linus McGregor seated himself next to her and favored her with a smile. "I must say, your little town has shown me a great deal more than I expected."

Cecil Percy took his seat on the other side of McGregor just as Joe led Sheriff Hagan and Deputy Conner to the last remaining chairs.

"Where could Caleb be?" Tom whispered.

Katherine swallowed and answered honestly, "I don't know."

Joe Perry stood behind the podium, tossing a smile over his shoulder at Katherine as the crowd cheered even louder. He let them applaud just a bit more before raising his arms in a plea for silence. Slowly the cheers faded and Joe began the opening speech.

"Ladies and gentlemen, welcome to Belle Plain, the fastest growing city in Texas!"

A hearty cheer went up from the crowd, and Katherine joined in the applause. Joe thanked the crowd for their enthusiasm and began introducing those seated behind the podium, each person receiving a round of applause.

"And last but not least." Joe smiled at Katherine. "Someone we all owe a debt of gratitude. When this town needed a leader, she was there. Without thinking of herself, she stepped in and did what needed doing. Ladies and gentlemen, the best mayor a town ever had, Katherine McBride!"

The crowd cheered louder than ever, and Joe motioned for her to join him at the podium. Under normal circumstances, Katherine would have been flattered by Joe's accolades, but she was in no mood to make speeches today. Still, she had to get through the ceremony without rousing Sheriff Hagan's suspicions.

Tom and the other men stood as she made her way to

the podium. Joe shook her hand, and she smiled out at the crowd that seemed larger than ever. She waited until the cheers ended before saying, "Thank you for your kindness. I can only say that I love Belle Plain, and that I can never give back what this town has given me."

She remembered to smile, looking out into the sea of expectant faces, and caught sight of Luke Cantrell making his way to the front of the crowd. He smiled up at her and folded his arms across his chest, and she gripped the podium to keep from stumbling.

Panic seized her, and she dared not look back at Sheriff Hagan. Perhaps, she thought, he would not recognize Luke. Still, she wanted to scream for Luke to run, to get away, but she could only stare at the man who was suddenly a stranger to her.

"What is it, Katherine?" Joe whispered.

She glanced at Joe, desperately wishing she had taken him into her confidence. Joe was an attorney, and he would have known what to do. All she could do now was pray the marshal would remain hidden in the crowd and not call attention to himself until she could warn him.

When she turned back to the crowd, she found Luke standing at the bottom of the steps, and his smiled faded when their eyes met. He knows, she thought, so why doesn't he leave?

Luke swore he'd never seen a more beautiful woman than Katherine McBride. As he neared the gathering at the courthouse, he caught sight of her seated beside Tom at the top of the steps. This was how he wanted to remember her. Cool and serene, not tearful and promising him she wouldn't cry anymore.

Joe Perry stood before a podium, speaking to the cheering crowd. A consummate politician, the bright young attorney soon had his audience applauding each statement he made, and Luke even joined in the applause when Joe bade Katherine to join him at the podium.

She spoke to the crowd, her voice so soft that the crowd hushed, straining to hear each word. A stark contrast to Joe's rousing proclamation, nonetheless, the people loved her and hung on her every word.

He shouldered his way through the crowd toward the base of the courthouse steps, close enough that Tom would see him and know that he was there for the ceremony. He had, however, arrived conveniently late to escape being part of the presentation.

Katherine was still at the podium by the time he reached the front of the crowd. Her hair shimmered in the mid-morning sun; she had worn it pulled back by a simple ribbon the same shade of blue as her dress.

She smiled at their cheers, caught sight of him, and her smile vanished. Her eyes grew wide with horror, and she gaped at him as if he were a stranger aiming a rifle at her. The crowd remained silent, waiting for further words. When she remained mute with fright, murmurs of concern became audible.

Joe whispered something to her, and she gave him a startled glance. Luke didn't miss the way she gripped the podium, her knuckles white.

A buzz of whispers rose above the crowd. Too late, the instincts Luke had long ignored took over, and he read the warning in her eyes. Danger! Run!

The crowd thronged around him, and there was no escape without shoving bodily through the mass. Before he could even turn away, Joe caught sight of him and made a desperate attempt to save the moment.

"Marshal Johnson," he called out in a calm voice. "Now that you're here, why don't you join us for the ceremony? After all, if it weren't for you we wouldn't be having this moment."

The crowd broke into applause and several men standing

nearby clapped him on the shoulders, urging him toward the steps. Two men seated behind the podium rose to their feet, quickly followed by the others. A flash of recognition passed through Luke's mind, but when he heard the voice he knew he was doomed.

"Johnson? Where?"

The sheriff from Cutter's Creek!. Luke hadn't hung around that town long enough to make introductions, but he remembered the gravely voice shouting for men to arrest him.

"Caleb Johnson." Tom pointed toward Luke. "Right there."

"Son of a bitch." Hagan swore loud enough for most of those gathered to hear. "That's not Caleb Johnson, you damn fool, that's the man he was bringing back for hanging."

The crowd fell silent and looked toward their marshal for a contradiction. Hagan didn't wait to be countered. "That's Luke Cantrell, a wanted killer, and he had the gumption to put in for the reward on his own head! I'll bet he murdered Johnson."

Gasps of shock and disbelief raced through the crowd, and Luke met Katherine's stricken gaze.

"Don't be ridiculous!" Joe found his voice first. "Luke Cantrell is buried in our cemetery. This man brought him to the doctor, but he died just the same."

"I don't care who's buried in your boneyard," Hagan sneered, drawing his pistol. "I'm carrying *his* ass back to Cutter's Creek for hanging."

"No! No, you're not."

Katherine rushed down the steps, and Luke caught her before she could throw her arms around him. "Stay back, Katherine."

"This is all my fault," she sobbed, struggling against his grip. She managed to catch hold of his vest, clinging as if to a lifeline. "I thought you had already left town. I thought you were safe."

"Damn, Conner, get him in irons," Hagan ordered his deputy. "Don't just stand there!"

The smaller man hurried down the steps. "Step aside, ma'am," he said with as much authority as possible, but Katherine stood her ground.

The deputy gently grasped her arm and tried to pull her away. Luke would have loved nothing more than to toss the bastard flat on his face, but Hagan would seize any opportunity to put a bullet in him. The last thing Luke wanted was a lot of shooting with so many onlookers gathered around.

"Get your hands off my sister." Tom McBride wasted no time in getting down the steps and jerking Conner back by his collar.

"Tom, get her out of here," Luke ordered, turning Katherine toward her brother.

"No, no." She tightened her grip, sobs racking her body. "This is my fault. I should have warned you."

He hushed her heartsick words with gentle fingers against her trembling lips. "No, it's not your fault."

Tom gently laid a hand on his sister's shoulder, his face stricken when he asked, "Then this is true?"

Luke could only nod, forcing himself to meet the accusation in Tom McBride's eyes. Tom gently tried to pry Katherine away from Luke, but she held on. Luke smoothed his hands over her arms allowing her to press her lips against his face, and he could feel the warmth of her tears.

"I'm the one who's sorry," he whispered, firmly pushing her back. Tom was waiting to take her arm. "I should never have lied to you."

"Come on, Katherine," Tom's voice was flat and his movements were stiff. "I'm taking you home."

"Don't let them do this," she pleaded, still reaching for Luke as Tom began pulling her away. She would have fought her brother, but he circled her shoulders with one arm, holding her against him. Still, she begged, "Please, Tom, don't let them take him away."

"Don't just stand there, deputy," Hagan made his way down the steps. "Get the prisoner in irons. Do I have to show you how to do everything?"

Luke never saw Hagan raise his pistol, his only concern was Katherine and the stricken look on her face as Tom led her away. The sickening thud barely registered as the sound of the butt of a revolver connecting with his skull, sending him headlong into unconsciousness.

The last thing he remembered was a woman screaming, "My God, he's killed the marshal!"

Katherine awoke slowly, unsure of her surroundings. She tried to remember going to sleep, but nothing made sense. Slowly her eyes began to focus, and she recognized her own bedroom, but something was terribly wrong. She tried to think what it could be, but a dull pounding at her temple made that impossible.

She glanced toward the door, finding Tom stationed just outside in the hall. He looked so solemn, so miserable. Just like the day their father died. Then she remembered.

"Luke!" she cried, swinging her legs off the bed.

"Hold on there, young lady." Dr. Sullivan appeared from nowhere, pressing a cold compress against her forehead. "You lie back down. You've had quite a shock, and the last thing you need is to be up running around."

"How long have I been asleep?" she demanded.

"You were very upset, my dear," Dr. Sullivan peered into her eyeball, first the left then the right. "You were nearly in shock, so I gave you a mild sedative."

"I didn't need a sedative." She shook her head, fighting the grogginess that threatened to swallow her up again. The oblivion was tempting, but she had to stay awake. "Where is he?"

"Katherine, you need to rest now."

She accepted the glass of water Dr. Sullivan held out to her and took a deep swallow. Bitterness filled her mouth and she spit the water back into the glass. "What is this?"

"Sis, you need to rest." Tom finally entered the room, kneeling beside the bed. "The doctor knows what's best."

"Best for who?" she asked, rising to a sitting position. She took her brother's hands in her smaller ones. "Please tell me where he is?"

"I tried to stop them," he began, looking down at their joined hands. "I even offered to arrest him myself and hold him here for trial. Joe threatened to file a lawsuit against the whole state of Colorado, but they just laughed. They said he was their prisoner and they'd do as they pleased."

Her grip tightened on his hands, and he winced slightly. "What did they do?"

Tom's eyes filled with such anguish that Katherine feared Luke had already been hung. His voice was thick when he said, "They left town about three hours ago. Said they wanted him out of Belle Plain.

"Three hours?" she cried. "Where were they going?"

"Colorado, eventually," he guessed. "But I heard Hagan say something about getting to Abilene by tomorrow."

"And you let me lie here asleep while this was going on?" she demanded, anger taking precedent over heartache. "Three hours have gone by and we've done nothing!"

"There's nothing we can do now," Dr. Sullivan assured her, once again offering the drug-laced glass of water. "Now drink this so you can get some rest."

"We have to try." She tried to think, but the drowsiness made the task difficult. There had to be a way, some way to save Luke from Hagan, but first she had to clear her head.

Katherine rose to her feet with such force that both men took a step back. The sudden movement made her light-headed and she was forced to accept Tom's assistance. Once her legs were steady, she crossed the room heading for the stairs.

"What are you doing," Tom demanded on her heels.

"We are going to do something about this," she informed them both. "I'm calling an emergency meeting of the town council—right away. Dr. Sullivan, you make sure everyone is at the jail in half an hour."

"The jail?" Still holding the glass of water, Dr. Sullivan exchanged such a look of concern with Tom that she feared they might actually attempt to pour the contents of the glass down her throat.

"Yes, the jail," she snapped. "And I don't want any excuses. Drag them in by their collars if you have to!"

Catching her by the arm, Tom leveled his gaze with hers. "Katherine, he lied to us."

Her eyes narrowed. "What would you do to keep from getting yourself hanged?"

Tom's expression softened first. "All right, big sister, what have you got in mind?

∗ 14 ∗

Blood mingled with dust was the most disgusting taste Luke could imagine, and once again he found himself gagging as Hagan reined the horses to a stop. They had ridden hard the last few miles, and Luke had no doubt Hagan had deliberately chosen the roughest terrain. Despite his handcuffs, Luke hung on, unwilling to give the man one additional bit of satisfaction.

"Get started making camp," Hagan barked to his deputy. "I want a pot of coffee. What about you, boy? You ready for supper?"

Leering at Luke, he laughed out loud at his own humor before dragging Luke from the horse without warning. With his hands shackled, Luke fought to gain his balance, but Hagan roughly shoved him to the ground. Unable to break the fall, Luke landed hard in the dust, gravel grating against his face. Hagan laughed again before delivering the toe of his boot to Luke's already aching side.

"You sorry piece of trash," he growled, kicking a good amount of the gritty dust into the face of his prisoner. "Eat all the dirt you want, it's all you'll be getting."

Luke rolled onto the side that hurt the least, ruing the fact that the bastard wouldn't kill him tonight. Like Johnson, Hagan wanted him delivered for hanging.

He watched with little interest as the two men hovered over the newly built fire and argued over the amount of coffee needed for a strong enough brew. Nothing from their conversation gave him the slightest hint as to their location, and Luke wondered how far they had ridden before he had regained consciousness.

Dimly, he recalled leaving Belle Plain. He had heard angry voices. Joe's voice had been stern and hard. "We'll take this up in court. I'll go to the governor, if need be." Finally, Hagan's ultimatum was that he either leave with the prisoner or hang him right there in Belle Plain. Amid the arguments on his behalf, Luke had not heard Katherine's voice, and he was glad. He couldn't stomach the thought of her seeing him this way, a common criminal shackled like an animal.

Rolling to a sitting position, Luke scanned the dark expanse of prairie in hopes of getting his bearings, but he couldn't even determine in what direction they had been traveling. The last thing he remembered after leaving Belle Plain was stopping to water the horses and stumbling to the stream to ease his own thirst. He had splashed his face with cool water, a little shocked to find his fingers stained with blood. Even now as he felt his forehead, he found the deep gash bleeding anew.

"Don't worry about getting cleaned up." Hagan had loomed over him, his fists clenched. "I doubt there will be much of a welcome home party for you in Cutter's Creek. Folks there don't cotton to murderers."

"I didn't murder anyone." Luke knew better, but he had spoken his piece anyway. "I cleaned a man out in a card game, and he was fool enough to pull a gun on me."

"That's not how the boy's Pa sees things." Hagan had gripped him by the collar, dragging him to his feet. "And

Ed McClain has made my life a living hell since you got away.''

Luke didn't doubt it. ''Big Ed'' McClain owned everything and everyone in the tiny mining town.

''It couldn't have been too bad,'' Luke's temper had gotten the better of him, as usual, ''or else you would have been man enough to come after me in the first place.''

Hagan's face turned red, and Luke was gratified by his ability to rile the sheriff. But his satisfaction had been short-lived, as Hagan had felt no compunction over beating a man in irons. Luke groaned inwardly, wondering if he would ever learn to mind his sharp tongue. With the slightest movement, Luke could still feel Hagan's fists pounding against his flesh, and the foul taste of his own blood served as yet another reminder of the man's violent temper.

The camp fire was burning brightly now, and the aroma of frying bacon filled the air. Hagan and Conner were at ease, each man savoring a cup of coffee. Conner tended the skillet while his boss searched a saddlebag, producing a whiskey bottle.

''How 'bout a little cream in your coffee?'' Hagan offered the bottle to his deputy after pouring a liberal amount into his own cup.

Conner forked the bacon from the skillet, glancing in Luke's direction. ''Shouldn't we feed him?''

''And waste good food?'' The lawman hefted the whiskey and guzzled straight from the bottle, wiping his mouth with the back of his hand. ''Let him have what's left, if you like.''

Luke wondered how drunk they would get before going to sleep. Always a survivor, he couldn't help but think about escape. He didn't dare hope for the same luck that had gotten him away from Johnson, and he secretly feared luck had finally abandoned him. No, this time he would have to look for any opportunity, for any carelessness on

Hagan's part, and this time he would be damn sure to leave his captors behind . . . dead.

And where would he go? He knew of only one place, but that was impossible. If he returned to Katherine, Hagan's cronies would follow, and the lives of others would be at risk. Besides, the good folks of Belle Plain would not welcome the man who had cost them their hope of being a whistle-stop on the Texas & Pacific Railroad. Luke didn't miss the look of shock on McGregor's face, and he had no doubt the man was not accustomed to being duped.

"Hey, Cantrell." Hagan's voice drew his attention. "That sure was a pretty little gal cryin' over you back yonder."

He ignored the taunt, knowing that the whiskey would only make Hagan bolder, crueler.

"I reckon she'll be mighty lonely now that you won't be tossing her petticoats." The sheriff spooned his mouth full of beans and chewed thoughtfully. "Maybe I'll just ride down there every once in a while and keep her company myself. I hope you got her broke in good, 'cause I hate it when they holler too much."

Never looking in the man's direction, Luke said, "You'll never touch her."

"Oh, and just what makes you so damn sure?" Hagan demanded. "You'll be hung and buried by then."

Luke levelled his gaze on his enemy. "Her brother will kill you, you son of a bitch."

Hagan tossed his plate aside and sprang to his feet, his angry features distorted in the flickering light of the campfire. "Maybe, that's what I ought to do to you."

"You won't do it," Luke taunted, desperation making him brave. "You've got to make a good show of bringing me back for a hanging. I'm sure Big Ed will be happy to know he has a lawman who can actually bring a man in every now and then without a bullet in his back."

Hagan's eyes bulged with fury. "You bastard, I'll kill you myself."

The horses, picketed nearby, suddenly raised their heads and nickered in alarm. One mare, her ears pricked against the night air, whinnied loudly.

"Someone's coming," Conner called after Hagan.

"No shit," Hagan sneered, turning in the direction in which the horses had their ears at attention.

Both men stood and gazed out toward the expanse of darkness, their weapons drawn. The wind picked up, bringing with it the sound of approaching riders. Luke turned as best he could in direction of the pounding hooves, catching sight of flickering light, a torch of some kind.

"A lynch mob!" Conner voiced Luke's worst fear. "What are we gonna do?"

"They mean *us* no harm," Hagan assured the deputy. "In fact, they'll be saving us the trouble of a hanging. As long as he's dead, the matter is settled."

He turned toward Luke, his anger replaced with a gloating smile of satisfaction. "I reckon I won't have to listen to your smart mouth much longer."

By the time the masked riders reached the tiny camp, the tethered horses were frantic, rearing against their leads. Luke felt the chill of fear race up his spine as he took in the sight of torch-wielding henchmen wearing crude masks made of flour sacks. Gaping holes had been slashed for their eyes and noses, giving them all leering expressions.

"Evenin', gentlemen," Hagan called. "What can we do for you?"

As if in military drill, the riders each raised rifles and Hagan's bravado waned. "Now wait a minute. If you've come for Cantrell, there he is, but I've got no argument with you."

"Get your hands up and step aside," the rider in front ordered. "Or I'll blow enough lead in you to sink a steamship."

Hagan hesitated, but Conner's arms shot up immediately.

"We're taking your prisoner—and there's no need trying to be a hero."

"Take him," Hagan spat out, raising his arms reluctantly. As if on second thought, he asked, "What's he to you?"

"He made a fool of our whole town, and we don't intend to let that go unanswered."

Hagan's eyes narrowed. "What about all that talk about me having no right to arrest him?"

"We don't hold with those bleeding hearts, and we're going to see that justice is done." When Hagan made no reply, the leader pressed, "You want him hung, don't you?"

"Hell, yes."

"Then we agree on one thing."

Our whole town. The words rang in his ears, and Luke felt bile rise in his throat, unwilling to believe the vigilantes were from Belle Plain. He had betrayed the town, that was true, but the knowledge that they could turn on him so viciously hurt more than anything he had suffered at Hagan's hands.

The masked rider brandished his rifle in Conner's direction. "Mount him up on the sorrel there and be quick about it."

Conner didn't need to be told to be quick. He spooked easily enough and rushed to lead Luke toward the waiting mob. It just wasn't in Luke's nature to surrender, and he couldn't stifle the urge to resist Conner's efforts.

Despite the irons, he managed to land an elbow in the deputy's soft belly, rending a groan from the man. Hagan rushed forward, seizing a great handful of Luke's hair. He raised a fist, but the mob's spokesman was quick to protest.

"I told you he was ours." The rifles were instantly trained on the sheriff. "Now mount him up on that damned horse and be real easy about it."

Hagan reluctantly loosened his hold on Luke's scalp, and transferred his grip to his arm. "Get on with you."

Luke didn't go easy, his steps halting. Of all that he dreaded, this was the worst: being led off by a bloodthirsty band of vigilantes intent more on gore than justice. Even a public hanging would be better.

As he was shoved past the first horse, he was suddenly aware that each rider was armed with the exact same type of rifle. No pistols or shotguns, just blue steel carbines, gleaming in the moonlight.

"Be sure to hand those keys over," the leader ordered. "We want him to claw at the rope a little."

Hagan laughed at the thought. "All I ask is that you leave him for the buzzards. I want to be sure he's dead this time."

Hagan gave Luke a shove. "Get up there." Luke hoisted himself up behind the slim figure on the sorrel.

The moment he was astride the horse, realization slammed into his gut. It was Katherine. He shifted forward just enough to let the wall of his chest brush the delicate curve of her shoulders, his thighs encircling the flare of her hips. It was all he could do not to bury his face against the nape of her neck.

His movements were limited by the irons, but he managed to cup the dip of her waist and felt her shiver beneath his touch. Her grip tightened on the reins, and he could feel her heart pounding beneath the fabric of the oversized shirt she wore.

Confusion and hope surged in his mind. He refused to believe that she could hate him to the point of wanting him lynched, but he couldn't comprehend her thinking him worthy enough to risk so much danger to save him.

"All right, we're on our way," the spokesman shouted. "Get back to your fire and back to your business. We want no trouble from you, just the satisfaction of knowing this man gets what he deserves."

Conner wasted no time returning to the camp, and Hagan lingered only long enough to say, "Much obliged, fellas. Just hang him with a new rope, is all I ask."

Katherine turned her horse and the rest followed, riding fast. When he was certain of their distance from Hagan, Luke let his face fall against her shoulder, drinking in the sweet scent of her body.

He was too tired, too sore to ask or even wonder where they were going. He loved her, and he was willing to go wherever she was taking him.

Katherine had not ridden in several months and the furious pace of her horse jarred every bone in her body. Still, she urged the sorrel on faster, away from Hagan, toward the only safety she'd been able to find. Luke was slumped against her and she feared he was badly injured.

She had barely glimpsed his face in the flickering light of the torches, but she had seen enough to know he'd been beaten badly. Killing Hagan was out of the question, as too many people would wonder about him when he failed to return to Colorado, but she had wanted to do just that.

Just ahead, she caught sight of a grove of trees, and she could make out the figure of a man waiting with two horses.

She reined the sorrel to a halt and quickly dismounted. "Someone help me get him down. I'm afraid he's hurt badly."

Tyler Martin stepped forward first, gripping Luke around the waist and hoisting him down. Katherine removed her mask, as did the others, and knelt beside him. She traced the battered lines of his face with her fingers.

"Let me get a look at him." Dr. Sullivan turned Luke's face to the light, holding a canteen to his bruised mouth. "Son, wake up. Drink some water."

Katherine held her breath as the water ran away from his slack mouth. Dr. Sullivan pressed the canteen firmly against his lips. "Son, wake up!"

More water ran over his face, and Luke grimaced, turning away from the deluge. Dr. Sullivan withdrew the canteen and shook him slightly. To Katherine's relief, he did open his eyes, though one was nearly swollen shut. She leaned forward, "Luke, can you hear me?"

He turned at the sound of her voice and she gripped his hand. "Can you ride?"

He nodded, raising himself to a sitting position without help. Dr. Sullivan again offered the canteen, and he accepted, this time drinking deeply. Still holding the canteen, he glanced around the group hovering over them and then back to Katherine.

"You people scared the hell out me," he managed a tight grin. "You could hire out to ward off train robbers."

Everyone laughed softly, and Preacher Meeks stepped forward, still brandishing the rifle he wielded so well. "There's no sin worse than the sin of omission, and we weren't about to see you railroaded into a hasty hanging. I will have to pray for forgiveness for myself, however. I'm afraid I purely enjoyed the fear in that heathen's eyes."

Cecil Percy peered over the pastor's shoulder, clearly amused. "Maybe you ought to start delivering your sermons with a rifle rather than a Bible."

Everyone laughed again, and Katherine felt her heart turn over at the sight of Luke's weak smile. Their plan had been thrown together so hastily, based on a story Mr. Percy had read in a dime novel! It was a miracle they had found Luke still alive and an even greater miracle no one had been hurt.

"You'd better get moving," Tyler Martin's stern voice cut through the laughter. "The cabin's at least an hour away, and those men might decide to come looking for his body."

"He's right," Dr. Sullivan's face grew serious, and he reached down to help Luke to his feet. "Are you sure you can ride?"

Luke nodded, shrugging away the doctor's hold. He

turned toward Martin and demanded, "What cabin?"

"We're already on Tyler's land," Katherine explained, taking his arm. "There's a line shack about an hour from here. His men use it in the winter, but no one will know we're there."

"We?" He shook his head. "You're not going."

"Try and stop me." Katherine was in no mood to argue. "You're hurt, and you don't know where this place is. I'm going with you."

"Better ride now," Ty Martin cut in, leading two fresh mounts toward them. "You can do your talking later."

Katherine took the reins and tossed the other set to Luke while Preacher Meeks unlocked the handcuffs. The pastor pocketed the irons, and placed his hand on Luke's shoulder. "You'll be in my prayers."

Luke shook the pastor's hand. "Believe me, I'll need them."

He then turned to Martin. "Why are you helping me?"

The two men faced each other, and Katherine couldn't believe they had chosen to discuss their differences now.

"I did it for Katherine," Martin insisted stubbornly. "I can be a horse's ass when I want to be, but I'm man enough to admit when I'm wrong about someone."

Luke offered his hand, and Martin accepted, offering a smile in return. "Good luck to you."

Katherine wasted no time in mounting the smaller of the two horses. "Luke, please, we've got to hurry."

"You can't go with me."

"Yes, I can and I am, and that's that. I'm taking you to a safe place." She turned to the others, sensing their reluctance to allow her to take off alone with a wanted man. The concern was touching, but this was hardly a time to consider propriety. "You all get back to town and make sure things look as normal as possible. Tell Tom I'll be home as soon as possible."

Luke, at last, had mounted the large roan, and she man-

aged a tight smile as she turned her horse east, hurrying
away from danger.

Luke guided his horse behind Katherine's. The path had
narrowed considerably and he could hear a gurgling stream
just ahead.

"Just down there," she whispered. "Not much further."

The cabin came into sight, its weathered boards gleaming
silver in the moonlight. Worn by the elements more than
by use, the cabin looked utterly abandoned. Katherine dismounted and motioned for him to do the same.

They put the horses in a crude lean-to behind the cabin,
where an ample supply of hay and grain was kept.

Once inside, Katherine scurried to light a candle that sat
over the fireplace. The cabin was nothing more than a one
room shack, offering shelter and little else. The only window remained shuttered, and Luke wondered when was the
last time anyone had been in the cabin.

"Here . . . you sit down." She drew a small chair from
a crude wooden table. "I've got to do something about that
cut."

She heaved one saddlebag onto the table, hastily searching its contents. She placed several tiny bottles on the table
and turned toward the hearth. She poured a generous
amount of water into a basin and resumed sorting though
the saddlebag.

The content of one tiny bottle was added to the water,
and Katherine reached into the saddlebag, producing a
larger bottle he recognized immediately. She handed the
whiskey to him without a word and placed a folded cloth
in the basin to soak.

He raised the bottle to his battered lips, disheartened to
learn that good whiskey stung just as much as rotgut. Still,
he drank deeply, savoring the smoky flavor and the warmth
that surged through his insides. "I suppose I should introduce myself."

She flicked a smile at him. "Let me guess. You're Luke Cantrell, the most wanted man in Texas."

He raised the bottle in salute. "And you're Katherine McBride, the bravest woman in Texas."

"I'm not brave." She began wringing out the cloth and the cloying scent of disinfectant filled the room. "I was scared to death. That Hagan is a pig."

He corked the bottle and set it aside. "How long have you known who I am?"

She turned toward him, brushing the hair away from his forehead with trembling fingers. "A while. Since the day you turned down Stuart Carey's contract."

She placed the cloth against the gash on his forehead and fire shot through the wound. He cursed, turning away from her touch. "Damn it, what are you trying to do?"

"That's a nasty cut, and it has to be cleaned." She caught his face with her palm and made him look at her. "I'm sorry if I hurt you."

Luke could have kicked himself. After all that she'd done, he had to snap at her over a little sting. He reached for her other hand, bringing her knuckles to his lips. "I'm the one who hurt you, and I'm the one who should be sorry."

He held still while she ministered to his wounds. Once she was satisfied that he was safe from infection, she produced another bag, this one filled with food—bread, cheese, jerky, and cookies.

"Ty said it would be best not to start a fire," she explained, pouring water from a canteen into a clean cup. "Smoke from the chimney is an invitation to anyone passing by, and we certainly don't want company."

"Martin is a good man," Luke observed, reaching for a cookie. "A better man than I am."

"You're not a bad person," she insisted. "I think I knew that the first time I saw you. I just didn't want to admit it."

"You're not angry at me for lying?"

"You had no reason to trust me in the beginning," she answered, taking a seat across from him. "Had you told me who you were, I would have no doubt turned you in. Then when I knew, I chose not to demand the truth."

"How did you know?"

"I found an old newspaper from Denver, and there was an article written about Caleb Johnson." She kept her eyes on her hands, folded tightly on the table before her. "The man they described was nothing like you."

He covered her hands with his, finding her trembling. "Why didn't you say something?"

"I should have. Then you would have left right away and avoided this awful mess." She raised her face to his, her eyes filled with guilt and remorse. "But I kept quiet, because . . . I wanted you to stay just a little while longer."

"Katherine," he said softly.

"You're the one who should be angry." Her eyes grew bright with tears. "I should have realized the danger you'd be in if someone discovered your identity. Instead, I let you go on pretending to be marshal, so that I could pretend you cared about me a little while longer."

Luke leaned forward and kissed her. "There was never any pretending on my part, not when it came to caring about you."

It seemed a small token to him, but his assurance brought a warm smile to her face. Luke traced the line of her face. He kissed her again, this time gathering her in his arms, and her lips parted beneath his, welcoming him.

The rickety chairs were awkward, and Luke rose to his feet, gently pulling her up as well. He drew her fully into his embrace, her slight figure fitting perfectly against him. He smoothed his hand over the faded chambray shirt, and asked, "Where on earth did you get these clothes?"

"The shirt is Tom's," she replied, looking up at him. "I had to have boy's denims. Mr. Sneed donated a pair to the cause."

"The cause?" he whispered, grazing his lips against her forehead.

"Saving you," she managed before his lips covered hers.

Katherine sank against him, reveling in the feel of his solid strength. He was alive and safe, and she had promised God never to ask for anything again. It didn't matter that this was all she would ever have of him.

He broke the kiss, and studied her face, his eyes dark with passion. Without asking, he reached for the buttons of her borrowed shirt. She tried not to quiver when the garment slid from her shoulders, but the feel of his hands on her bare arms sent tremors coursing through her body.

Her chemise was thin, and the feel of his palm against her breast burned, making her feel more alive than she had thought possible. His lips trailed the line of her throat, and she made no protest when he slid the delicate material away, baring her to his eyes.

His touch was light, but her nipple pebbled against his thumb. He lowered his head, taking the darkened peak in his mouth, and Katherine felt her knees weaken as waves of sensation washed over her. He caught her weight against him and increased the pressure, his tongue unrelenting in the exquisite torment.

Without warning, he raised his head and actually took a step back. A strangled cry rose from Katherine's throat, and she felt dazed from the sudden loss of contact. She reached for him, and he caught her hands, keeping her at a distance.

"Do you know what this will mean?" he asked, his voice gentle but unwavering. "I can stop now, but the choice is yours. If I taste you again, I will take you, Katherine."

With a love in her heart that she had not known possible, she closed the distance between them. "You don't have to take what is freely given."

He brushed his lips against her knuckles and raised her

hands to the buttons of his shirt. Her fingers trembled but she managed to work the buttons free, unwilling to look away when he tossed the garment to the floor. He drew her against him, her breasts settling against the sprinkling of hair on his chest, and his mouth claimed hers.

He took her hand and led her to a narrow bed wedged in the corner of the room. The faded quilt and lumpy mattress were of no consequence as they sank to the bed, and Katherine was only slightly aware of the groan of the sagging bed frame as Luke's weight covered hers.

His kiss was no less ardent, but the pace was less demanding. She felt his fingers tug at the buttons of her britches, and she suddenly felt awkward and wished she were wearing a nightgown of flowing white silk. Luke knelt above her, and the look in his eyes as he slid the denims down her bare legs assured her that he loved what he saw.

"I wish we were in a hotel in New Orleans," he whispered against her breast. "Or even San Francisco. You deserve better than this."

She wanted to tell him that she had no regrets, but he silenced her assurances with a deep, drugging kiss. His hand smoothed over her belly and stroked her thighs, startling her when he slid his fingers between her legs. She gasped slightly, but his touch deepened and all thought of protest or modesty left her.

As if he knew her body as well as his own, Luke soon had her straining against his touch. His lips left hers to find the throbbing pulse at her throat and to whisper heated promises of pleasure and gentleness. He rose from the bed, causing her eyes to fly open in alarm, but he returned to her arms as soon as his remaining clothes were shed.

The feel of his hair-roughened thighs settling between hers was a welcome comfort that quickly vanished at the feel of his hardness probing her flesh. She shrank back from his touch and the invasion ceased. He lifted his head to study her face, his expression one of understanding.

"Don't be frightened," he whispered, reaching between them. He stroked her moist flesh, and slipped one finger inside her. Using his thumb, he brought her back to the state of mindless need. "You're ready, kitten. Let me love you."

All she could do was whimper and nod her head slightly, hooking her arms around his shoulders as he spread her thighs even wider. This time she didn't pull away, but the fear was still there. Her body didn't accept him easily, but the relentless pressure continued until her flesh gave way and they were joined completely.

They both lay still, but she could hear his ragged breathing. The pain began to ease, as did her grip on his shoulders, and only then did he begin to move within her. Her body was limp, and he cupped her bottom and guided her into his rhythm.

Heat began to pool in her belly, and she felt her stomach muscles clench in anticipation of something she couldn't name. His shoulders were slick with sweat, and by the tension in his corded muscles she knew that he was restraining his passion for her sake. His thrusts grew deeper, and she felt her own flesh grip him tightly.

A mewling cry escaped her lips, and her body suddenly shattered into a million pieces. Dimly, she was aware of his whole body going rigid and the warm rush of his release. He fell, sated, into her arms, and an unexpected hope filled her heart.

Perhaps, she would have his child.

Tonight was all they would have together, but a baby would always serve as a precious reminder that she had known love the way few people ever do. Her arms tightened around him, and tears stung her eyes.

A baby wasn't much to ask when she had waited so long to fall in love—only to lose him forever.

• 15 •

A RIM OF light framed the shuttered window, and Luke could only guess the time. He had been awake for better than an hour and in that time, the narrow band of sunlight had gone from a soft grayish hue to the bright shade of gold now dappling the dirt floor of the cabin.

He scanned the interior of the cabin, finding it even more lacking in the pale light of day. Along the bare board walls hung an assortment of coiled ropes, harnesses, and other necessities for tending cattle. The cabin was meant for nothing more than sheltering cowboys weary from trailing a herd far from the main bunkhouse. The only furniture was the rickety table and chairs, an ancient cookstove stacked with rusted skillets and dented pans, and the narrow bed where Katherine still slept.

Even the scant light wasn't needed to see how beautiful she was, and Luke cursed himself for the hundredth time. She was a lady, and she deserved better than a borrowed bed in a ramshackle cabin. He also cursed the fact that, given the chance, he would have done nothing differently. She had given herself to him, and he had gladly taken her innocence and her love, neither of which he deserved.

Luke was unaccustomed to comparing himself to other men, and certainly wasn't pleased to find himself lacking. Stability and reliability were traits he would have scoffed at had he ever considered the need for them. He always got along, sometimes by the skin of his teeth, but his own welfare was all that ever mattered.

He'd done quite a bit of thinking in the last hour, and for the first time, he had really considered the direction his life had taken. In seventeen years, he'd accomplished little besides living well when he could. Rarely had he done without anything, but whatever money he'd had was spent for fine clothes, lewd women, and room service. All that had ever mattered was getting to the next town and the next game.

Now that he was free, the last thing he wanted to do was return to that life. He had no desire to spend the rest of his days at the mercy of the turn of a card or hustling drunks and greenhorns when times were lean. He wanted something permanent and real, without deception or trickery.

He wanted Katherine.

Not just for a night, but for always.

He turned to find her watching him, her eyes half open. She stretched beneath the quilt, her bare arms pale and delicate. Pushing her tousled hair from her eyes, she asked, "What time is it?"

He shrugged. "I'm not sure. The sun's been up about an hour."

"An hour!" She sat straight up, pulling the quilt around her. "You should have been gone before now."

She swung her legs over the side of the bed, wrapping the quilt around her shoulders. Padding across the room, she began a hasty attempt to gather the food for his saddlebag. The heavy blanket hampered her movements and she abandoned the task, scanning the room.

"Where are my clothes?" she asked.

He motioned to the chair where he had placed her neatly folded shirt and denims. "There's no hurry."

"No hurry?" She shook her head, grabbing the shirt and turning her back to slip her arms into the too-long sleeves. "The sooner you start for Mexico, the sooner—"

She started when he placed his hands on her shoulders. "Katherine, I'm not going to Mexico."

She hesitated, almost turning her head, before reaching for the long row of buttons down the front of the shirt. "Perhaps, it would be best if you don't tell me which direction you're going. Someone might ask, and I won't have to worry about giving you away."

He covered her trembling hands with his larger ones. "You don't understand."

"Yes, I do. Hagan may think you're dead, but someone else might be after that reward." She let her head fall back against his chest. "Maybe in a few years, you could write to me . . . just to let me know you're safe."

He turned her around and forced her to look up at him. "The only place I'm going is back to Belle Plain . . . with you."

She gasped. "You can't! Luke, they'll come after—"

He silenced her protests with gentle fingers against her lips. "Katherine, I can't spend my life running away from this problem. I shot the man in self-defense, but I'll never clear my name by running."

She shook her head. "It's too dangerous. What if you can't prove it was self-defense?"

"There's a fine lawyer back in Belle Plain I know can help me."

"Joe," she concluded. "Yes, he's good, but what about Hagan?"

"He's a problem," Luke agreed. "He wasn't in the saloon when the shooting happened, but he'll probably have a half dozen witnesses against me."

"Then you can't risk it," she insisted, pulling out of his

embrace. She quickly buttoned the shirt and reached for her denims. "There's plenty of food and you can take both canteens. I also brought your guns and two hundred dollars in cash. That should get you to Mexico."

"What about you?"

She stepped into the dark britches. "I can get back to town by myself."

"And then what?" he asked. "We just forget each other? Pretend the past few weeks never happened?"

Her head snapped up at that, and he didn't miss the anger in her eyes as she buttoned the fly. "You picked a fine time to get sentimental."

"Do you want me to leave?"

"Yes," she answered without hesitation. Turning away from him, she crossed the tiny room and began gathering the items strewn across the tabletop and cramming them into the saddlebag. He advanced on her, bracing his arms on the back of a rickety chair facing the table. "Well, I'm not. I'm going back to Belle Plain and settle this thing once and for all."

"And risk your life?" she asked in a cool voice. "Luke, the game is over; we lost."

"You don't think I'm innocent!" The realization hit him and he pushed away from the table with such force the chair toppled over, splintering against the hard-packed floor. "You think I deliberately killed that man, don't you?"

"I'm sure you didn't mean for anyone to die," she assured him. "But when men have been drinking and gambling, tempers sometimes flare."

"He drew a gun and pointed it at my face." Luke couldn't keep the anger from his voice. The last person he should have to explain or defend himself to was Katherine. "I thought he might be bluffing and kept my pistol out of sight. When he cocked that hammer, I fired and blew a hole through the top of the table and through him. Would you feel better if I'd let him kill me?"

She didn't flinch. "How do you think I'll feel if they hang you?"

He backed away, toward the door. "I'm saddling the horses. You can ride with me or not, but I'm going back to Belle Plain."

Katherine reined the gentle sorrel toward the back of the livery, anxious to get home to clean clothes and hot food. She had ridden the entire distance without looking at Luke, afraid she would be unable to keep from crying. She held onto her anger as a shield against her fear and panic. Why did he dare to risk his life on the slim chance of clearing his name?

It was still early when they reached town, but many were already milling about. The tattered red, white, and blue parade banners hung like funeral wreaths, and the remains of discarded paper popcorn bags and cardboard lemonade cups waited for the push broom. The odor of roasting meat lingered in the air, and Katherine could picture the solemn crowd filing toward picnic tables. Tom told her the festive atmosphere of the barbecue quickly became the somber mood of a wake after the marshal's arrest, and the food became a source of comfort rather than revelry.

She wondered if Luke had any idea what the people of Belle Plain had risked to come to his rescue. He was doing them a great disservice by risking the freedom they had all conspired to give him.

Silas Matthews stepped out of the livery to greet them, obviously surprised to see Luke. "Miss McBride, I was expectin' you alone."

"There's been a change in plans," she said, offering no further explanation. "I can't thank you enough for the loan of the horses."

"Anytime." Silas studied Luke intently as he swung down from his mount. "Do I still call you marshal?"

"Luke is fine."

Katherine watched the two men shake hands. "Have you seen Tom?"

"Yes, ma'am. He's waiting for you at your place." Silas wagged his head. "He's mighty worried about you. Came by here not half an hour ago and told me if you weren't back by noon that he was going after you."

"Well, I'd better let him know that I'm safe." Katherine placed a hand on the old man's arm. "Mr. Matthews, I'm trusting you not to tell anyone that we came back together. There's still a lot of danger, and for the time being only a few people need to know Luke is back in town."

"Of course," he assured her. "I would never want to cause you a moment of grief."

She smiled and thanked him, turning back to Luke. "We'd better get back to my house before anyone else sees you."

"Your house?"

"Yes, until you have a chance to talk with Joe, you'd better keep out of sight."

They managed the brief distance to Katherine's house without encountering any neighbors, well-meaning or otherwise. The back door swung open at the first sound of their boots on the steps. Tom rushed outside, his expression one of concern and surprise, and Katherine welcomed his embrace. Her exhaustion and shattered nerves had taken their toll, and she hurried everyone inside and closed the door before her brother could begin questioning her.

Tom regarded Luke openly. "I didn't count on seeing you again, at least not so soon."

"I'm much obliged to you and the town."

For the first time, Katherine noticed Luke's haggard countenance. No doubt he had slept less than she, and had his own share of worries. She glanced toward her brother. "Is there any coffee?"

Tom filled two cups as she sank into a chair at the table. Luke remained standing, somewhat wary, and accepted the coffee. He drank deeply and crossed his arms over his chest. Tom joined Katherine at the table, placing a cup before her, and she couldn't keep from glancing up at Luke's hesitant figure.

"Why don't you join us?" she asked quietly. "We have a lot to work out."

"Maybe I should just get back to the hotel."

"You can't," she exclaimed in a voice strangely hoarse. "Who knows who might see you and send a wire to Hagan?"

"She's right," Tom said. "That reward is hanging over your head, and there were a lot of visitors in town overnight. Any one of them might not think twice about putting your life in danger for that money."

Luke muttered a curse under his breath and set his coffee aside. "I just want this thing behind me."

Tom nodded. "I understand that, but you've got to be careful. Hagan won't take you back alive the next time."

Katherine felt the color drain from her face. She hadn't considered that Hagan might be vengeful, only the danger of Luke facing charges in an unfriendly town. "My God, what can we do?"

"I've already sent a wire to Judge Drinkard in Abilene." Tom didn't look at either one of them. "When I was putting the rifles up last night, I remembered what Pa always said about him. Honest as the day is long and twice as ornery."

Luke rolled his eyes. "Sounds like just what I need."

Tom stiffened at the sarcasm. "If you're going to fight this problem, you've got to do it on the side of the law."

"You mean the same law that offers rewards for innocent men . . . dead or alive?"

Tension hung in the air, and they were all startled by a sudden knock at the door. Tom rose to his feet and crossed the room, peering through the lace curtain. "It's Joe."

Tom opened the door and ushered him inside. Joe easily

assessed the situation, glancing first at Katherine, then at Luke. "I hope you realize this will be an uphill battle all the way."

"And a losing one," Katherine added, her only hope now was that Joe could convince Luke there was no chance of proving his innocence.

"Not necessarily," he replied, producing a folded piece of paper from his pocket. "Tom, Judge Drinkard answered our telegram, and I think you'll all be interested to know that there was never an arrest warrant issued for Luke Cantrell."

Katherine shot an accusing look at Luke. "If you haven't told us the truth by now—"

"I took the warrant from Johnson myself," Luke insisted.

"Only a federal warrant would allow him to take you across state lines." Joe sat down at the table, a calming presence. "You may be wanted in Cutter's Creek, but nothing was ever filed with the U.S. Marshal in Texas or Colorado."

Luke neared the table. "What are you saying?"

"This casts doubt on Hagan more than you. And Judge Drinkard will want answers that Hagan won't be prepared to give."

They all remained quiet for a moment, until Joe looked up, his eyes widening with realization. "Do you know if Johnson could read or write?"

Luke shook his head. "We didn't exactly get to know each other."

"I suspect that he was hired by Hagan to bring you in under false pretenses. I'd like to see that warrant."

"It was in my gear," Luke explained. "I had my bags stashed at the livery."

"Silas found them when he was cleaning the stall." Tom stood, turning toward the next room. "I put your things in the dining room."

Tom returned to the kitchen with the saddlebags and Luke wasted no time in locating the arrest warrant. Joe scanned the paper, a smile touching his lips. "This is nothing more than a crude statement of intent written out by Hagan; it's not worth the paper it's written on."

"Then how can there be a reward for his arrest?" Katherine asked.

"A reward can be offered without formal charges being filed, saying that the person is wanted for questioning," Joe explained, his eyes scanning the warrant. "Hagan probably knew about the reward before it was announced, and he hired Johnson to return Luke to Cutter's Creek."

"Poor fool Johnson, a thousand dollars was a fortune to him. But it was Hagan who would collect the full reward, and the bounty hunter—none the wiser—would be paid off with a mere pittance," Luke concluded. "And I would have been eliminated with a quick hanging."

"I'd bet even now Hagan is on his way home planning how he's going to spend his reward money. He'll have a thousand dollars more than he expected, now that Johnson's share doesn't have to be paid up." Joe was pleased with his reasoning.

"Then Luke is free," Katherine glanced up. "If Hagan collects his reward money, believing Luke is dead, there's nothing to worry about."

"Except, I'm alive. I played a dead man once—I won't do it again."

"But if Hagan finds out we've tricked him, he'll come back for you." Katherine didn't want to hear any more about Hagan, warrants, or hangings. She wanted Luke to be free and safe, and he could be neither as long as he remained in Belle Plain. The scornful look on his face, however, gave her no hope that he was willing to leave with the question of guilt hanging over him.

"I'm tired of hiding, and I aim to prove my innocence,"

he countered. "The fact that no warrant has been issued shows that Hagan has no case."

"Which will only give him more reason to kill you rather than arrest you." Katherine rose from the table, resenting his stubbornness. "Dead men take little pride in being right."

Neither Tom nor Joe would comment, and Katherine suspected their silence was more out of support for Luke than any desire to remain neutral. She shook her head, refusing to make accusations or enter into further debate. Before turning toward the stairs, she did warn them, "Whatever comes will be on your heads. I want no part of it."

Luke's eyes narrowed. "Katherine, I'm innocent and I intend to prove it."

"This isn't about guilt or innocence!" she cried, gripping the banister for support. "This is about money, and Hagan has already proven he's willing to kill you to keep that reward. Is it going to take a rope around your neck to convince you?"

Katherine slept fitfully, curling away from the afternoon sunlight streaming through her bedroom window. She dreamed of lynchings, of her mother burning with fever with only two frightened children to tend to her, and of her father's funeral. She awakened with her stomach in knots and her heart slamming against her chest, wishing she had allowed Dr. Sullivan to sedate her after all.

Exhaustion had finally driven her to seek rest in the middle of the day. She had lain wide awake for the last half hour, her neck and shoulders stiff, listening to the constant commotion downstairs.

The front door had been opened and closed at least a dozen times, and the sound of muted female voices and footsteps drifted upstairs. She strained to hear what was being said but could only make out snatches here and there.

"Is she asleep?"

"Poor thing."

"What an ordeal."

"Bless her heart."

Pity. She flinched at the thought. No matter how good their intentions, in the end they all felt sorry for her. The poor spinster who was so lonely she let herself be duped by an outlaw. That's what they would all think, and she wasn't sure the truth was much different.

Katherine stretched her aching muscles, wincing at the unexpected twinge between her legs. The last thing she needed was yet another reminder of all that had happened in the last twenty-four hours, but the backlash of emotions swept over her, causing her to hug her pillow as if to shield herself from the pain.

For all the whispered accounts of lovemaking, her married friends had hardly prepared her for the passion she had found with Luke. It had been so easy to give herself to him without shame or doubt.

Their night together had been beautiful, and her only regret was that those memories stood the chance of being spoiled by Luke's untimely sense of nobility. If the world were a perfect place, she would be delighted that he had returned to Belle Plain, but the stakes were much too high.

She reminded herself that he had returned to town with the intent of fighting the charges against him, and nothing had been said about a future with her. He could still leave, returning to the decadent lifestyle of a gambler while she eked out a life as a spinster . . . a ruined spinster.

Hypocrite.

She had rallied the town to save him from the gallows, not to set a marriage trap. She loved him and seeing him alive had been all that mattered; everything that followed had been as much her choice as his. Besides, only another man would consider her ruined, and she couldn't even begin to contemplate giving herself to anyone other than Luke.

Mother had always said there was "being in love" and then there was loving someone. Loving someone was much harder because true love was selfless. Katherine smiled at the thought of her mother, a soft-spoken woman who read to them from the Bible by the light of the evening fire. The words came to her, warm and soft from childhood.

Love beareth all things, believeth all things, hopeth all things, endureth all things.

Could she endure loving someone only to lose him? Before, there had been no choice; send him away or see him hang. Now other possibilities loomed before her.

Finally, she slipped down the stairs to the kitchen. She opened the door to find Charlotte hovering over a table loaded with food. Platters were perched on top of bowls of every kind of vegetable imaginable. The counters were lined with jars of pickles and preserves, and a wide assortment of cakes and pies.

"What in the world is all of this?" she asked.

Charlotte shrugged. "People didn't know what else to do, so they brought food."

Katherine had often been a contributor during times of illness or grief, preparing large quantities of rich, satisfying food. Chicken and dumplings for funerals, chicken and dressing for sick neighbors, and, without fail, she would bake a ham when a new baby arrived. Nothing but habit, but a sincere gesture nonetheless.

Charlotte, being her close friend and soon in-law to be, had the honor and responsibility of accepting the offerings in Katherine's stead. Still in her dressing gown, Katherine padded barefoot across the kitchen floor. She lifted lids and sniffed the tantalizing array, suddenly famished.

"Think you could eat a bite?" Charlotte asked.

"For some reason, I'm starved." She reached for a slice of freshly baked bread and slathered it with strawberry preserves.

"Nerves, I guess."

"Here, sit down and eat a proper meal," Charlotte instructed, pulling out a chair at the only bare spot on the table. "The men will be back soon and I'll see that they're all fed."

Katherine ate the jelly and bread while Charlotte loaded a plate with chicken, green beans, potatoes, and corn bread. A cold glass of buttermilk, her favorite, completed the meal.

"Where have the men gone?"

"Joe sent another telegram to that judge in Abilene," Charlotte explained, preparing a plate for herself. Spooning gravy over her potatoes, she added, "They're waiting for his answer."

Katherine tasted the green beans and made a face. "Mrs. Tate, right?"

"Too much salt," Charlotte declared after sampling her own portion. "But her intentions were good."

Katherine nodded, digging her fork into the potatoes. No disappointment there; Mrs. Newman had a way with potatoes, and Katherine thought it would be a sin to drown them in gravy. The chicken was just as good, and they ate in silence. Usually, Charlotte chattered like a bird, but the weight of the situation kept her quiet.

Sated, Charlotte cleared the dishes and, finally, wiped her hands on a dishrag. She plopped herself into the same chair, facing Katherine and said, "Well?"

Katherine didn't have the strength or the patience to be coy. "What do you think?"

Charlotte practically beamed. "I don't blame you. Is that why he came back to town?"

At that, she could only shrug. "Partly, but he believes he can prove his innocence."

"Can he?" Charlotte asked. "I mean, *is* he innocent?"

"He must be. Why else would he risk everything?

The back door rattled and both women glanced up ex-

Lisa Higdon

pectantly. Joe Perry stepped inside the kitchen, his face taut with worry.

"Aren't Tom and Luke with you?"

He shook his head. "They're at the jail. Luke Cantrell has been placed under arrest."

Luke and Tom faced one another in the narrow hallway separating the row of cells. The keys dangled from Tom's fingers, keeping time with the tick in his jaw muscle.

"I guess I can take my pick." Luke scanned the first cell and shook his head. "I'd better take the one in back with a window. I always prefer a room with a view."

"You're taking this all with a rather casual attitude, don't you think?" The keys jingled as Tom moved to unlock the cell in the far corner. "I don't see anything funny about being arrested."

"Well, you're the one who wired the judge," Luke countered in a tight voice. He didn't think Tom would really go through with locking him up, but the young deputy considered the judge's orders unquestionable. "I suppose I'm lucky he didn't tell you to hang me."

The matter of Luke Cantrell was now under consideration by the U.S. District Court, and the judge had ordered Tom to place Luke in custody pending the jurist's arrival in Belle Plain. Despite Tom and Joe's assurances that the decision was in his best interest, Luke resented being jailed.

Tom threw the cell door open, causing it to bang against the concrete wall. "I had no idea he'd tell me to arrest you. Besides, you're the one who wanted to take this to trial. And Judge Drinkard wanted you jailed until your innocence or guilt could be determined. The judge always goes by the letter of the law."

Luke passed through the open doorway into the tiny cell, and an overwhelming feeling of confinement pressed down on him. The air seemed heavier, and he felt that the six by six room was closing in on him.

Tom slammed the cell door between them, the hollow clang reverberating in the pit of Luke's stomach. "The way I figure it, I'm doing you a favor."

"By having me arrested?"

"No." Tom gripped the bars. "By protecting you from Hagan. That man wants his reward money and won't think twice about killing you before the trial to get it. But he can't touch you as long as you're in my custody—not without Judge Drinkard's permission."

"How much faith do you have in this judge?"

"He's fair and honest," Tom assured him. "And he won't tolerate Hagan's lying ways."

The last statement was of little comfort to Luke, and he asked, "How do you think he'll feel about an outlaw wearing a badge under a false identity?"

❖ *16* ❖

KATHERINE HAD NEVER been past the front office of the jail; when the building was first completed, she had opted not to view the new facilities. She had only caught glimpses of the cells after the bank robbery, and those gruesome scenes had squelched any curiosity she might have had.

Even now, she hesitated outside the law office, doubting the wisdom of seeing Luke behind bars. Could she maintain the brave front she'd put on for everyone else? She kept telling herself the visit was to offer him support and encouragement, but what she really wanted was to have him promise her that all was not lost.

Tom glanced up when she entered the marshal's office, the expression on his face a painful mixture of surprise and shame. "Katherine, I had to—"

Raising a hand to silence him, she only nodded. Tom owed her no explanation. "Joe already explained about what happened with the telegram."

Tom rose from the desk. "Once Hagan learns that Luke is alive, he'll be back."

"You can't let him take Luke away this time." She crossed the room, welcoming her brother's embrace. She needed the comfort that only kin could offer. "Hagan will kill him before they reach Colorado."

"Hagan can't touch him as long as he's in my custody," Tom assured her, stepping back just enough to gauge her expression. "Not unless Judge Drinkard says different."

"Oh, Tom, he wouldn't." Katherine couldn't even consider the possibility of Luke being turned over to a sheriff who surely wanted him dead. "Once he hears Luke's side of the story, he won't do that."

Tom nodded, but he voiced no agreement. They both knew that Hagan's word would hold more weight than that of a drifting gambler who had lied to an entire town, but Katherine held fast to her father's high opinion of the judge.

Glancing toward the one empty cell visible from the front office, Katherine asked, "Is he all right?"

"He'll be fine, Katherine." Tom kept his hand on her shoulder, his touch comforting. "I'm staying right here, and I won't let anything happen."

She nodded and managed a convincing smile. "Of course, you won't. I'd like to see him for a moment."

Tom looked away but not quickly enough. Katherine didn't miss the reluctance in his eyes, and her stomach lurched at the possibility of what he didn't want to tell her. She squared her shoulders and asked, "Tom, what's wrong?"

"He doesn't want to see you."

Katherine flinched as if she'd been slapped. "What?"

Tom shrugged. "He said he didn't want you down here."

She couldn't believe what she was hearing. It hadn't even occurred to her that Luke wouldn't want to see her, and she tried to understand. Being jailed was a disgrace and he wouldn't want anyone gawking at him, but she wasn't just anyone. She loved him, and nothing could disgrace him in her eyes. If anything, she should be the one person he would want to see.

At last, Tom met her gaze with his own, and she asked, "Are you going to try to stop me?"

By way of token resistance, Tom warned, "He won't like it, sis."

With a nod, she turned toward the narrow doorway leading to the cell block.

Katherine held her breath as she approached the tiny room where Luke was being held. The cell was plain and ugly but thankfully clean, and he sat slumped forward on the narrow cot. At the sound of her footsteps, he glanced up, and his expression grew cold and distant behind the gleaming steel bars.

He rose to his feet but kept his distance. "I told Tom not to let you back here."

"I'm the mayor, remember?" she reminded him. "I outrank him."

He made no comment, and she neared the bars hesitantly. "Joe told me what happened. I'm so sorry."

"Well, don't be." He ran a hand through his dark hair, and she could see the worry he was trying to conceal behind his arrogance. "I told you once before that I didn't need your pity."

"Yes, you did," she agreed, hurt by the dismissive tone of his voice. "Standing over a grave with your name on it, as I recall."

"You have a good memory." He turned away from her to stare out of the tiny window. "Looks like I'll be claiming that marker after all."

"Surely, you're not giving up?"

His back stiffened. "I can't put up much of a fight from in here."

"What about your family in Santa Fe?"

He whirled around as if she had slapped him. "I don't have any family."

"You said your mother had other children," she countered. "They must still live there. Perhaps, I could send a telegram or write—"

"And tell them what?" he demanded. "That Lucinda's Anglo bastard is about to be hung? Why don't they come down to watch?"

"What a hateful thing to call someone."

"Yes, I thought so, too. Especially standing over her grave."

Katherine gripped the bars. "Who said that?"

"Her grieving husband," he said, shrugging off the remark as if it were nothing. "Don't feel sorry for me, kitten. I suppose I should be grateful he let me go to the funeral."

Tears stung her eyes at the thought of a young Luke enduring the painful loss of a parent with no one to offer him comfort or reassurance. Losing each of her parents had been painful, even with the love and support of remaining kin. She couldn't imagine enduring that loss along with such scorn and resentment.

"I'm so sorry," she managed. "I didn't know."

"It's nothing to cry over." He neared the bars and reached to stroke her cheek. A hint of a smile softened his features. "It wasn't me he really hated. My mother broke an engagement to him to marry my father, and he never forgave her. I always suspected he married her out of spite when my father died, but he took everything out on me."

Katherine shook her head. "If he loved her, he wouldn't have mistreated her child. You should have told her."

"She was always so fragile, especially after my brother and sister were born. I didn't want to upset her or cause him to turn on her." His hand lingered against her face. "I wish she'd been more like you. You're a strong woman, Katherine."

"Not as much as you might think," she confessed. "I'm more frightened now than I've ever been in my life."

His mouth hovered over hers, the cold bars allowing that

much intimacy, and she raised her lips to his. Slipping one hand through the bars, she gripped his shoulder as the kiss deepened. She ached to feel his arms around her, to have him hold her and promise that everything would be fine, but she knew in her heart that he didn't believe that anymore than she did.

Abruptly, he ended the kiss, pulling away from her touch. "I want you to promise me something."

Startled by the sudden loss of contact, she held the bars to steady herself. "Anything."

"Don't come back here." He stepped back, just out of her reach. "I don't want you to see me like this . . . behind bars."

"No." She shook her head. "You can't ask that of me."

"Look, we don't know how this will turn out," he crossed his arms over his chest. "Joe says that even if I prove it was self-defense, I could still be facing time in the state prison."

"I don't believe that."

He only shook his head. "We may have run out of miracles, and I don't want to leave you spinning a lot of dreams about what might happen when I get out. Face it, Katherine, I have nothing to offer you."

Stung, she let her hands fall from the bars. "The only thing I asked of you was that you take your one chance at freedom and leave. You're the one who insisted on proving your innocence."

"You asked one other thing of me," he corrected her. "You asked me to convince your brother that he didn't have what it takes to be a lawman. In view of my situation, I should have listened to you on both counts."

"Yes, you should have," she agreed before turning to leave. She had to get out of the jail before she gave way to the choking sobs caught in her throat. "We would have all been better off."

*   *   *

"Stand aside, deputy! I'm here to claim an escaped prisoner, and I'll kill you if you get in my way."

The sound of Hagan's voice propelled Luke to his feet. Jesus, the bastard would kill him on sight! He quickly glanced around the tiny cell, finding nothing he could use as a weapon.

"You're in my jail and my jurisdiction, sheriff." Tom's voice was cool and level, holding no trace of fear. "You're not taking anyone without a court order. A *legitimate* court order."

"Did you hear that, Conner?" Hagan's voice held an unmistakable sneer. "This snot-nosed brat says I ain't taking my own prisoner."

"I didn't say that," Tom corrected. "Judge H.L. Drinkard, U.S. District Court of Abilene, did."

"Judge Drinkard." Hagan spat. "How the hell did he get involved in this?"

"You'll have to take that up with Cantrell's attorney."

"His attorney?"

The door to the cell block burst open, and Hagan marched toward Luke's cell. "You slippery bastard, looks like you're caught now."

"I've been caught before." Luke glared at the man through the bars. "Doesn't mean I'll stay caught."

"You'll stay caught," Hagan countered. "I'll kill you myself before anyone saves your hide this time."

"You must have felt like a jackass." It was almost worth getting arrested, if it meant foiling the sheriff's carefully laid plans. He shook his head in mock sympathy. "Aiming to collect a reward on a dead man, only to find out he wasn't dead—again."

"Makes no never mind to me," Hagan said. "Now I can deliver you to McClain myself, and he can hang you from his front porch if it suits him. Just so long as your worthless life is over."

"And who will get that reward?" Luke could see that

his death, or rather the lack thereof, was the only thing standing in the way of Hagan collecting a fortune. "It damn sure wasn't going to be Johnson, was it?"

"Johnson would have hauled you in for a bottle of rotgut," Hagan said. "He was never one to ask questions, as long as he got paid what he was promised."

"And as long as he couldn't read for himself that he was being cheated." Luke shook his head. "You had things all worked out, didn't you? Well, I didn't feel like dying to accommodate you."

"All I want is to see you delivered to Cutter's Creek," Hagan assured him. "Whether you're alive or dead is of no matter to me."

The sheriff's determination to return him to Cutter's Creek baited Luke's finely honed instinct to spot a bluff, and he decided to ante. "Are you saying you've nothing to gain by taking me in?"

Hagan swallowed hard, and Luke knew he was right. "Son of a bitch. You've already spent the damned reward."

Finding his voice, the sheriff attempted to turn the danger back on Luke. "You'd best be worried about your own neck and quit meddling in my business."

"That's why you never answered those telegrams you thought were from Johnson," Luke concluded, stunned by the irony of the situation. He had been holed up in Belle Plain, waiting to learn that the reward would be paid, while Hagan was already busy enjoying the money. "Maybe I should ask Deputy McBride to send a wire to your boss . . . what was his name? McClain?"

Hagan's arms shot through the bars, but Luke anticipated the move and sidestepped the hands grappling for a hold on his collar. The sheriff only succeeded in grabbing a handful of shirtfront but yanked hard, dragging Luke up against the bars. "Let him go!" Tom yelled.

Luke didn't spare even a glance toward the deputy, keeping his eyes level with Hagan's. "How about it, sheriff? Think you can beat a man who isn't handcuffed?"

Luke didn't hesitate to take the one chance he might have, reaching through the bars to sink his fist into Hagan's soft belly. The sheriff staggered backward and barely kept his footing on the smooth floor of the jail. Clutching his gut with one hand, Hagan groaned and shuddered, and Luke thought for a moment the man was going to vomit.

"You bastard," Hagan wheezed, palming his revolver. Righting himself on shaky legs, he faced Luke. "I'm through toying with you."

"Drop your weapon, sheriff!" Tom McBride shouted, his pistol drawn and cocked. Leveling the barrel with Hagan's forehead, he ordered, "Get out of my jail."

The sheriff paled and let his pistol clatter to the floor. "What the hell kind of town is this? You just saw him assault a lawman and you draw on me?"

Tom didn't flinch, kicking the weapon aside. "I saw you attack my prisoner, and I'd be well within my rights to lock you up. You'd better get out while I'm in a forgiving mood."

Hagan straightened, glaring at Tom in disbelief, but he made no further argument. His gaze followed the path his weapon had taken into the outer room, and he summoned what little authority he had left. "Conner!" he barked. "Damn it, don't just stand there. Get my pistol!"

Luke watched him stalk out of the cell block and out of the jail, all the time haranguing Conner for his ineptitude. When the door slammed behind them, Tom glanced back at Luke and asked, "How did he ever come to be a sheriff?"

"He's like everything else in a mining town," Luke offered the only explanation he could think of. "Bought and paid for, but never worth the price."

*   *   *

"Ah, little Katy, you're the image of your sainted mother."

"Judge Drinkard." Katherine smiled as the little man stepped off the stage and took her hand. "How nice to have you back in Belle Plain. You remember Joe Perry, our attorney, don't you?"

Joe offered his hand. "Nice to see you again, judge."

Once the pleasantries were exchanged and the judge's luggage taken from the stage, Judge Drinkard pinned Katherine with a sharp eye. "Suppose you tell me about this young man of yours who's caused such a commotion."

Katherine flushed. "Well, I'm not sure where to begin."

Touching his throat, the older man suggested, "How about over a nice glass of your father's Scotch whiskey?"

She smiled. "Of course, and you will have dinner with us, won't you?"

By way of accepting the invitation, he took her arm and they began walking down the street toward the McBride house. "Just like your mother. Always a fine meal and warm welcome for a guest."

Joe tossed a coin to a boy from the hotel and instructed him to see that the judge's luggage was taken to his room. The judge glanced up and down main street, noting the many changes in Belle Plain since his last visit.

"The town is coming right along," he observed as they passed the row of merchant shops. "Your father had big dreams for this place, and I see you're not going to disappoint him."

"I've done my best," Katherine managed the vague answer, hoping to avoid any talk of the railroad. She felt that the events of the past few days had put a damper on any hope Belle Plain had for becoming a railroad stop.

McGregor's team had made the customary survey of the land, but she knew it was all a formality. The governor's aide had left town without apology or explanation, tossing

Tom his medal while boarding the stage, and she was surprised the railroad men hadn't done the same.

Katherine feared dinner would drag on the entire afternoon, and the judge insisted on discussing no legal matters while eating, saying, "Such talk always gives me a nasty case of indigestion."

Instead, he fondly recounted stories of her parents and how they had met on a wagon train not long after coming to America. "The bloody fools put us all together, saying there was no difference between Scots and Irish."

The judge laughed at that, and Katherine gently kicked Joe under the table when he didn't join in the exchange. Their feigned delight only encouraged the judge to elaborate on the adventures of traveling by wagon train.

"I'll never forget the first time I saw your mother." The judge's laughter faded, and his voice took on a reverent tone. "I had no family traveling with me, and your father insisted I take meals with them. I can still see her hovering over that fire to stir a kettle, and you, Katy, were just a wee bairn on the way."

Joe cleared his throat as if to say something, and Katherine shot him a warning look. Judge Drinkard was their only hope, and if he wanted to drone on about ancient history she would listen as long as was necessary. She rose to clear the dishes, and stirred the coals of the older man's memories. "Mama used to tell the story of the time you and Papa both shot the same deer, one on either side of a clearing."

"I'll always believe that my shot hit first," Drinkard maintained. He hefted the glass decanter of amber whiskey and poured a generous amount into his empty water glass. "It was a miracle we didn't shoot each other."

Katherine took her seat and slid the sugar bowl within the judge's reach. He gave her a thankful smile and spooned a generous amount of sugar into the glass and stirred.

Drinkard took a swig of the mixture and nodded in appreciation. "Why didn't your brother join us?"

"Tom is afraid to leave the jail," Katherine confessed. "It seems Sheriff Hagan is determined to take Luke Cantrell back to Colorado."

Drinkard was taken aback. "Against my orders?"

"Yes, indeed, your honor," Joe spoke at last. "He claims that you have no jurisdiction over him."

"Oh, he does, does he?"

Katherine nodded in confirmation and Joe continued. "He threatened to remove Mr. Cantrell by force, if need be."

"Did he?"

"Tom was forced to draw his weapon," Katherine continued, shaking her head. "Against another lawman! He was quite shaken by the experience."

The judge sipped his drink and considered the situation. "Why is that sheriff so determined to take Mr. Cantrell back to Colorado when he agreed to return him to Belle Plain for a hearing?"

Katherine glanced anxiously at Joe, unsure of what to say next. She cleared her throat and wished she had kept her mouth shut about Hagan. "Well, Sheriff Hagan didn't exactly agree to return Luke to Belle Plain. We, more or less—took him back."

"Took him back?" The judge's eyes narrowed. "How?"

"It became apparent that Hagan's arrest of Mr. Cantrell was not legal," Joe reiterated. "More than likely he would have been lynched upon arriving in Cutter's Creek, if he survived the trip."

Judge Drinkard never took his eyes off of Katherine, his expression stern and disapproving. "What did you do, Katy?"

In a voice little more than a whisper, Katherine related the account of banding together a group of masked riders and pretending to have Luke Cantrell abducted by a lynch mob. Deliberately, she omitted her intent to send him to Mexico to escape the law altogether.

Drinkard sat back, his whiskey forgotten. "It's never wise to take the law into your own hands. I'll have to give this matter some thought."

❖ 17 ❖

The Belle Plain jail was cleaner, newer, and safer than most. Luke tried to be grateful for that and the fact that there were no other prisoners sharing the cell block. Still, the cement walls and steel bars pressed in on him, and he felt smothered.

An untouched tray of food sat on a bench shoved against the far wall of the cell: Luke had yet to muster enough of an appetite to consider eating. Since noon, different townsfolk had brought food to the jail—enough to feed ten prisoners. Even Ruby Alston delivered a cake and a stern lecture to Tom on how disappointed she was that Luke had not trusted them enough to confide his plight.

"Given the circumstances, we would have understood," she insisted, somewhat miffed that Luke would accept no visitors. "I would have done whatever I could to help, and this unpleasantness might have been avoided."

Luke considered the statement, wondering just what would have happened had he revealed his true identity to anyone. That first night in town his only thought had been to escape, deceiving only Tom and Katherine long enough to get Johnson buried and make his escape. He certainly never dreamed he would become so tangled up in the town.

He breathed a curse and mentally corrected himself. The *town* had gotten tangled up in *him*. In a very short time, Belle Plain had become home, and he had made excuse after excuse not to leave.

Dusk had come and gone and now darkness hung behind the tiny barred window. He was grateful for that. The night had sent the concerned and the curious home to their dinner tables. For hours, he had been painfully aware of a shifting crowd milling about in the lot behind the jail. Their hushed whispers had darted through the bars like wasps, stinging his pride and his conscience.

"The marshal is in jail?"

"He killed a man in Colorado . . . they say."

"Poor Tom had to lock him up."

"Poor Katherine, you mean."

Poor Katherine, indeed. Luke sank back on the thin mattress, folded his hands behind his head and stared up at the smooth white ceiling. He had wronged her in every way possible, but she didn't hate him.

Twice he had heard her voice outside, pleading with Tom to let her see him, but Luke had made the deputy swear not to let her near the cell. It was bad enough she would see him tomorrow being led into the courtroom in chains; he simply couldn't endure the sight of her tear-streaked face staring at him through those damned bars.

Closing his eyes, he let another image form in his mind, remembering the feel of their naked bodies joined in passion. She had been so shy and innocent, but her eyes had shone with love as she gave herself totally to him. That was the picture of Katherine he'd carry to his grave.

Voices rose just outside the cell block door, and Luke strained to hear what was being said. The heavy wooden door swung open, and McGregor's stocky frame filled the doorway. Luke let his eyes close again. If McGregor had come to gloat or verbally abuse him, he would have to do it without the satisfaction of a response.

"Luke Cantrell," McGregor quietly mused, and Luke heard the door shut with a heavy thud. "I've heard of you. You're the man to beat, they say."

"Well, you beat me." Luke purposely kept his response disinterested, as if dismissing a waiter offering more coffee.

"I hardly think so."

"Luke! I'm sorry about this. Mr. McGregor, I asked you not to barge in here."

At the sound of Tom's voice, Luke opened his eyes, finding McGregor peering down at him through the bars. The deputy hovered nearby, prepared to bodily escort the visitor away if necessary.

"It's all right, Tom." Luke only shrugged. "Let him have his say."

McGregor didn't waste words. "You let me win, didn't you?"

Luke swung his legs over the side of the cot. "My pride wasn't worth this town's future."

McGregor chuckled. "You calling me a sore loser?"

"You tell me," Luke countered. "Have any of your flunkies ever beaten you?"

"Point well taken," he conceded. "But you weren't playing on your pride. As far as I was concerned, you were nothing more than a tinhorn lawman in a dusty little town. Now, I look like a fool, bragging about beating a man who let me win when he could have cleaned me out."

Rising to his feet, Luke wondered what the man was up to. "Like I said, the town's future isn't worth my pride."

McGregor smiled slightly. "What is this town worth to you?"

Luke's eyes narrowed, and he watched the man pull a deck of cards from his pocket. McGregor held them up for Luke to see. "What do you say, Cantrell? Ever played for something that really mattered?"

"Belle Plain isn't mine to gamble with."

"I wouldn't say that," McGregor said. "These people have already gambled quite a bit on you. You owe it to them to make it worth their while."

"And the odds are . . ."

"A stop on the Texas & Pacific Railroad," he replied in a matter-of-fact tone. "I give the word and the tracks are laid, no questions asked."

Luke rose to his feet and crossed the cell. "Why would it matter to you, McGregor?"

"I like knowing who the better man is."

Luke grinned. "Then it's your deal."

McGregor moved quickly to the cell, calling out for someone to bring a table. His ever-present flunkies moved even more quickly, despite Tom's protest, and dragged a wooden table into the narrow space separating the cells. The table was placed flush against the iron bars, and a chair was positioned for McGregor. Luke seated himself on the stool provided for prisoners and motioned for McGregor to deal the cards.

"It's your game," he said.

"We'll see about that." McGregor began shuffling the cards, shooing away the flunky who delivered the bottle of whiskey and glasses along with a box of poker chips. "Just the two of us, Cantrell. You name the game, and we'll play five hands. Whoever ends up with the most money wins, and the winner takes all."

Luke slipped his glass through the bars and downed the whiskey as the cards were dealt. "Let's keep it simple. Five card draw, jokers wild."

"You disappoint me." McGregor refilled their glasses. "I had expected more of a challenge than that."

"The game isn't the challenge," Luke reminded him as he took up his hand. "The skill is in winning."

McGregor chuckled at that, drawing a thin cigar from his vest pocket. He searched another pocket for matches and soon the acrid scent of sulfur mingled with the sweet odor of tobacco. McGregor studied his cards, but Luke studied his opponent. McGregor's face remained impassive, but the cigar rolled easily between his fingers.

"I'll open for twenty."

Luke nodded, tossing two of his own blue chips alongside those already on the scarred tabletop. He didn't miss the subtle smile that caused McGregor's lips to lift ever so slightly. He considered his cards—two queens, a ten, seven, and three—and tossed the seven and three aside.

"Two for the dealer as well," McGregor commented as he selected cards from his own hand. He dealt two cards to Luke and then a pair for himself.

Luke tucked the new cards into his hand: a ten and a nine. Now he had two pair, ladies high, but there were a number of hands that could beat that. The cigar was still twirling in McGregor's hand, and he didn't reach for his glass. Luke hoped winning the first hand would give McGregor just enough false confidence to bet more heavily on the next hand.

McGregor glanced up, and Luke wasn't surprised when he tossed two more blue chips into the pot. "I'll raise twenty."

Luke shook his head and placed the cards face down. "I'll have to fold on this one."

The disappointment was plain in McGregor's eyes, and Luke knew he'd been right about the man's cards. Nothing was said as the winnings were collected and the cards reshuffled, and Luke felt his luck improving as he gathered his second hand: two sevens, two nines, and a four.

After they each anted, McGregor studied his own hand and tossed out three cards, and he scowled slightly when Luke only laid one card aside. The cards were doled out, and Luke wasn't sure which made him happier, the third nine he needed to make a full house or the way McGregor began puffing on his cigar.

"I'll raise twenty." Luke pretended not to notice the way McGregor's eyes darted accusingly to the pot. "That would make us even."

The taunt worked, and McGregor saw the twenty and raised Luke's bet by ten, a cloud of cigar smoke swirling about his head. Luke met the ten, and said, "I'll call."

McGregor scowled and placed his cards on the table. "Three tens; beat that."

Luke laid the full house in plain view. "Happy to oblige."

The next two hands proved no different, as McGregor struggled both with his temper and mediocre hands. He filled his own glass with whiskey and then Luke's, gulping the liquor as Luke scraped more winnings to his side of the table.

"Last hand," McGregor declared as he dealt the cards, the cigar clenched between his teeth reduced to a glowing stub. "Winner take all."

Luke took up his cards and felt vindicated by the joker grinning up at him beside a pair of kings. Somehow it was fitting that he should win the railroad for Belle Plain with a wild card, and he downed his whiskey before requesting two cards from the glowering dealer. The six and three he set aside were replaced with a pair of tens—a better hand and McGregor would shoot him.

McGregor took two cards for himself and studied his hand. He glanced up once at Luke and then back at his card. Swearing under his breath, McGregor shoved all his chips toward the center of the table and growled, "I call."

Luke didn't hesitate, pushing his collective winnings toward McGregor's and placed his cards atop the pile. "Joker's wild. That gives me a full house."

McGregor swallowed once and tossed his hand in the center of the table. "That's the first flush I've had in two years, and you beat it with a damn joker."

"Belle Plain still gets the railroad?" Luke demanded.

McGregor refilled their glasses. "I never welsh on a bet."

"That's good to know." Luke raised his glass. "A toast then, to Belle Plain and the Texas & Pacific Railroad."

Their glasses clinked but McGregor hesitated before raising the glass to his lips. "I'd like some advice, Cantrell. What can I do to improve my game? I mean, what would you do differently if you were me?"

Luke thought for a moment and said, "I'd give up smoking."

"Congratulations, Miss McBride." The pleased expression on Linus McGregor's face only grew in response to the shocked silence following his announcement. "You seem a little surprised."

Stunned, was more like it. Without thought to decorum, Katherine slumped back against the sofa and raised clasped hands to her face, as if in prayer. "You wouldn't tease about this, would you?"

At that he laughed. "No, ma'am. They'll be laying track in a month's time, and I'll have a man here by summer's end to start on the depot."

The depot. Katherine let her hands fall to her lap, still clasped to hide their trembling. The town was saved! Merchants would remain in Belle Plain, and others would come seeking prosperity.

Suspicion caused her to ask, "I thought you still have two more towns to visit. What about them?"

"I've already sent wires apologizing for any inconvenience," he assured her. "The decision was mine, and I've made up my mind."

Katherine hesitated. "Luke Cantrell wouldn't have anything to do with this, would he?"

"The man loves his town, Miss McBride," McGregor rose from the chair. "You'll be receiving correspondence from my office over the next few weeks, but rest assured, the stop is yours.''

''You said he loves his town?''

''More than you know.'' He put on his hat and started toward the front door. ''Miss McBride, I do hope things work out for Cantrell. This town is going to need a good marshal.''

She nodded. ''All we can do is hope.''

He wagged his finger at her. ''Young lady, don't ever bet against Luke Cantrell.''

Before she could discern his meaning, a knock sounded at the door. Katherine reached to open the door and found a solemn-faced Joe Perry standing on the porch, his hand raised to knock again.

''Katherine.'' He made no move to step inside, glancing at her guest. ''Good day, Mr. McGregor.''

''Joe, you won't believe it.'' Taking his arm, she led him into the front parlor. ''Mr. McGregor has brought the most wonderful news. We have the rail stop!''

Joe nodded and managed a weak smile. ''I hope I won't be spoiling such a good day, but Judge Drinkard has called for a hearing . . . this afternoon.''

''This afternoon?'' She glanced back at McGregor. ''I thought everything was set for tomorrow.''

''I'll be honest with you. Judge Drinkard spent the morning with Sheriff Hagan.'' His lips thinned as if he had just swallowed a spoonful of bitter medicine. ''It was after this meeting that he decided to call the hearing early. I'm afraid it doesn't look good.''

''All we need now is the railroad, and Belle Plain will become the biggest town in west Texas!''

''Well, Papa, you have your railroad,'' Katherine whispered, staring at the framed photograph of her father. She'd hung the portrait in the mayor's office to serve as a reminder to herself and others of all that her father had done for the town.

For years, she had resented his dreams, silently accusing him of being foolish and irresponsible. Only now did she begin to realize that he had never sought wealth or riches for himself, but that he strove to make life better for others. He had wanted the railroad for the town, not for his own benefit.

For the first time in her life, Katherine wished she were more like her father. She stared down at her hands folded atop the massive desk and tallied her selfish acts. She wanted the railroad so that she wouldn't have to answer for the town's failure. She wanted a marshal so that she wouldn't lose her brother and be left alone. And she went along with Luke Cantrell's false identity so that she wouldn't lose the man she loved sooner than necessary.

Now she had lost him forever.

A knock sounded at the door, startling her from her morose thoughts. Rising from the chair, she steeled herself against the inevitable. No doubt someone had come to tell her the hearing was about to begin.

Katherine opened the door and felt her resolve crumble at the sight of Patsy Reynolds standing before her, cradling her son. Without a word, Patsy stepped inside the room and slipped her empty arm around Katherine's shoulder, offering empathy and understanding.

"Justin was in town and came for me as soon as he heard about the hearing," Patsy said, gently patting her friend's shoulder. "Why didn't you let me know?"

Katherine stepped back and managed to smile at the baby, tickling him under the chin. "You've got enough on your hands with this little fellow."

"Don't be silly," Patsy countered. "I'm never too busy for my best friend, especially when she's in trouble."

"I'm not the one in trouble." Katherine motioned for her to take a seat in one of the leather chairs facing the desk. Sinking into a chair across from Patsy, she swallowed hard against the tears. "Oh, Patsy, I'll never forgive myself if they . . . if something happens to him."

"This isn't your fault."

She shook her head. "Yes, it is. I suspected who he was but kept silent. If I had warned him, he would have been long gone before Sheriff Hagan came to town."

"But you didn't want him to leave town," Patsy concluded.

"I was only fooling myself." Katherine gazed at the baby cradled in her friend's arms. "I just wanted to pretend a little while longer. Just once in my life, I wanted something . . . special."

"Oh, honey." Patsy's eyes shone with tears as she reached across the table to clasp Katherine's hand. "You just fell in love; there's no pretending to it."

Luke heard the sound of boots in the outer office and he rose to his feet. Tom had said the hearing was to be today, but no one knew why the date had been moved.

The heavy door opened and Tom McBride stood peering at him, the keys to the cell hanging from his fingers. He moved to unlock the cell, looking at Luke almost apologetically. "The judge wants everyone in the courthouse."

Luke nodded at the brief explanation, not sure if he wanted further elaboration. Tom reached for the set of cuffs hanging from his belt, and Luke couldn't help asking, "Are those really necessary?"

"I'm afraid so." The young deputy wouldn't meet his eyes. "Not because I don't trust you, but . . . well, that's the law."

Luke held out his wrists. "Would you stop me if I escaped?"

"Hagan would," Tom reminded him as he snapped the iron bracelets in place. "He'd shoot you in the back and haul you back to Colorado . . . dead. Here, we'll go through the back hall." Tom led the way toward a door leading into the recesses of the courthouse. "There's a crowd gathering out front."

Luke and Tom stepped into the shadowed hallway leading to the main courtroom. Their boots made a hollow sound, echoing down the long corridor. A door at the end of the hall opened, and Katherine stepped out of the mayor's office, followed by her friend Patsy Reynolds. She froze in place at the sight of them, startling Patsy with the sudden halt.

"Luke," she breathed.

"Hello, Katherine."

Patsy gave her a shove toward him, and he glanced back at Tom. "Is there a law against me having a little privacy?"

"I'll go look that up." Tom and Patsy ducked inside the mayor's office, leaving the door open slightly.

Luke knew arguing with her was pointless, but he did say, "I wish you wouldn't come to this hearing."

"I had to see you," she said in a tremulous voice. "It might be my last time."

"It will be if this judge of yours sends me back with Hagan."

She raised a hand to her lips, squeezing her eyes against tears. Luke damned himself for not thinking before he spoke so harshly.

"Shh," he whispered, leaning forward and silently cursing the bonds that kept his arms from encircling her. Instead, he took her hands and pressed his forehead against hers. Her arms went around him and he heard the soft catch of a sob in her throat, even as he brushed his lips against hers.

"Oh, Luke," she breathed. "I can't lose you."

"You'll never lose me," he swore, lifting his shackled hands to her face. "No matter what happens, my heart will always be with you. I love you, Katherine, and I deserve hell for making you cry."

"That's not true," she whispered, pressing her lips against his palm. "Tears are a small price to pay for love."

"Promise me something," he breathed against her forehead. "If things don't work out . . . if they hang me . . ."

"No," she cried. "Don't say that."

"Shh . . . it could happen, Katherine, and I've been thinking about you. I don't want you to spend your life grieving for me." He paused, forcing a steady tone. "Just promise that you'll have me buried here in Belle Plain."

She paled and tears spilled down her cheeks, but she managed to nod. He wiped her damp face with his thumb and smiled down at her. "Save your tears. I might need them later."

A strangled cough drew their attention to where Tom stood in the open doorway. "I reckon it's time to get going."

Luke nodded and kissed Katherine one last time, the sweetness of her mouth tainted by her salty tears. He turned to follow Tom toward the courtroom. He could hear Patsy trying to console Katherine, but the sound of her muffled sobs followed after him and tore at his gut.

To Katherine's dismay, the courthouse was filled with people, and more kept filing in. Soon, every seat was taken, and people began lining up along the walls. The din of conversation pressed down on her, and the mood grew heavy with the worry and concern of those assembled for the hearing.

Flanked by Charlotte and her mother on one side and Patsy and Justin Reynolds on the other, Katherine was grateful not to be subjected to the well-intended expressions of concern from friends and neighbors.

Joe Perry made his way down the center aisle and seated himself at an oak table stacked with law books. He glanced over his shoulder and gave Katherine a reassuring smile.

She leaned forward and whispered, "Have you spoken with the judge?"

Shaking his head, Joe said, "He's been in the chambers all morning. He asked to borrow two law books and then sent me away."

Before she could ask any further questions, Sheriff Hagan and his deputy entered the courtroom, marching confidently down the aisle. Katherine glanced toward Joe, who refused to so much as look in the sheriff's direction.

To the left of the judge's bench, a door opened, and Katherine caught sight of Luke entering the courtroom, followed by Tom. They both glanced in her direction, and Katherine grasped onto Charlotte's hand. Tom took the lead and ushered Luke to the table where Joe sat waiting. The men shook hands, taking their seats.

A twin door on the opposite side opened and the judge emerged. Tom and Joe rose to their feet, as did Luke and those gathered for the hearing. Reluctantly, Hagan and his deputy also stood.

Judge Drinkard scanned the crowd and glared first at Hagan, then at Luke. Once he was seated, everyone else took their place. Silence fell over the courtroom as the judge leafed through several papers stacked on the bench.

He glanced pointedly at Hagan. "You claim this man murdered someone in your town. Suppose you explain that to me."

Hagan cleared his throat, obviously unaccustomed to being doubted. "Well, sir, he was playing poker at the Red Horse Saloon with three other men. He was winning and had been winning since he got there. One man finally had enough and called him out for cheating. Cantrell refused to return the man's money and started dealing a new game. When the man protested, Cantrell shot him."

Joe rose to his feet, his confidence and education showing. Luke never took his eyes from the judge's face. The old goat was probably one hell of a poker player, as Luke couldn't begin to guess whether or not he believed Hagan.

"Your honor, with all due respect to Sheriff Hagan, I must remind the court that he was not present when the shooting occurred and his testimony is based on hearsay."

Hagan shot to his feet. "Hearsay, my ass! I'm telling you, that's the way it happened."

Judge Drinkard slammed the gavel against the desk. "Order! That means shut up!" He leaned forward, studying Joe with great interest. "Where did you go to school, young man?"

Joe was somewhat taken aback by the question, but answered anyway. "Baltimore, your honor, in Maryland."

"I know where Baltimore is," the judge snapped. "And I know there is a difference between hearsay and the testimony gathered by a lawman investigating a crime."

Luke slid a palm over his eyes. It was all over.

"Yes, your honor." Joe took his seat.

"You there"—Judge Drinkard pointed the gavel at Luke—"tell me what happened."

Joe motioned for him to stand.

"There's not much to tell, judge. I was in the middle of a winning streak that wouldn't quit. I had sixteen hundred dollars in the pot and three queens and a pair of tens. If I was going to cheat, I wouldn't give myself that good of a hand. McClain called with two pair, eights and sixes. He went wild when I laid those ladies on the table."

"It's his word against two witnesses!" Hagan shouted.

"And you have statements from these witnesses?" Drinkard demanded.

"I can get 'em," Hagan growled before he could stop himself. Sheepishly, he added, "Your honor."

Drinkard sat back, surveying Hagan with open distaste. "You've made quite a commotion in this town, making trouble with the deputy and knocking on my door before breakfast. All that and you have no statements?"

Quickly dismissing the irate lawman, he turned toward

Luke. "What about you? Any witnesses that can back up what you say?"

Luke glanced at Joe then back at the judge. He nodded. "Anyone there can tell you I did what I had to do to save my own life."

Pointing the gavel toward Joe, he pressed, "Can you get statements? Anyone who'll testify that they saw what happened?"

Joe cleared his throat and hesitated. Finally, he said, "I'm sure I could, if I—"

"I was there, your honor!"

All eyes turned to where Ruby Alston stood, regal as a queen. She tilted her head defiantly. "I saw the whole thing."

"So did I." Cecil Percy was on his feet, hands folded across his wide girth. "Mr. Cantrell acted in self-defense, I'll swear to it."

"Me, too."

"Same here."

One by one, the entire population of Belle Plain, at least all that could fit in the courthouse, stood in unified testimony.

Drinkard surveyed them, his disbelief betrayed by a single raised eyebrow. He turned his attention to Hagan. "That's more witnesses than you've got."

"You can't believe these people!" Hagan's face was mottled with anger. "You daft old coot, there ain't a one of them that's ever been to Cutter's Creek!"

"Daft, am I?" Drinkard leaned forward, the gavel dangling between his fingers, and smiled. "Suppose you prove who was in your town or not."

Hagan faltered, and in that moment lost his argument. Drinkard turned toward Joe. "It seems there is not enough evidence against your client to make a case. The charges are dismissed."

He banged the gavel against the oak desk and a wave of

cheers rose from the assembly. Joe clapped Luke on the back and Tom shook his hand.

Luke was dimly aware of people swarming around him to offer their congratulations and good wishes, but he was intent on finding Katherine.

She stood waiting for him, just behind the railing that separated the spectators from the court. Her eyes sparkled with unshed tears and the smile on her face was like sunlight fighting its way from behind a cloud.

The well-wishers grew quiet, and the crowd parted like the Red Sea before Moses. The only audible sound was that of Luke's boots on the polished floor as he made his way to Katherine, his love—his life.

"Oh, Luke," she began, but he silenced her tremulous words with a gentle touch of his fingers against her mouth.

The banging of the judge's gavel barely registered, but Katherine finally glanced up at the judge's shout. "This courtroom has not been dismissed!"

Hagan was on his feet and Joe turned toward the bench. "Please forgive my client's exuberance, your honor."

"Perfectly understandable," Judge Drinkard said with a wave of his hand. "There is still the matter of the reward. It seems, Sheriff Hagan, that you've been playing it fast and loose with the law. The way I understand it, you were paid quite a hefty sum on the head of this young man. Now, we can all see that he is alive and well here in Belle Plain."

"But your honor, I received a wire saying that he was dead."

"Which you learned not to be the case," the judge countered. "Why didn't you inform the authorities?"

"I was going to, in Abilene. But he was taken from my custody—"

"In an attempt to save his life . . . ," Joe added.

"Mr. Perry, your client has been exonerated. This is no longer your concern. However, I am most concerned with Sheriff Hagan's misuse of legal authority, not to mention the fact that he failed to report that his prisoner had been abducted.''

"He was abducted by people from this town!" Hagan shouted, brandishing a hand in a sweeping gesture. "They should be charged with obstruction of justice!"

"You should have seen to that as soon as you arrived in Abilene," Judge Drinkard said. "I'm going to send for the U.S. Marshal to take you into custody. You will answer these charges in accordance with the law."

He glanced toward Tom. "Will you take the prisoner into custody until the marshal arrives?"

"Yes, sir." Tom moved forward. "With pleasure."

Stunned, Hagan offered no resistance as Tom snapped the handcuffs on his wrists. Steering the prisoner aside, Tom turned back toward Luke and Katherine, waiting.

Luke winked at the deputy before turning to the woman in his arms. "Katherine McBride, will you marry me?"

No one moved, the assembly held its collective breath as if all depended on the answer. She nodded, even as tears spilled down her face. "Yes, oh yes."

He kissed her then, and the crowd cheered again.

❖ EPILOGUE ❖

SILENCE FELL OVER the crowd gathered at the depot, and Luke smiled at Katherine before turning his gaze toward the empty expanse of tracks snaking into Belle Plain. The first train was due to roll into the station at seven minutes past two in the afternoon, marking the beginning of a new era for Belle Plain.

Katherine smiled at him and glanced down at the baby dozing peacefully in her arms. She tickled the child's chin, but their daughter only turned her head against her mother's shoulder. "Miss Lucy," Katherine cooed, "you're going to miss the choo-choo train."

Tom grinned down at his niece. "The daughter of the mayor shouldn't sleep through such an important occasion."

"The daughter of *both* mayors," Charlotte corrected.

Katherine laughed. "Luke is the politician in the family, not me."

Luke grinned at her. "Does that mean you won't be running against me in the election?"

"I'd say we make a pretty good team," she assured him. "Just don't switch tickets on me."

Right on time, they heard the whistle blow, long and loud, and a cheer went up from the crowd just as the smokestack came into view. The shrill blast of the train whistle startled the baby, and her face puckered beneath the frilly white bonnet.

The locomotive chugged into the station, and the squeal of brakes was smothered by the jubilant cheers of the crowd. The conductor stepped out onto the station platform placing a wooden step on the ground below. In a loud voice, he called, "All those departing at Belle Plain, please take your leave."

Luke glanced at his wife. "Did you know about any passengers coming to Belle Plain?"

Before she could answer, an elegant looking man and two women appeared in the narrow doorway. They scanned the crowd before the man stepped down, offering his assistance to the ladies. Once again, they glanced over the crowd, only this time the man pointed toward Luke.

Smiles broke on their faces and the trio marched directly toward him. The man spoke first. "Brother, I have waited a long time for this day."

"Brother?" Luke took a step back, but Katherine caught his arm and urged him forward. He stared at the stranger, disbelief clear in his eyes. At last, he breathed, "Raphael?"

"You remember little Teresa?" he prompted, drawing one of the women forward. "Come, say hello to your brother."

"Lucien." Her voice trembled. "It has been too long."

Luke offered his hand in welcome to her, uncertainty marring his features. Raphael clapped a hand on his brother's shoulder, and Katherine couldn't say who moved first but suddenly the three of them were caught in an embrace. The young woman clung to Luke's broad shoulders, her body trembling with mute sobs, while Raphael reassured her in Spanish.

Luke turned toward his brother, and the men embraced while Teresa dabbed at her eyes with a handkerchief.

"My wife is also here." Raphael motioned for her to come forward. "This is Angelina."

"My mother knew your mother when they were girls," the newfound sister-in-law explained. "She sends her love."

Still holding onto his newly reunited family, Luke turned toward Katherine. She only smiled when he said, "Why is it I don't feel the need to explain to you who they are?"

"This must be Katherine." Raphael rushed to clasp her hand, his eyes shining with gratitude. "Thank you. Thank you for your letters."

"Thank you for coming," she replied. The baby squirmed against her shoulder, wailing in protest of the commotion. "This is your niece, Lucy."

Raphael and his sister exchanged a knowing look before Teresa reached to stroke the baby's downy face. "Lucinda? For our mother?"

"That's right," Luke answered as he returned to Katherine's side, slipping an arm around her waist.

The hushed on-lookers gathered on the platform quickly transformed into a welcoming party, swarming to shake hands and lay claim to Luke both as friend and neighbor. Tom and Charlotte began directing the crowd toward the town hall for the reception in honor of Luke's family, and Katherine didn't miss the admiration on Joe Perry's face as he watched Teresa gracefully descend the steps of the depot.

"You did all of this for me?" Luke shook his head in disbelief as he led her toward the town hall. "How did you know?"

Katherine only smiled. "I wrote a few letters to Santa Fe. Evidently, they had given you up for dead years ago and were thrilled to learn you were alive and well."

The baby continued to fuss, reaching chubby arms out to her father. Luke hefted her to his shoulder, and Lucy quieted right away. He grinned at his wife and said, "And it didn't hurt that you managed to get them here today . . . on the first train to Belle Plain!"

"Just good politics," she explained. "Anything that's good for our family is naturally good for our town."

Our Town...
where love is always right around the corner!

● ● ● ● ● ● ● ● ● ● ● ● ● ● ● ● ● ● ●